THE
MERDE
FACTOR

Stephen Clarke lives in France, where he divides his time between writing and not writing. His first novel, *A Year in the Merde*, originally became a word of mouth hit in Paris in 2004, and is now published all over the world. Since then he has published three more bestselling Merde novels, as well as *Talk to the Snail*, an indispensable guide to understanding the French, and *1000 Years of Annoying the French*, in which he investigates what has *really* been going on since 1066. A *Sunday Times* bestseller in hardcover, *1000 Years of Annoying the French* went on to become one of the top ten bestselling history books in paperback in 2011.

Also by Stephen Clarke

Fiction
A Year in the Merde
Merde Actually
Merde Happens
Dial M for Merde
The Merde Factor

Non-fiction
Talk to the Snail: Ten Commandments for
Understanding the French

1000 Years of Annoying the French

Paris Revealed: The Secret Life of a City

Digital Short
Annoying the French Encore!

Stephen Clarke

THE
MERDE
FACTOR

arrow books

Published by Arrow Books 2013

2 4 6 8 10 9 7 5 3 1

Copyright © Stephen Clarke 2012

Stephen Clarke has asserted his right under the Copyright, Designs
and Patents Act 1988 to be identified as the author of this work

First published in Great Britain in 2012 by
Century
Random House, 20 Vauxhall Bridge Road,
London SW1V 2SA

www.randomhouse.co.uk

Addresses for companies within The Random House Group Limited can
be found at: www.randomhouse.co.uk/offices.htm

The Random House Group Limited Reg. No. 954009

A CIP catalogue record for this book
is available from the British Library

ISBN 9780099580546

The Random House Group Limited supports The Forest Stewardship
Council® (FSC®), the leading international forest-certification organisation.
Our books carrying the FSC label are printed on FSC®-certified paper.
FSC is the only forest-certification scheme supported by the leading
environmental organisations, including Greenpeace. Our
paper procurement policy can be found at
www.randomhouse.co.uk/environment

Typeset by SX Composing DTP, Rayleigh, Essex SS6 7XF
Printed and bound in Great Britain by Clays Ltd, St Ives PLC

This novel is dedicated to everyone who has written to me over the past three years saying, 'When's the next Paul West novel coming out?'

Merci for asking.

'The English have corrupted the mind of my kingdom. We must not expose a new generation to the risk of being perverted by their language.'

Louis XV, King of France 1715–74

'Die Erde hat mich wieder.' ('The Earth has reclaimed me.')

From *Faust* by J. W. Goethe

'Die Merde hat mich wieder.' ('The *merde* has reclaimed me.')

From *Watt* by Samuel Beckett

Un

'Le printemps à Paris – il me donne suffisament d'énergie pour conquérir le monde. Ou au moins l'Angleterre.'

Springtime in Paris – it gives me enough energy to conquer the world. Or, at the very least, England.

Paul-Ovide-Robin Desclous, general in Napoleon's army and alleged lover of Josephine, killed at Waterloo by a stray French cannonball

I

THE SUN came out, and springtime hit Paris like a tsunami of hormones. Suddenly every life form in the city, from the preening pigeons to the usually sullen street cops, seemed to grow a grin on its face.

The morning pavements were as crowded as ever, but now the Parisians looked as though they were enjoying their walk to the Métro station instead of doing their usual head-down rush. The rental bikes at the Vélib' stations disappeared early as occasional cyclists opted to take the scenic route to work. Almost overnight, girls decided that the season for tights was over, and the men in the streets mutated into owls, their necks suddenly capable of 360° rotation in search of bare legs.

The first tourists were just appearing, tiptoeing in like guests who arrive early at a party and feel embarrassed until they notice that the plates on the buffet are all deliciously full. And their timing was perfect – the café awnings had been winched away to expose the terraces to the sun, transforming the city into one big open-air theatre.

The tall plane trees that lined the streets, their spindly new branches waving like over-excited children, were sending out a blizzard of pollen that swarmed through the air, the particles as big as insects and as spiky as a Parisian waiter's morning conversation. There were even tufts of plant life poking up through the round metal grilles at the bases of the tree trunks. These absurdly optimistic little sprigs would soon be pecked out by birds or peed on by dogs, but for the moment they were raising their heads through the drift of pollen and cigarette ends, and enjoying springtime in Paris.

Why couldn't I do the same?

Well, the immediate reason was that I was sitting in a café in the posh 6th *arrondissement* suffering from palpitations. I'd come indoors to avoid paying extra for a drink on the terrace, but it hadn't done me much good. The waiter had just deposited a coffee on my table, accompanied by a toothpick-sized complimentary chocolate and a bill that suggested I was being asked to help refund the eurozone debt. Surely he'd mixed me up with the table across the aisle, where a family of tourists were grazing on a mound of croissants?

'Excusez-moi,' I called out, but the waiter was on his way to inflict some pain at another table. I heard an American woman ask for a cappuccino. No, I thought, don't do it.

'Un cappuccino? Ce n'est pas San Francisco ici, madame,' the waiter guffawed.

But the woman wasn't backing down. She looked around the place, taking in the leather banquettes, the flitting waiters in their long aprons, the clink of spoon on china cup.

'C'est un café ici, non?' she enquired in an extreme American accent.

'Off course,' the waiter mispronounced. 'You want un café crème?'

'Non, un cappuccino.'

It would have been fun to watch them battle it out – the waiter trying to tame the intruder, the woman naively expecting to get exactly what she wanted in a French café – but just at that moment, in walked my reason for being here, a loping figure who stood out in the chic environment like a cigarette butt on a dish of oysters. Even the waiter flinched.

My American friend Jake looked, as usual, as if he was auditioning for the role of a corpse washed up on a beach: his clothes had apparently been gnawed at by a shoal of sardines and his long blond hair styled by the rising tide. Only the huge grin on his erratically shaven face showed any sign of symmetry.

'Hey, Paul, beau weather, huh? Merci for having come, man,' he said in his unique brand of Franglais. He was one of those people who learn a new language by ejecting bits of the old one from their memory. In the ten or so years he'd been living in Paris, he'd managed to stew his French and English into a lumpy linguistic *soupe à l'oignon*. You never knew what you were going to get: broth, crouton, or a soggy mix of the two.

'So how did it go?' I asked as he joined me at the table.

'Oh, formidable, man, she adored them.'

I nodded, but found this very hard to believe. The 'she' in question was a literary agent, the 'them', Jake's poems, and 'adoring' was not usually something you did with Jake's poems. Surviving them was more like it, or taking them on the chin. There was something about his combination of excruciating rhymes and explicit pornography that made you want to go and put your finger in an electric pencil sharpener to ease the pain of listening to them.

'You say she *invited* you to come and see her? I mean, *after* you'd sent her a sample?' I tried my best to banish the incredulity from my voice.

'Oh, oui, man,' Jake said, getting out a packet of rolling tobacco and some papers. He had never quite managed to get his head around the no-smoking rule in French cafés. 'I heard of her from this guy I know. He's a writer. Well, he says he's a writer but he hasn't yet finished anything – he's Français – but he telled, tolen, uh . . .'

'Told?' I prompted. Once Jake got caught up trying to extract English grammar from his French-soaked mind, conversation could grind to a halt for several hours.

'Yes, voilà – he told to me that this agent makes the Français writers famous in all the world. You know, she is the one who selled, uh, sailed this French writer to Hollywood. You know that movie about the guy who meets the girl but really it's her spirit because she's in a coma?'

'Yes.' He was talking about France's biggest-selling author, whose first novel had been signed up by Spielberg before it was even published, thanks to this Paris-based literary agent. 'And you think Spielberg will be putting in a bid for your poems?' I asked Jake. Unless Hollywood was about to start a fashion for hard-core porn with verse dialogue – rhyming couplings – I couldn't see it happening. But Jake ignored practicalities and stampeded on with his story. I hadn't seen him this excited since he'd bumped into a group of female delegates from a conference on saving the world's endangered languages. Given that his aim in life was to sleep with a woman of every nationality in the world, to him it had been like stumbling on a stockpile of free cigarette papers.

'I written a poem spécialement for her, you know, inspired by the coma story. You want to hear it?'

'Well . . .' How did you say 'please God no' politely? But I wasn't given the choice.

'Girl, you may be in a coma, but I love your hospital aroma . . .'

'Yes, Jake, I get the picture.' And I wanted to erase it.

'Who cares if you're comatose, cause you got sexy underclose.'

'So you sent her *that*, and she agreed to *see* you?' I asked.

In reply, Jake just grinned and nodded. By now his cigarette was in his mouth and he was looking round for someone to give him a light, frowning at the inexplicable absence of smokers.

'She even rassembled all her colleagues in her bureau to listen,' he went on, 'and they understood all my ironies. They were non-stop laughing.'

I bet they were, I thought.

'She *adored* them, man. She has said me to, uh . . .' Jake gazed into mid-air as if to capture the magic of the moment when someone told him they liked – or could even endure without painkillers – his poems. '. . . to go away,' he concluded.

'She told you to go away?' A glimmer of sanity had suddenly entered the room.

'Yeah, and come back when I have traduced them.'

'Traduced?'

'Yes, you know, into other langues. To come back when I have traduced them into ten other langues. Then she can sell them to the world.' Now I understood. Translate his poems into ten languages? It was like telling a seven-foot-tall aspiring jockey to come back when he was five foot five. As in, never.

'I can ask some of my ex-girlfriends to aid me,' Jake ploughed on. 'Li, the North Korean, and Yamani, the Saudi, and, oh, monsieur?'

I was afraid that Jake might be about to enquire whether the waiter fancied translating some risqué verse, but he only asked if he could have some *feu* for his cigarette.

'Non, monsieur,' was the candid reply. Jake still didn't get the message, though, and kept the ragged tube between his lips in the hope that someone with a lighter would turn up.

'She only ended our interview because she said she was obliged to go to a party,' he told me proudly. 'It is her birthday, or we would still be there listening to my oeuvre.' He paused, a new idea making the cigarette twitch in his mouth. 'Merde!' he exclaimed, attracting the attention of everyone in the café. 'I must write her a birthday poem, an improvisation. Oui!'

I couldn't stop myself wincing.

'I must do it,' he declared, rummaging in his shapeless jacket for a pen. 'I will go to her now!' He was gathering momentum, like a landslide about to bury an unsuspecting village.

'Send her an email,' I pleaded.

'No, much better if I perform it en direct. I will return at her office – they have an intercom. I will rap it to her from the street.'

'You sure that's a good idea?'

'Oh oui. What rhymes with birthday? Surfday, Smurfday . . .'

He stood up, the glow of a mission burning in his eyes. As he walked away, his soggy cigarette was bouncing up and down in his mouth to the rhythm of an emerging poem.

Poor lady, I thought. Until today, being a literary agent must have been fun. Putting the squeeze on publishers, the endless lunches and cocktail parties. Now she was going to see the dark side. And on her birthday, too. I shook my head to try and clear it of the suffering Jake was about to unleash. But no, it wouldn't go away. What, I wondered, was the equivalent of putting my finger in an electrical pencil sharpener? Oh yes, a fight with the waiter in a snooty French café.

'Monsieur?' I hailed him as he walked by. He ignored me and sauntered towards the lady who'd tried to order a 'San Franciscan' coffee. He stopped beside her table, swivelled and ceremoniously delivered a textbook, white-capped cappuccino in a tall glass mug. It was a work of art in shades of cream and beige. I had to laugh. He'd complained, but given her exactly what she wanted, even if he had made her wait several punitive minutes.

'Ah, merci,' the woman cooed, delighted.

The waiter now came and looked down his nose at me. So he'd heard me after all.

'Monsieur?' he asked.

I'd prepared my fighting talk. 'I ordered an espresso,' I had planned to tell him in my best French, 'but you gave me the bill for the menu du jour, non?'

But somehow, I couldn't bring myself to do it. It was the way he'd given the tourist her cappuccino, the way he'd appeared to ignore me and then come straight to my table. He wasn't such a snooty bastard, after all. He was just doing things his way.

'Je voudrais payer, s'il vous plaît,' I simpered.

Springtime was turning me soft.

II

My personal *printemps* got even cloudier a few minutes later when my phone buzzed.

'Pool?'

Only one person called me that, the halfway house between the French pronunciation of my first name – 'Pol' – and the correct one.

'Bonjour, Jean-Marie,' I answered. 'We're not due to meet till next week, are we?'

'No, but I am free now. Can you come to meet me? I'm in the Sixième.'

'Oh, so am I.'

'Excellent, come to . . .' And he dictated an address.

'Right, OK. Be there in about ten minutes, then.'

If I sounded unenthusiastic, it was because I'd been trying to squirm out of meeting Jean-Marie, in the same way I always put off going to the doctor to get a flu jab. Both of them, I suspected, would give me a pain in the same place.

Jean-Marie was the man who'd hired me for my first job in Paris. He'd then unfairly fired me and muscled in on the tea room I started, taking advantage of a temporary cash-flow problem to grab 50 per cent of the business. A meeting with him was never pleasant. He was a French cross between Silvio Berlusconi and a used-car salesman, but slightly less honest than either. And with a Napoleon complex thrown in. He was the kind of guy who, as a Parisian friend of mine once put it, should never be allowed to borrow your goat. (Parisians have long left behind their rural roots, but they still have

10

subconscious memories of the horrors that can be inflicted on livestock entrusted to the wrong type of person.)

The problem was that a meeting with the least trustworthy man in Paris was a necessity if, like me, you were jobless and subletting a top-floor garret so small that you had to ask the woman at the *boulangerie* to cut your baguettes in half so you could fit them into the kitchen. One thing Jean-Marie had was contacts, and contacts are what you need in Paris to get yourself out of a cheap garret and into some money.

He'd summoned me to an address just off the boulevard Saint-Germain. His office was nowhere near the Quartier Latin, but he loved to hang out there to give himself an intellectual sheen. There was nothing very intellectual about his meat-wholesaling business.

It was even more typical of Jean-Marie to give me an address instead of the name of a café or office. Why the secrecy?

The mystery deepened when I found the place. It was a New York-style diner called American's Dream. That had to be wrong, surely. Not just the pointless apostrophe S but the whole address. Jean-Marie, French owner of a multi-million-euro company and wearer of suits so sharp they could slice cheese, in a fake American diner?

I walked in and was hit by a warm fug of food smells and conversation. The place was almost full, mainly of teenage and twenty-something Parisians. Strange, I thought. These were posh people from one of the snootiest neighbourhoods in the city. What were they doing sitting at these canteen-like plastic tables? It felt like stumbling across a crowded champagne lounge in a riot-torn housing estate. Totally incongruous.

And there, in one corner of a booth for four, was Jean-Marie, his fist clamped around a big white mug of coffee. He was grinning at me, and obviously exchanging some wisecrack with the gorgeous dark-haired girl sitting next to him. She laughed politely, giving him an excuse to squeeze her shoulder. Oh God, I thought as I walked towards their table, she's even younger than his daughter. The girl was twenty-five at the most, a classy *Parisienne* with her hair tied back in a tight ponytail: efficient but sexy. She was wearing bright red lipstick and a white blouse that was buttoned up almost to the neck as if she was determined not to let anyone get a glimpse of her cleavage, which, ironically, only made her even more alluring.

'Ah, Pool, you have found me!' He grabbed my outstretched hand and almost dragged me across the table.

'Yes, well, you gave me the address,' I admitted modestly.

'This young Englishman knows me very well,' he told the girl in the kind of soft French accent that makes

English ladies go gooey at the knees. 'Too well.' He laughed loudly and clapped me on the shoulder. 'This is Amandine,' Jean-Marie announced, and before I had time to wonder whether I should shake hands or kiss her on the cheek, she held out a slim, perfectly manicured hand and gave me the briefest of squeezes. 'Amandine is my, how do you say, stagiaire?' Jean-Marie said.

'Intern. Hi, Paul,' she said in a slightly transatlantic accent. I guessed Mummy and Daddy had probably sent her to an American business school.

'Yes, intern. There is no need to trouble yourself with your terrible French, Pool,' Jean-Marie said. 'Amandine speaks perfect English. She is only an intern now, but she is already the new star in my company.'

Starlet more like, I thought. Poor girl. I tried to smile sympathetically at Amandine but she had her eyes cast down, and seemed to be fiddling with something under the table.

Jean-Marie was smugger than ever, if that was humanly possible. Even at normal times he wore an expression that suggested he'd just shagged a Hollywood actress and found a winning lottery ticket under her pillow. Now he looked as though he'd discovered how to turn Parisian pigeon poop into gold.

He was looking good, though, I had to admit it. Slimmer than when I'd last seen him, and sleeker, with his balding pate carefully shaven, giving him a slightly menacing edge. In the past he'd just looked sleazy. Now he was dangerously so.

'How are things at VianDiffusion?' I asked, and had the malicious satisfaction of seeing him twitch. Jean-Marie had never forgiven me for pointing out that the brand name he'd come up with when he'd decided to go international had not been quite right for a food company: VD Exporters.

'We supply the meat for this diner, you know,' he said. 'And with Amandine's help, we will conquer the world.' He patted Amandine's hand again.

This time, though, with me as a spectator, Amandine didn't laugh so hard. She went through the motions, but her eyes caught mine and I got a sudden flash of 'don't think I enjoy having him do this'.

'Talking of meat, why don't we order?' she said, impressively deadpan.

'Ah yes.' Jean-Marie held up a heavily Rolexed hand and waved to the guy standing by the till. 'Kevin is the owner of the diner,' he told me. Of course, Jean-Marie wasn't going to deal with any underling.

Kevin came over. I saw immediately that he wasn't a Kevin. He was a 'Kev-EEN', a French guy with an Anglo-Celtic name, like the many Brendans ('Bren-DAN') and Dylans ('Dee-LAN') I'd met. And, like all trendy Parisian guys between about eighteen and thirty-five, he had bushy hair, a boyishly unshaven face, and the air of being unsure whether to be gay or straight.

'Bonjour, Monsieur Martin,' he gushed, shaking Jean-Marie's hand with all the gratitude of a café owner towards his meat supplier. We were introduced, and he lingered just a little when it was Amandine's turn. Not gay then.

'Alors, que prendrez-vous?' Kevin asked, pen and pad at the ready. 'Voulez-vous juste coffee and toast, ou pancakes avec bacon? Ou peut-être le total breakfast?'

I was stunned. I'd never heard French and English slapped together like that by anyone except Jake.

'Moi, je prends pancakes avec maple syrup,' Amandine said without batting an eye. 'Je n'ai pas pris de breakfast ce matin.'

I hadn't eaten anything before going out to meet Jake, so I decided to join in with the culinary Franglais.

'Deux slices de toast, s'il vous plaît,' I said, 'avec beaucoup de butter. Et scrambled eggs avec deux pieces of bacon, très well done.'

'OK.' Kevin simply wrote it all down.

Even more weirdly, Jean-Marie didn't react at all. This was the man who'd got himself elected as a local councillor on an extreme right-wing platform of obligatory *pétanque* at school, no mention of Waterloo in history books, and defence of French traditions like shooting any endangered species of bird that flew into its airspace. I expected him to insist on seeing a French-language menu but he simply ordered 'toast avec butter', adding that he had to watch his weight, 'unlike the lovely Amandine, who is naturally perfect'. He squeezed her upper arm, and again I saw her messing with something under the table. A Taser, I hoped.

When Kev-EEN had gone, Jean-Marie began to reminisce fondly about the last time we'd both discussed Anglo-French menus. Fondly for him, that is. For me, it was ripping out the stitches in a deep financial wound.

'You remember, Pool, when you got that immense, what do you call it – amende?'

'Fine,' I grunted helpfully.

'Yes, thirty thousand euros, wasn't it? Hoo!' He grimaced in badly acted pain. 'When Pool started his tea room,' he told Amandine, 'his menu had too much English with no translation. You see, on this' – he held up the diner's double-sided plastic menu – 'they are careful. They translate everything in little French letters. French letters? Isn't that something naughty?' He exploded with laughter.

'Yes, it means condoms,' Amandine said, managing to smile. 'What we girls need to protect us against careless men.'

'Oh, you are right,' Jean-Marie said, suddenly serious. 'I hope you carry them with you. Do you have some in your bag?'

Instead of Tasering him or poking a fork through the back of his hand, Amandine smiled as if her boss was being oh-so-witty. What these French office girls have to put up with, I thought.

'Pool did not translate his menu at all,' Jean-Marie went on. 'They attacked him for, what was it, "cup of tea"?'

'Yes,' I confirmed. 'They were afraid that if I didn't put "tasse de thé", French people might confuse it with "mug of sulphuric acid".'

'Thirty thousand euros for that?' Amandine looked genuinely shocked, as well she might.

'Luckily, I saved him with money,' Jean-Marie trumpeted, and paused as if he expected me to get under the table and show my gratitude. 'Pool was not very happy at first, but, what do you say in English? Every cloud has a golden shower?'

'Exactly,' I confirmed.

'Anyway,' Jean-Marie went on, 'since I have bought half of the business, we are in the position where today, we want to expand.'

This was why we had been due to meet – to discuss opening a second tea room, an idea I loved but couldn't afford.

'Is that why you wanted to meet here?' I asked him. 'To show me how to write a menu?'

'No, not at all. Well, almost not. I wanted to present

17

you to Amandine, who will work with us on the dossier.'

'Great,' I said sincerely. With two of us there, meetings with Jean-Marie might be easier. A pain shared is a pain halved, although he was also capable of doubling it.

'Yes, I hope it will be fun,' Amandine said, with just a tad too much emphasis on the hope. 'We must think what to call the second tea room. I had some ideas—'

A grumphing noise came from Jean-Marie's corner.

'We will talk about this at our next meeting,' he said. 'Today I want you to think of something different.' He lowered his voice conspiratorially. 'You know about this American businessman who decided no more olives in the airline salads?' We nodded, remembering the famous story of the guy who saved millions with this one menu change. 'He was called a genius, yes? But he was not. He did not, how do you say, think without his box?' I didn't correct him. 'The answer was not to take out the olives,' Jean-Marie went on. 'It was to cut the whole meal. No more free food on aeroplanes! That was the genius idea.' He sighed at the brilliance of it. 'Now they want passengers to stand up, and they take away the toilets, even. Soon they will take out the pilot, no?'

'Yes, and then probably the wings,' I agreed. 'So what you're suggesting, Jean-Marie, is a tea room with no seats, no toilets and presumably no tea?'

'No, no, no,' he said seriously. 'But I want you to think of this principle for our next meeting.'

Before I could ask him what the hell he was talking about, Kevin came over with the food, reciting a porridge-like mixture of English and French as he slid each plate on to the table. I tucked in, and had to admit it was good. Not as tasty or generously portioned as a real diner in real America, but definitely edible. I understood why the place was full.

'Voilà. Tout va bien?' Kevin asked.

'Très bien,' Jean-Marie answered, putting one arm around Amandine's shoulders and the other on my hand. 'Tout est parfait.'

'I have a question,' I told Kevin in English. 'Why did you call it *American's* Dream? Why not *American* Dream?'

'Ah yes.' Kevin smiled philosophically. 'We 'ave decided eet is mush more rich in signeeficance. It is American's Dream, so is it ze dream *of* an American, or *by* an American, or maybe *about* an American? Who is ze dream's subject and who ze object? And what is ze dream?'

Ask a Frenchman a silly question and you'll get a silly French answer.

'You see?' he asked me.

'Yes,' I said. 'All too clearly.' As Kevin left, I looked across at Amandine and we shared a moment of eye contact before Jean-Marie leapt in.

'By the way, Pool,' he said, 'you are searching for work, yes? And you don't want to help at the tea room?'

I nodded. There were five staff, and I didn't want to steal one of their jobs.

'Well, call this lady.' With a flourish, Jean-Marie produced a large white business card and slid it croupier-style across the table. There was a multi-barrelled name on it: Marie-Dominique Maintenon-Dechérizy, and a French government logo: the tricolour, decorated with the profile of Marianne, the symbol of the Revolution, who was looking fresh and wrinkle-free, as if the République was a frisky teenager rather than a haggard 200-year-old.

'Ministry of Culture?' I read. 'What would I do for them?'

'Call Marie-Dominique and ask. Oh.' He put a finger to his temple in a bad mime of pretending to remember something. 'And Benoît told me some interesting news.' Benoît was Jean-Marie's son. He was managing the tea room. 'Apparently he saw Alexa photographing the place.'

I dropped my fork.

'Alexa is Pool's ex-girlfriend,' Jean-Marie informed Amandine. 'She left him for . . . who was it? An Irishman? Or a Japanese lesbian? Oh no, it was both, wasn't it?'

In fact he was Irish-American and she was Cambodian, but I couldn't be bothered to argue.

'Is Benoît sure it was her?' I asked.

'Oh yes. He talked to her.'

'Why would she be taking photos of the tea room?'

'I don't know. She hasn't called you? Perhaps she is too busy with her boyfriend and girlfriend? That must take a lot of energy, no? No?' Jean-Marie gurgled suggestively towards Amandine, and suddenly I had to get out of the diner as fast as possible.

Why, I thought as I stepped outdoors into a group of loudly flirting teenagers, does every meeting with Jean-Marie leave me feeling as if I've just been minced in one of his meat machines?

III

I hardly had time to cross the street before my phone started ringing. I took a grudging look at the screen. It was a number I didn't recognise. Or was it? I pulled out the business card Jean-Marie had given me. And there was the number – the woman from the Ministry. Bloody hell, I thought, she's keen. Or maybe Jean-Marie had just told her to call me. Either way, I decided to play hard to get, and thrust the phone into my deepest pocket as I chose a narrow, car-free street and headed towards the river.

I was aiming for the île de la Cité, the macaroon-shaped island in the middle of the Seine where the city of Paris was born. It has come a very long way since it was inhabited by a small tribe of mosquito-bitten Gauls, and today it houses not only a Gothic cathedral but also surely the most impractically positioned flower market in Europe. If you want to buy an immense potted olive tree, where better to come than a market in the very centre of a city where it's impossible to park?

I've always been very fond of the Marché aux Fleurs, though, with its long glasshouses and miniature jungle of urban plants. Whenever you cross the Seine, it's always worth a detour to sniff the orange blossom, fig leaves or whatever is in season. And today I knew I was going to need several nostril-loads of perfume to get me through my ordeal.

I was on my way to the Préfecture, just opposite the flower market, to swap my UK driving licence for a French one. The changeover was compulsory, so I'd been reliably informed (by Jake), if I wanted to avoid having to retake the test in France, as he'd had to do. It had taken him months of revision for the fiendish French highway code exam ('When approaching a red light, should you (*a*) brake, (*b*) accelerate, (*c*) what's a red light?'), and three failed attempts at manoeuvring his way through Parisian traffic jams. In the end, he'd found a driving school out in a new-town suburb ringed with wide boulevards and American-style roundabouts, and taken the test with an examiner who was a 'good friend' of his driving instructor. And Jake came from a country where they drove on the right. I preferred to do the licence swap.

The only bad news, Jake had told me, was that it meant a visit to the Préfecture.

This news alone was enough to make me want to get drunk and crash a Citroën. The Préfecture was the scene of my first brush with French civil servants just after I arrived in Paris, about two years earlier. I'd been sucked into the familiar whirlpool of 'you can't get a residence permit without a recent electricity bill' and 'you can't get an electricity bill without a residence permit', and had ended up photocopying so many documents that Xerox offered me shares in the company.

At least this time I needed only my driving licence, passport, two photos (which, the official website said, had to be 'identical', as if someone might turn up with one picture of themselves and one of their dog) and a completed driving licence request form, which was available from the Préfecture. I guessed that putting the form online would have made things much too easy. Still, I reasoned, I ought to be able to ask for a form and fill it in while I waited. France is a logical country, *n'est-ce pas?*

After an energising sniff at the tangy leaves of a potted kumquat tree, I crossed the square towards the imposing, double-towered grey chateau that houses Paris's police HQ. It looked as though Napoleon had wanted a building grand enough to represent his ideal of imperial order, but had told the architect that it also had to embody the spirit of French bureaucracy: impenetrability. I joined the line of suitably gloomy people standing outside the fortified main entrance.

For the next twenty minutes I edged closer to the two security men in blue blazers who were rummaging in people's backpacks and handbags. From what I saw, the secret to smuggling a gun or bomb into Paris's central police station was to hide it right at the bottom of your bag, where the guards wouldn't bother to delve. Either that or be a reasonably attractive female. Girls with cute faces or curvy figures seemed to be beyond suspicion.

After the symbolic terrorism test, an arrow sign directed me into a room that had obviously been decorated by psychologists to be as soulless as possible. Colour scheme: pus yellow and hypothermia blue; seats arranged in two facing semi-circles so that everyone was staring at everyone else and multiplying their misery; ceiling hanging low over the scene like stormy cloud cover. Here, thirty or more stressed-out men and women were waiting, their eyes flicking from watch to phone to neon countdown sign. A red number flashed every time one of the two consultation windows was free. I took a ticket from a machine on the wall. It was number 888. Held on its side, the ticket read three times infinity, a pretty long wait even by French waiting-room standards. The neon counter was flashing 851. Brilliant, I'd have time to grow a beard.

A few people, I noticed, were going straight up to the

windows to ask a question. A Parisian attitude I'd seen before: 'You expect me to queue? *Moi?* There must be some misunderstanding.'

All of them came away frustrated, though, and were forced to sit down, staring in disbelief at their number as if it was a death sentence.

A mere twenty games of solitaire and ten or so 'guess what I'm doing' text messages later, 888 came up. I made for the glass window, trying to banish all impatience from my mind. In my experience, you only get one chance with a French civil servant. Lapse into exasperation and you're out the door for ever.

'Bonjour,' I said to the middle-aged Caribbean-looking lady sitting behind the fingerprint-smeared glass window.

'Bonjour,' she replied. So far so good. As she checked and then crumpled my 888 ticket, she looked quite friendly. This was going to be a doddle.

'Je viens changer mon permis de conduire anglais,' I told her, smiling as though in three minutes we'd both be at Saint-Michel having a celebratory cocktail.

'Ce n'est pas ici, ça,' she told me. It's not here. So much for our *kir royal*.

'Pas ici?'

'No, you have to go to your préfecture,' she said.

'Mais ici, c'est la Préfecture,' I argued.

'Oui, ici, c'est la Préfecture.'

25

By some miracle we seemed to be in agreement.

'Well, here I am.'

She groaned and gave a quick glance upwards for divine help.

'No, this is *la* Préfecture,' she said oh-so-slowly. 'You want *votre* préfecture.'

'But I live in Paris. This is my préfecture.'

'No, your local antenna is in your arrondissement. Where do you live?'

'In the Eighteenth,' I told her. I was currently subletting Jake's tiny apartment, which he'd vacated to move in with one of his girlfriends.

'OK.' She typed something into her computer, copied down an address on the back of a police-recruitment flyer and pushed it through the slit underneath her window. 'You have to go here,' she told me.

By this time, after ninety minutes in various queues and one ludicrous conversation, the exasperation was bubbling up in me like an Icelandic volcano, threatening to erupt and prevent aeroplanes landing in Paris for a good fortnight. But, unlike Iceland's mountains, I kept a lid on it.

'Could I have one of the forms?' I asked.

'Oui, oui.' She got up, walked out of her little office and came back a minute later with a small sheaf of papers. 'Voilà,' she said, stuffing them under her window. 'Bonne journée,' she wished me.

Journée? I thought. Can it really still be daylight out there?

IV

The nearest Métro station was Cité. It's on line 4, which is only gradually being upgraded. On a bad commuter morning in one of its rattling old carriages, your only chance of getting a seat is to sleep there overnight. Usually you have to stand up and take the elbows in the kidneys and the sneezes in the face. Now, though, in late morning, most Parisians were entrenched in their offices, and things were quiet. Breezy, even. At their worst, Parisian Métro passengers can make a dead salmon look cheerful, but today they'd been hit by the opposite of seasonal affective disorder. They weren't suffering from SAD. It was more a case of SOD: springtime overdose. Bright T-shirts and serene expressions were the order of the day.

No one even moaned when the lights went out and the train wrenched to a halt in mid-tunnel. There was a deafening screech from the PA followed by what sounded like a robotic alien announcing that Earth had just been conquered. It was the Métro driver, apparently keen to inform us in his loudest voice that 'kakashinafak pishiwishi gawakak'.

'Merci, vous aussi,' a lady passenger quipped, and all the people around her giggled.

27

We jerked back into motion a few minutes later and, comfortably settled in a corner seat, I filled in the driving-licence form. Despite its thickness, it wasn't that difficult. There were no trick questions asking me to name French Grand Prix winners or put Renault car models in chronological order. And I had all the necessary photocopies with me. I'd got off to a false start, but surely now I was on the home straight?

Coming out of the Métro, I checked the back of my police-recruitment poster for the address of the Police de Proximité – the local cops on the beat. There'd been a big media campaign about this idea of proximity – an attempt to mend the rift between the French police and the public by bringing law-enforcement officers closer to the people, and not just so they could throw stones at them. Strange, then, that the station was shut at eleven thirty in the morning. A metal grille blocked the door, and the barred windows were shuttered. So much for proximity.

A notice taped to the metal grille said that this station was only manned in the afternoons, and gave the address of the nearest Commissariat, ten minutes' walk away. Quite a hike, I thought, if you were being chased by muggers or had just found a suitcase full of cocaine. (Yes, Jake's area wasn't the kind of Parisian neighbourhood that gets filmed for Hollywood movies about young Americans falling in love while wearing designer clothes.)

At least the Commissariat was open – though 'open' was a relative term. In this neighbourhood, the only entrance, apart from a large gate that rolled sideways to let police cars in and out, was a thick glass door leading to yet another reinforced window. I rang the bell, gazed innocently into the security camera above the buzzer, and the door clicked open.

I stepped inside, and a policeman appeared on the other side of a glass panel, a thin, pasty-faced guy of about thirty in white shirtsleeves. I didn't think he was the kind who'd be fond of too much *proximité* with the locals.

'Bonjour,' I said into the microphone, and he looked surprised, as though people usually came here to insult him.

'Bonjour, monsieur.'

I told him why I'd come, and gave him my forms. Or rather slotted them into a metal drawer that he opened and then shut so he could retrieve the papers without giving me an opportunity to bite off one of his fingers.

'Vous êtes anglais,' he noted.

'Oui,' I confessed.

'We don't get many of you doing this. It's mainly Eastern Europeans.'

'Perhaps because it's more difficult for us to drive to France. Under the sea.'

The policeman frowned at my geological wisecrack.

'How long have you been resident in France?' he asked, perusing my forms.

'About two years.'

'More than a year?' Ominously, he stopped flicking through my forms.

'Oh, you mean non-stop?' I asked. 'Non-stop, I have only been a resident here for about six months. Before that, I was in America. Sorry, I did not understand. I'm English, you see.'

He nodded. It's a lesson you learn early with Parisian officialdom: when in doubt, play the foreign idiot. The policeman opened my form again.

'Give me your English licence,' he said, and the metal drawer clanged open. I dropped it inside, and the metal clanged shut, almost taking off my arm. 'We'll keep it while your application is processed.'

'What? How long?' I asked.

He shrugged. 'It depends. Three weeks?'

I groaned. 'Why can't I keep it? You have the photocopies.'

The only reply was another shrug.

'We will phone you when your licence is ready,' he informed me, with a tiny grin of amusement at my distress about being separated from my beloved English document. 'Bonne journée, monsieur.'

*

V

'Merde,' I told the pigeons as I walked back to Jake's flat. Instead of fluttering away, they only cooed at me, making me feel guilty about not joining in with the seasonal mood of hysterical happiness.

But I had good reason to be sulking, and not just because my driving licence had been taken into police custody. I'd been back in Paris for a few weeks now, watching all my plans get blown away like so much pollen. The mobile catering business I'd hoped to set up had never recovered from the fiasco of Jean-Marie's daughter's wedding reception down in the south of France. Though it was hardly my fault if the dinner was late. Proceedings in the kitchen had been disrupted just a tad by the attempted assassination of the star wedding guest, le Président de la République. And I couldn't really be held responsible for the subsequent outbreak of food poisoning, either – as any caterer will tell you, it is difficult to maintain food hygiene when the kitchen has been invaded by French secret servicemen demanding to test the sea bream for booby traps.

So I was cashless, which was why I'd gratefully accepted Jake's offer to squat at his place. It was a double-edged sword of an offer. Jake was a great friend of mine, and had helped me out of various catastrophes, but a homemaker he was not. Living in his apartment was a bit like having to borrow someone else's unwashed underpants. No, that's unfair. He wasn't dirty, he was just unaware of his surroundings, so that he probably didn't even notice that the saucepan on one of his two electric rings was half full of cigarette ends, floating in stagnant black water. He must have stubbed one out in the saucepan, and then subconsciously decided that that was where his half-smoked roll-ups belonged. All of which explains why it took me a whole day of scrubbing to get the place fit for someone with all five senses functioning to sleep in.

The good thing about the apartment was that it was high up, so the racket made before dawn by the binmen and street cleaners on the wide boulevard rarely woke me up. I was usually able to snooze on until the first insane drivers began hooting and revving their way to work.

I was on the top floor, the sixth, in a converted maid's room, or *chambre de bonne*. Well, I say converted, but all that had happened was that some thoughtful property speculator had slotted a dwarf shower cubicle in one corner, a toilet of sorts in another and a sink against the wall, making the remaining floor area just about big enough for a maid to curl up in. This was where the landlord had jammed an antique fold-out sofa bed that rightfully belonged in an orthopaedic torture museum. As soon as I had enough money to bribe a Parisian estate agent to consider my request to rent a decent-sized apartment, I was out of there.

After climbing the stairs, I flung open the single window in my ongoing campaign to get a few particles of oxygen into the studio to dilute Jake's Old Tobacco air freshener. Down in the street, a car driver was alternatively hooting and shouting at the whole neighbourhood in the vain hope that the guy who'd blocked him in by double parking would come back and free him. Meanwhile, undeterred by the noise, the two ladies on the second and fourth floors were tending their plants.

They were in the apartments known as *deuxième droite* and *quatrième droite*, meaning that their doors were on the right as you arrived on the second and fourth-floor landings.

Both of them had typically Parisian fake balconies – the cruel architectural trick of putting elaborate iron-work railings outside a window to give the impression that the building has *balcons*. The two middle-aged ladies had both hung their ironwork with plant pots, and today they were working away at the soil as if they were tilling a rice paddy, even though their only crop was red geraniums, the ever-present Parisian flower. A harmonious spring scene. Until, that is, the woman on the fourth floor produced a plastic watering can and began drowning her pots, sending a monsoon down on to the second-floor lady's plants (and, on this occasion, her head).

The respectable-looking woman yelled up an accusation about deliberately causing a waterfall, and got no answer, which prompted her to embark on a series of insults every bit as colourful as her geraniums. On previous days, I'd begun making a list of her favourite swear words, and today she sent me hunting for a pen with a new one: *pisseuse de chiottes de merde*, which, if I'd heard it correctly above the hooting car, meant something like shitty toilet pisser. Impressively graphic.

This barrage of insults had its usual effect of rousing the old guy below me on the fifth floor (*cinquième gauche*) from his lair. He was a recluse whose only activities in life seemed to be yelling out of his window and feeding pigeons, which regularly gathered around his window like an over-excited, feather-moulting fan club.

Sure enough, I saw his tousled grey head pop out at the fifth-floor window.

'Enculé!' he shouted, a crude French term for a recipient of sodomy. 'Pétasse!', which could be translated as farting woman. 'Va chier!' Literally, go and shit – a more solid version of the English 'piss off'.

Luckily, Jake had told me how to curtail his outbursts.

As 'Enculé!', 'Pétasse!' and 'Va chier!' continued to ring out from below, I leant over my window ledge and shouted, 'Connard!', a word meaning something like male vaginal idiot.

And miraculously, it always put a stop to the *enculés*, although on this occasion it also seemed to convince the driver doing the hooting down in the street to give up and find an alternative solution to his double-parking problem.

All of which made me feel a twinge of conscience about not taking the call from the Ministry of Culture woman earlier. So much abuse was being hurled about, and I'd refused a polite conversation about finding me work.

I dug out my phone and hit callback.

'Allô?' The reply was instant, female and very loud.

'Bonjour,' I said. 'J'aimerais parler avec . . .' Damn, what was the woman's name? Anne-Valérie something, or Jeanne-Bernadette maybe.

'Avec qui?' the voice barked at me.

I would have loved to answer but I had my jacket between my teeth and was tugging at the pocket in an attempt to extract her business card.

'C'est Pol Wess?' It sounded like an accusation.

I spat out the jacket and said yes. My accent must have given me away.

'Bonjour, c'est Marie-Dominique Maintenon-Dechérizy.' Of course, I thought. How could I have forgotten that?

'Bonjour, you called me?' I said in my shaky French. 'Je n'ai pas . . .' But I didn't know how to lie and say I'd missed her call. 'Er, you called and I didn't answer.' A bit blunt, but at least it had the merit of being true.

She asked me very slowly whether I had a few minutes to talk.

'Bien sûr,' I assured her, my French improving with every sentence.

'Excellent. What has Jean-Marie already told you about me?' she asked.

I was just preparing a speech about her being someone important at the Ministère de la Culture when the old guy on the fifth floor beat me to it.

'Pétasse!' he yelled.

'Pardon?' Marie-Dominique sounded surprised.

'Sorry,' I apologised, trying to work out how to explain that my neighbours were suffering from a sort of communal Tourette's.

'Enculé!' came the voice from outside.

'Monsieur Wess?'

'Va chier!'

'Uh?'

'One moment,' I told Marie-Dominique, and leant outside. 'Connard!' I shouted, and was relieved to see the tortoise-like head disappear indoors.

'Tout va bien?' Marie-Dominique asked me, clearly regretting that I'd returned her call.

'C'est pas moi,' I improvised. 'Well, the connard, c'est moi, but the enculé and the pétasse, c'est pas moi.'

'Who was it, then?' she demanded.

'L'homme au cinquième. Il est crazy.'

Fortunately for me, mad-neighbour syndrome was common enough in Paris for her to forgive me and suggest that we might be able to have a more satisfactory conversation if I came to her office.

'Très bien,' I said. With any luck, face to face she wouldn't need to yell quite so loudly. We agreed to meet the next day, and, just out of curiosity, I had a go at asking what kind of work she had on offer.

She said I'd see, but that from what Jean-Marie had told her about me, it was 'parfait pour vous'. She hooted a laugh.

'Ah, did Jean-Marie say that I am un peu excentrique?' I asked. It's an English stereotype that reassures the French. 'Is that how you recognised me?'

'No. Your number showed up on my phone.'

'Oh yes, of course.' What a dickhead. How to screw up a job interview in one easy lesson. We said 'au revoir' and I went over to the window.

'Connard!' I shouted at myself. 'Enculé!'

It felt surprisingly good.

Deux

'Mon père était fonctionnaire et ma mère ne travaillait pas non plus.'
My father was a civil servant, and my mother didn't work, either.

Coluche, French comedian, who died in 1986 in a
motorbike accident. Or so they say . . .

I

NEXT MORNING, I got a call from Jake. He told me that he'd had no luck declaiming his birthday poem into the agent's intercom the previous day. Apparently, it had gone dead after only two or three lines – no doubt, I thought, when she ripped her receiver out of the wall socket.

Jake had decided to 'take his day', he told me, meaning he was bunking off work. He earned his baguette crust teaching English of sorts to French adults, which I couldn't help thinking was a bit like taking lessons from a drunk in walking straight.

'I think I've found what you're researching,' he said.

'I'm not doing any research,' I replied.

'No,' Jake said, 'I mean, what you're – you know – looking after, for, at.' He often thought it best to hedge his bets with English verbs.

'You've found what I'm looking for?' Did he mean a job, a decent apartment, a life?

'Yeah, man, I'm in le Marais taking a coffee with some belles filles.'

'But I thought you were living with that girl, what is she, Libyan? Syrian?' His latest girlfriend belonged to a new motherlode of female company that Jake had recently stumbled upon: refugees arriving in Paris from troubled Middle Eastern and North African countries.

'Yemeni,' he said.

'You told me just the other day you were crazy about her.'

'I'm not seeing her any more,' he said.

'You're moving out of her apartment? You mean I have to find somewhere else to live?' Against all expectations, my life had just got even more complicated.

'No, not yet. It's her quitting the apartment.'

'She's leaving her own apartment? Why?'

'She received a letter. She is in danger to be deportée. She is an exile but they say she's an illegal immigrant. France is the merde for them, man. Luckily for me, she paid six months' rent en avance. Anyway, I'm with some belles filles now, and one of them would be perfect for you.'

'Why?'

'She's got a massive apartment. Paid by her parents, man. *No rent*.' For Jake, those two syllables – no rent – were the equivalent of most people's *je t'aime*. They were the keys (literally) to a meaningful relationship with him.

'So why don't you go after her?' I asked. 'For when your Yemeni lease runs out.'

'I did, man. I even wroten her a poem. A sexy one.'

'And she didn't like it?' I tried to conjure up some disbelief.

'She told me it was too powerful for her. But you, Paul,' he went on, 'you like these sexually repressed girls, n'est-ce pas? Anyway, she's from Nouvelle Zealand and she's got this totalement fascinating project – you must come and check it out. Like, maintenant.'

With a growing sense that the day was getting way too exhausting for me already, I agreed to let him text me the address.

II

You have to love the Marais. Not necessarily the heart of it, which is overrun by tourists dashing from the BHV department store to the place des Vosges, but the northern part, where the Marais's narrow medieval streets become dark and peaceful, occasionally almost shabby. There are plenty of art galleries and boutiques to remind you that you're not in a deprived area, but no crowds or frustrated drivers to stop you ambling around, wishing you could afford to live in that chateau-like *hôtel particulier*, this cobbled courtyard or that rooftop medieval penthouse.

There's even a cool shopping street that pretends to be part of old Paris, and succeeds. The rue de Bretagne has real *boulangeries*, a *charcuterie* and even a cheese shop – alongside the inevitable estate agents, of course.

And it was just off the rue de Bretagne that I found Jake, smoking one of his droopy roll-ups. He was standing on a pavement so narrow it was more of a kerb than a sidewalk, chatting to a tall, elegant woman with her back to me. Not that I was complaining – it was a very picturesque back. She was dressed in the trendy *Parisienne*'s eternal uniform of short leather jacket (in this case, blood-red) and tight jeans, with bare ankles tapering into spectacularly high heels.

'Hey, Paul!' Jake waved his roll-up, scattering flakes of tobacco in the air, and the woman turned towards me. Her front view was even better. She was very slim, and wore no make-up except scarlet lipstick and an alluring dash of Cleopatra eye shadow. Her dark, curving eyebrows made her look as though she was permanently amused by life. A sort of cheerful existentialist – a very rare thing.

We were introduced with the obligatory kiss on each cheek, and I was glad that, despite my gloomy mood, I'd taken the trouble to put on clean jeans and a hip shirt: a leafy pink Paul Smith number that looked, in a subtle way, as if it was about to burst into blossom.

We exchanged names – hers was Marsha – and not for the first time I wondered how Jake got to meet these girls. Today, he was relatively well dressed (by his standards), in chinos and a white shirt that looked as though they'd just come through a car wash, but he was puffing on a cigarette that smelled as though it was made out of camel dung. I wondered if it hadn't been given to him as a joke by his departing Yemeni girlfriend.

'Can you point your stink bomb somewhere else?' I begged him as he tried to grab me for a Parisian man-kiss.

'Yeah,' Marsha said, 'we head to git him out of the shap,' or something like that. Of course – Jake had said she was from New Zealand.

'Is this your shop?' I asked her. If so, I was disappointed. The narrow shop window was almost empty, as all the trendiest windows have to be, and featured just three handbags of various sizes, from cigarettes-and-credit-card-only to yes-I-have-to-carry-Evian-with-me, all of them woven in colourful tartan wool. There were handwritten price labels beside each one, and frankly, given the choice, I'd have preferred to use the money as the down payment on a Marais apartment.

So I was relieved to hear her say no, it wasn't her shop, and offer to take me indoors and introduce me to Mitzi and Connie, the owners.

I let Marsha go in first, of course, and took the opportunity to give Jake the thumbs-up.

'How did you meet her?' I whispered.

'At the cultural centre of Bolivia.' A typical Jake answer.

There were no customers inside the shop, which was hardly surprising given the cost of the merchandise, and the long, narrow space was dominated by wall-hangings, blankets and clothes made of multicoloured tartans. The bright fabric contrasted with the deep brown of the gnarled wooden beams running along the ceiling. It all looked very classy, and like everything classy in Paris, there was a whiff of the nineteenth century about it.

Two thirty-something women were standing over a table, leafing through a book of cloth samples. They looked like twins who'd been born on different continents. Same height, same long black hair, one of them pale and Asian, the other a mellow South American. They were short, wearing jeans with jackets made out of the pink-and-yellow tartan of one of Scotland's more fashion-conscious clans.

Mitzi, it turned out, was the Asian – I'd have to ask

Jake what nationality exactly. Laotian, knowing him, or from one of those Central Asian republics I can never spell. Connie, short for Concepción, was Bolivian. They gave me mwa-mwa kisses, barely brushing my cheek, and explained that they ran a fabric business called Tissus de Vérité, designing patterns, selling them to fashion houses and making their own garments and handbags.

'What does the name mean?' I asked.

'Oh, it's a play on words.' Mitzi giggled. I'd guessed that already – practically every shop name in Paris is a pun.

'On what?'

'Oh come on, Paul,' Jake groaned. 'It's evident, man. Tissue of verities.'

'Right, thanks, Jake, but what does it *mean*?'

Neither Mitzi nor Connie spoke good enough English to enlighten me, so Marsha stepped in.

'Tissu de mensonges is a web of lies. And tissu is fabric. So tissus de vérité are like patchworks of truth.'

'Good one,' I congratulated them, and explained that I too was the part-owner of a pun, the My Tea Is Rich tea room. I added that I was going to have to think up a second tea-related play on words if Jean-Marie and I opened up a new café.

'Do you want to open it here?' Connie asked. 'We're leaving next week.'

This took me by surprise, but I instantly saw that it

might be a great idea. I'd already seen a little eatery further down the street: an oriental-themed sandwich place called Bread and Buddha. Yet another pun, and an English one at that. A bit of competition wouldn't be a bad thing, either. People often herd together in search of food, and if the street was getting a reputation for eateries, so much the better.

'Hey, no!' Marsha interrupted my reverie. 'Girls!'

The three of them began laughing, and I realised I'd been the victim of a female joke.

'*I'm* taking over this place,' Marsha explained. 'Opening a bookshop.'

'Yeah,' Jake butted in. 'And she will *publish* books, too. *Poems.*'

Suddenly I got the picture. Not only did Marsha have a free apartment, she might also publish him. Double jackpot. Or Jakepot.

'Not just poems,' Marsha corrected him. 'Everything. It's easy with e-books.'

'Is it a good spot for a bookshop?' I asked. 'Do people in this neighbourhood read anything except menus and price tags?'

'I'll need to bring them in,' she said. 'I'll have a drop-in café area down here, and the girls' workshop upstairs will make a great event space.'

'For *readings*,' Jake stressed.

'Yeah, starting with my launch party,' Marsha said.

'Right, the party de *launch*,' Jake repeated, nodding meaningfully at me.

Now I got it. I was meant to convince Marsha that Jake was the perfect headliner for her inaugural event. It was going to be tough. After all, she'd already seen one of his poems, so she knew they were capable of taking the fizz out of the finest bubbly.

I asked her why Mitzi and Connie were giving up the premises. 'Prices too high?' I pointed to a minute handbag and its three-figure price tag.

'No way,' she said, almost choking with incredulity. 'You kidding? They're opening a much bigger place in the Eighth. Going mainstream, big time. You think that's a lot for a designer bag?' She looked at me as though I was the kind of guy who'd take a girl out and then order a single glass of champagne to share.

'Don't get me wrong,' I hastened to say. 'I don't mind spending money. This shirt cost a ridiculous amount for a piece of printed cotton. But it's a shirt, not a bag. A bag is just a thing for carrying stuff around. I've got a four-wheeled suitcase that can perform pirouettes and survive getting beaten up by baggage handlers, but it only cost me half the price of the smallest bag in this shop. I've never understood why a handbag, any handbag, can be worth more than, say, fifty quid.'

When Marsha had recovered from her heart attack, she shook her head sadly at me.

'Sorry, Paul. It's like God. You either believe or you don't.'

'What if you're agnostic?'

'You buy one for your girlfriend who believes.'

Her eyebrows arched at me, and I knew that this was a cue to jump in with the old 'well, actually I haven't got a girlfriend at the moment' line. But I didn't want to play that game. Not yet, anyway. Truth be told, I was a bit scared of her. I've never had much luck with trendies. In my experience, they always try to doll you up, and then get angry when you revert to sloppy jeans and trainers.

'So you're planning to hold poetry readings?' I said.

'Well, I'd have to vet the poets first, of course.' She grimaced over towards Jake, who was chatting with Connie and Mitzi, but keeping one eye on me.

'Very wise,' I agreed, and we shared a chuckle.

'Listen, why don't we meet up for a drink sometime, talk a bit more about poetry?' she said, doing her raised-eyebrow trick again.

I surprised myself by hesitating. There was something of the rollercoaster about her. But I could see Jake watching me, as if he sensed what was going on. And I thought she'd be fun to go out with, even if it would mean raiding my already depleted funds to buy a second trendy shirt.

'Great, let's do the number-exchanging ceremony,' I said, miming two phones going head-to-head. We went over to the cash desk, where Marsha had left her own tartan handbag, and she was fishing inside for her phone when Jake suddenly grabbed my arm.

'Paul,' he hissed, dragging me towards the shop door. I signalled to Marsha that I wasn't leaving willingly and asked Jake what he thought he was doing, but he just kept on tugging until we were both outside on the pavement.

'Look.' He pointed along the shady street towards the bright sunlight in the rue de Bretagne.

The receding silhouette was an unmistakable sight, to give her wide hips swaying purposefully, her blonde head held high, gazing out at the world as if she was intrigued by every detail. She was wearing a loose skirt and flip-flops, but somehow looked just as classy as the girls in high heels. Sexy without even trying.

'It's her, n'est-ce pas?' Jake asked.

'I don't know,' I lied. 'What would she be doing here?'

'I saw her passing the shop. She stopped and made a photo.'

'She took a photo? Why?'

'Of you, maybe,' he said.

'No way. Why would she do that?'

'Who's the girl?' Marsha asked, arriving beside me.

'Alexa,' Jake said. 'His ex.'

'You've got a stalker ex-girlfriend, huh? Maybe we shouldn't go out for that drink.'

'Drink?' Jake asked, always ready to let someone buy him one.

'She's not a stalker,' I said, hoping this was true. 'She's a photographer. I guess she just liked the look of the shop window.'

'Well, if she's not going to murder us all, why don't we go and get a coffee, or something stronger?' Marsha suggested.

'Yeah, I'll see if Mitzi and Connie can come,' Jake said, dashing indoors.

I looked at my watch. It was nearly midday.

'Thanks, but I've got some stuff I need to do,' I told Marsha.

'So you're going to stalk *her?*' Her eyebrows gave me another of their sardonic looks.

'No, I'm headed the other way.' I pointed along the street away from the rue de Bretagne, even though I ought to have followed Alexa to get to the nearest Métro. 'I'll call you about that drink, OK? Soon?'

I said my goodbyes, leaving a shell-shocked Jake to escort Connie, Mitzi and Marsha along the road towards the café. Refusing a chance to be in female company was as inconceivable to Jake as ballet dancing is to a walrus. There just wasn't space for the notion in his head.

In this case, I kind of agreed with him. Was I really saying no to a sexy, witty woman who wanted to go and sit on a sunny café terrace with me? What better way to get in tune with springtime? And yet here I was, walking in the opposite direction, deeper into the shade of a narrow side street.

Something was seriously wrong with me. Something to do with Alexa. First she'd turned up at the tea room, and now here. Was she really stalking me?

And if not, did I wish she would?

III

The zoo at the Jardin des Plantes is famous for having once been a restaurant. Or rather a butcher's shop. It was first opened during the Revolution so that ordinary people could admire animals confiscated from private menageries. And this 'animals for the people' idea was taken a stage further during the uprising of 1871, when starving Parisians fed themselves on bear ribs and stuffed giraffe necks. Which, I guessed, explained the absence of big game when I went there once with Alexa. Alll I saw in the old animal houses, some of them designed by Napoleon, were small, mainly endangered species.

Not that I cared. I never enjoyed staring at caged lions and elephants, even as a kid. I always preferred those petting zoos where they let youngsters torture non-violent animals by hugging them, pulling their ears and generally doing things that would make a monkey bite your face off. Lambs would get shampooed with ice cream, rabbits thrown about like bowling balls and koalas almost suffocated with affection.

When I went to the Jardin des Plantes, though, things were slightly more modern, and the koalas were in a look-but-don't-touch enclosure. You could get close up and go 'aaahh' right in a koala's furry face, but you weren't allowed to so much as reach out a hand towards them. And one of the visiting toddlers couldn't take it. He was stamping his feet and wailing with frustration.

And the funny thing was that the Parisian koalas seemed to know what was going on. They sat on their wooden perches, gazing placidly out at their audience, apparently knowing full well that their only duty in life was to look cute and munch eucalyptus leaves. They had no predators and free food for life.

I didn't see that self-satisfied look again until the first time I came face to face with a French civil servant. It was the woman who dealt with my residence permit. Or rather, didn't deal with it. The koala-like motionlessness was there, as was the indifference to my wailing that I needed a *carte de séjour*. In a sense, the eucalyptus leaves had been there too, in that the lady *fonctionnaire* had seemed wholly occupied with the task of digesting her lunch. But the most remarkable thing of all about French civil servants was their look of sheer untouchability. 'Do what you want, say what you want,' their attitude said, 'you can't touch me.' The only thing missing was the cuddliness.

And now, for the third time in two days, I was about to throw myself on their mercy. First the Préfecture, then the police station, and now the Ministry of Culture. And this time I was due to meet a whole herd of them, or whatever you call a collection of koala bears. A smug, maybe.

I walked across town from the Marais, past the huge building site where the Les Halles neighbourhood was being torn down for the second time in fifty years: at the end of the 1960s they'd got rid of the beautiful old market halls, and now they were freeing the city of the 1970s eyesore that had been put up in their place. I wondered why they didn't just rebuild some vintage market halls. Everyone loves to think they're shopping at a market, even if it's air-conditioned and full of escalators.

I stopped in a small corner café for a beer and a cheese baguette. I even killed some time telling the waiter I'd like 'des cornichons en plus, s'il vous plaît' – extra gherkins, to liven up the slightly dull Gruyère cheese – but I still arrived much too early for my meeting. It was about half past one, and the appointment wasn't till two, so I went for a wander around the neighbourhood.

It was a beautiful place to wander, because the Ministry is right next to the Palais-Royal. Back in

Napoleon's day, the shady arcades running along either side of the gardens were where you came to pick up a prostitute. I knew this because Alexa had told me so, while reminiscing about how she'd once had sneaky sex up against one of the columns. Those were the days, when I had a French girlfriend who loved to tell me all about her horny exes.

It was also Alexa who first pointed out the Ministry of Culture to me. She had clambered up on one of its golden-spiked entrance gates and pretended to hacksaw through the black iron bars protecting its windows. She said they were there to guard French culture against invasion by foreign influences and to stop it escaping out into the streets where it might get polluted by non-intellectuals. The façade of the Ministry looked, she said, like a miniature Buckingham Palace, with the kind of balcony where royals gather to wave to the crowds. She imagined snooty French artists and writers gathering up there to look down on the philistine masses below. But she then ruined her speech by admitting that she'd love to be standing up there one day. Deep down, I realised, it was every French artist's dream to be misunderstood by the general public.

I remembered all this as I strolled around the outside of the building, stopping to dab a fingerprint on the brightly polished brass plaque that said 'Ministère de la Culture et de la Communication'.

I wandered into the inner courtyard and came face to face with one of the ugliest things I'd ever seen in Paris. I've got nothing against mixing the old and the new – the glass pyramid at the Louvre is spectacular, for example, as if the pharaohs in the museum had climbed out of their sarcophagi and built themselves a shiny new palace. But the Ministry of Culture's inner courtyard was a joke.

Here was a classical building, decorated with sculpted stone window frames, facing the gushing classical fountain and immaculately pruned trees of the Palais-Royal gardens, but in the centre of it all, dominating the otherwise timeless scene, was a courtyard full of black-and-white-striped columns, looking like fossilised toothpaste or the truncated remains of a cheap Greek temple. Some of the columns were a useful size – picnic-seat level or stand-on-that-and-I'll-take-your-photo height, but others were little more than pointless obstacles. As a work of art it was (in my humble, non-intellectual opinion) as exciting as a collection of empty tin cans, and spoiled the view just as badly.

By now it was one forty-five, so I thought I might as well go into the Ministry and see if they had a coffee machine.

'Bonjour,' I said to the doorman, who was slouching beneath a pair of miniature French flags, 'I have an appointment with . . .' Again I had to fish in my pocket for the visiting card. 'Marie-Dominique Maintenon-

Dechérizy.' When was I going to learn the bloody name by heart?

The doorman waved me through a smoothly revolving door into a small reception area dominated by an immense TV screen, which was showing silent footage of some kind of video art. A woman with a rock-solid blonde hairdo and an absurdly tight skirt suit was waving her arms around in front of a map of France. Dark clouds were streaming south across the Channel. Charming, I thought. It was obviously a message about English-speaking culture invading France. But then the credits came up, and I realised my mistake. It was the TV weather forecast with the sound turned down. Of course – the Ministry was also in charge of state television.

I went over to the receptionist's desk and told the woman – from memory, at last – why I was there.

'She won't be back till two,' the woman told me. 'Sit down and I'm sure you'll see her passing through.'

'I don't know what she looks like.'

'Then she'll see you.'

'She doesn't know what I look like,' I said, battling bravely with all this grammar.

The receptionist grimaced. 'I can't phone and tell her you're here because there will be no one in her office before two. Everyone's on lunch break.' Clearly I was screwing up the historic system of doing nothing except eat between twelve thirty and two. 'Why don't you go up to the second floor, where Marie-Dominique's office is, and wait outside her door till she comes back? Number 212.'

'Merci,' I said, and she pointed me through a small doorway towards the lifts and the stairs.

The staircase was in a wide, open hallway, like posh Paris apartment buildings I'd been in. Marble floor, polished stone steps, a swooping brass handrail leading to the upper floors. It struck me as all very bare for a ministry. There were no paintings on the walls, no sculptures leaping out from alcoves. It was chic and stylish but dull – not a great advert for French culture, I thought as I ambled along the corridor past large, open-plan offices equipped with rows of computer screens and identical anglepoise lamps. Again, most of the walls were strangely bare. Only one section of the office was colourful, a corner patchworked with photos of singers I didn't recognise, alongside a big poster announcing that it was '*L'Année de la Culture Francophone en France*' or 'The year of French-language culture in France'. A slightly bizarre notion, I thought, a bit like a special Pizza Week in Naples. But then I saw what they meant. The illustration was a burger bun filled with a Stars-and-Stripes pat of meat, crossed out by a large tricolour X. It was their old bugbear, the invasion of France by American culture. Alexa had been right – that spiked gate *was* intended to impale intruders.

With one hand clasping my passport in case I was accused of being American, I walked on and found a coffee machine surrounded by noticeboards. I bought myself an absurdly cheap espresso and tried to read the notices. On the main corkboard there was an official-looking announcement, entitled '*Restructuration des industries culturelles et théâtrales*', featuring a photo of a dozen or so grim-looking people in a grandly decorated meeting room. Their names were listed below the picture, each one followed by a long capital letter abbreviation, along the lines of 'Jean-Paul Le West, ADCAP, BADCAP, MADCAP'. These were their qualifications, I supposed. In any case, thanks to the abbreviations, the list of names was almost as long as the text explaining the budget-restructuring plan. I had a go at reading it, but gave up after the first sentence, which came out as something like, 'The central question for the working group is this: is culture part of the general economy, or is the economy part of our culture?' You needed at least a MADCAP to work that one out.

I had a look at the other official notices. One was an apartment to rent near Montpellier ('three rooms and barbecue'), another a country house for sale in Corrèze ('includes small tractor'), and the third an aged-looking card for a local Vietnamese restaurant.

On either side of the coffee machine were four more noticeboards in locked glass frames. Each one belonged to a trade union, and they all had a single, almost identical notice pinned up: an A4 sheet with each union's logo and a text opening with one word in red capital letters – 'NON!' A pretty clear message, I thought.

'We haven't given you a job yet.'

A female voice made me turn round to what appeared at first to be an empty corridor. Then, angling my neck downwards, I saw a tiny woman smiling up at me. Well, I exaggerate slightly, but she couldn't have been more than five feet tall, though she had a booming voice that sounded at least a yard taller.

'Bonjour, pardon?' I stuttered.

'You are choosing your union already?' she asked, and laughed deafeningly to show me that it was a joke. 'Marie-Dominique Maintenon-Dechérizy,' she introduced herself. 'Monsieur Wess?'

We shook hands and she explained to me, still in a voice that made the coffee machine rattle, that the union noticeboards had to be behind glass to prevent rival groups graffitiing each other.

'What are they saying "non" to?' I asked.

'Everything,' she boomed. 'As always. Come to my office.' It wasn't a command I would have dared to say 'non' to.

I followed her short, striding frame along the corridor, and wondered how old she was. Her hair was boyish and black, but could have been dyed, her face was

Mediterranean and ageless, and her stocky body was encased in a beige dress and black cardigan that could have been designed anytime since about 1965. So she was somewhere between thirty and sixty, then.

'Sit down.'

I sat, in one of four battered but tastefully designed chairs ringing a circular table. Marie-Dominique was obviously a lady of influence, because amidst all these open spaces, she had a glass-walled office of her own with a small meeting area.

'As you probably know,' she said in a voice that made me wonder whether she hadn't been walled in for the good of her colleagues, 'I direct the Bureau of Cultural Interventions within the Department of Artistic Development, which is of course attached to the Direction of Artistic Creation.'

I nodded, as if I probably did know.

'Jean-Marie tells me that you did the catering for his daughter's wedding. In fact it was also my cousin's son's wedding. He was the groom,' she added, in case I wasn't following. 'I thought the dinner was excellent, under the circumstances. I personally got food poisoning and spent two days in bed, but I realise that wasn't entirely your fault.'

I opened my mouth to agree, but she was off again.

'What I liked was your sensibility in choosing the ingredients. You are clearly a locavore.'

'I am?'

'It means a person who eats things that are produced in the region. Local, locavore,' she stressed.

'Ah, yes,' I said. 'I am very interested in—'

'That is the philosophy we want for our new project. Look.'

She thrust a folder at me, entitled '*Résidence d'Artistes Guy Étalon*'. It featured a computer mock-up of a gleaming white building that looked like a renovated monastery. There was also a densely typed report, ten or more pages long. All I could make of the text was a blur of grey.

'You know Étalon?' she asked me. 'No? A French performance artist, very avant-garde. Difficult but great. He was murdered by the Americans. Now, our project,' she went on matter-of-factly, 'is a residence in Brittany for up to forty artists, with studios, apartments and, of course, a restaurant where they can meet to exchange ideas. With a set menu five days a week. They will go home or eat elsewhere at the weekend. What do you think?'

'Well . . .' I was still a little shell-shocked, and not only because of the volume of her voice.

'Jean-Marie says that you are capable of visiting the local producers and negotiating prices.'

This was all very sudden, I thought. Why hadn't he warned me?

'If you think it is feasible, we can add your name to the working group,' she said.

She motioned to me to turn to a long list of names like the one I'd seen on the noticeboard. It was headed up by Marie-Dominique and her slab of initials, which included a BIC, a DADA and a DICA, whatever they were. She was presiding over a veritable printer's catalogue of her colleagues' capital letters. My own humble BA was going to look pretty pathetic down at the bottom.

'What I suggest is that you come to our next working-group meeting, and then visit the site in Brittany. What do you think?'

'Well . . .' I did have some questions about maybe getting paid for this, and what she might want me to do when I visited the 'site', but I didn't get a chance to ask them, because Marie-Dominique stood up and smiled as if she was going to bite my legs if I stayed any longer.

'Call me tomorrow to confirm that you're interested?' she commanded, shaking my hand. 'Or maybe it's best to email. In case your mad neighbours decide to join in the conversation.' She boomed a laugh at me and almost shoved me down the stairs. Meeting over.

As I went down, in something of a daze, I met several of her colleagues, all of them slightly posher versions of the people I used to work with in Jean-Marie's offices – a proliferation of light jumpers, pastel shirts and comfortable trousers. The women's necklaces were a bit heavier, there were more designer glasses, and a few of the men were wearing smooth suits and heeltap shoes. Not what I expected from civil servants, but these Ministry workers were obviously upper-crust koalas, at the top of the tree. All of them gave me a friendly 'bonjour' as though I was already one of the team or a colleague they couldn't remember meeting.

Outside the revolving door, four slightly less chic men were distributing leaflets to the post-lunch rush. When I emerged, going in the opposite direction to the returning workers, one of the men handed me a sheet of paper. It bore the four logos of the unions and their big red 'Non!' I wondered if it wasn't a message directed at me.

IV

Walking back through the Palais-Royal gardens reminded me yet again of Alexa, and I put in a call to Benoît, Jean-Marie's son, who'd supposedly seen her taking photos of the tea room.

The midday lunch rush was over, he told me, though I could still hear plenty of voices in the background. So business was still healthy, which was good news. That is, 50 per cent of it was good news for me personally, after salary bills, taxes, rent and various other outgoings. Not that I was raiding the tea room's bank account. It was my rainy-day fund. And if we were going to open another tea room, the rainy day would be coming pretty soon. All of which explained why I needed a job to have a chance of living anywhere decent.

'Yes, Alexa was photographing the façade,' Benoît said. 'First from across the road, then she came over and took some shots of the menu hanging up outside. That's when I went to say hello.'

'She was taking photos of the menu? What for?'

'For a website, she said.'

'What sort of website?'

'Don't know,' he said. Or rather, 'shaypa', the French way of pronouncing 'je ne sais pas' when they really don't care. This was typical Benoît. He was a bright guy when it came to managing the tea room, but he had the investigative instincts of a smoked haddock.

'What do you think of Papa's idea for this place?' he asked me.

I flinched. 'What idea?' Most of Jean-Marie's ideas made my head feel as though it had been set in concrete.

'My Diner is Rich,' Benoît said.

'Uh?'

'You know, turning the tea room into an American diner. Do you think it's a good idea?'

So that was it. The meeting to eat bacon and pancakes. The speech about thinking radically and getting rid of more than the olives. I'd literally crawled through wet paint and plaster to set up the tea room, and now he wanted to undo all my hard work? It occurred to me that maybe he was the one who had asked Alexa to take the photos and record the tea room for posterity. That bastard Jean-Marie – did he never stop trying to screw people, literally and metaphorically?

'Where is he, do you know?' I demanded.

'Pff.' This was another French sound indicating ignorance.

I rang off and called Jean-Marie, thinking how absurd it was for this *merde* to be happening in such a glorious garden. The Palais-Royal fountain was spurting out shafts of glinting sunlight, the birds were twittering, and tourists were trying to cram the whole scene into one perfect photo of Paris.

'Bonjour,' Jean-Marie said, before asking me to call him back 'après le bip'.

I speed-dialled his office.

'Le bureau de Jean-Marie Martin,' a croaky voice announced. Damn, I thought, he's got a new PA. His old secretary, Christine, had been a chum of mine. But now she had been replaced by someone older and more scary-sounding. Jean-Marie's wife had probably helped with the recruiting.

'Is Jean-Marie there?' I asked.

'Monsieur Martin is absent,' the PA replied, an iceberg sinking my over-familiar approach.

'I'm his *associé*, Paul West,' I told her. *Associé* is a nice

French word for business partner, vague enough to suggest dealings that PAs might do better not to ask about.

'Do you want me to pass on a message?' she offered, unimpressed.

'Yes, could you tell him he's a double-dealing shit and that he can blow his olives out of his arse and into his free refill of diner coffee,' was what I'd like to have said, but my French just wasn't good enough.

'Non, merci,' I told her.

Perhaps it was best to come at him when he least expected it.

V

Back in Jake's building, I found my mad neighbour loitering outside the door to his apartment. He was quivering with anger.

'Bonjour,' I said, but he wouldn't let me past.

'You piss on my head,' he said. *Vous me pissez sur la tête.* That was a new one, I thought, I'd have to write it down.

'Merci,' I told him. 'Bonne journée.'

'You think I'm mad?' he hissed.

Yes, as a schizophrenic hatter on acid, would have been the sincere answer, but I assured him that of course I didn't.

'Do you water your plants through my ceiling?' he

demanded, pointing to his head, which was, I now noticed, looking rather damp.

'No, I don't have any plants,' I said.

'So why is water coming through my ceiling? From *your* apartment?'

'Oh merde.' I ran up the stairs and saw a small lake forming outside Jake's door, slowly darkening the tiles of the corridor like the incoming tide on a Brittany beach.

'Chiottes de merde,' my neighbour said. 'Putain de chiottes de merde.'

I thought he was just having another outbreak of Tourette's but when I got indoors I saw that he was right. It was the *chiotte* – the toilet – that was leaking. It wasn't a real toilet. It was a horrific contraption that I'd never seen before I came to live in France: a *sani-broyeur*, a toilet bowl attached to a grinder that you can hook up to the smallest outflow pipe, so that (in theory) anyone can fit a loo in their converted attic, several metres away from the nearest toilet downpipe. It was an unnerving machine at the best of times. Every time I flushed, the wheels inside the white grinding box whirred, and the tiny waste-water pipe, originally designed to carry off the dainty trickles from a maid's sink, whistled like a whale's blowhole. At the best of times, it seemed about to explode. Now it had decided to spring a spontaneous leak.

'Shut the water off,' my neighbour barked, the first rational words he'd ever spoken in my presence.

I found a tap just inside the front door and twisted it until the flood began to ease.

For the first time I understood the only sign of organisation in Jake's life – the *Urgences Plomberie* card pinned to the wall above the toilet.

I called the number, signalling to my neighbour that he wasn't really needed any more, especially as all he seemed to be doing was tread the water around the apartment into all the corners it hadn't reached under its own power.

'Bonjour,' a jolly voice said, and went on to explain why it was so pleased with life – this call was costing me thirty-four cents a minute, or even more if I was calling from a mobile, which I was. I hit the hash key to agree to get fleeced still further.

'Bonjour,' an even jollier female voice said, and went on to inform me that a callout was going to cost me a minimum of a hundred euros, payable in advance by credit card.

'But you don't know my problem,' I protested.

'Is it a plumbing problem?' the woman asked.

'Yes, that's why I'm calling *Urgences Plomberie.*'

The subsequent silence cost me at least ten cents.

'And you want a plumber to come to your domicile?'

'Yes,' I confirmed.

'Then it's a hundred euros, payable in advance by credit card.'

I got out my plastic and paid.

'Merci,' she thanked me. 'Now what sort of problem is it?'

'Sani-broyeur,' I said, and I heard her wince.

'Blockage or leakage?' She sounded like a doctor with no bedside manner.

'Leakage,' I said.

She took the address and the door codes.

'When will he come?' I asked, looking at my watch. It was just after four.

'Between six and ten,' she said. 'Please stay at the address. If we have to reschedule an appointment, you pay the hundred euros again.'

What kind of 'urgency' was a six-hour wait? I wondered as I used a couple of towels to slop away the flood. Certainly not a hundred euros' worth.

In fact, if you took into account a pizza delivery and three phone calls to ask where the hell the plumber had got to, it must have cost me about 50 per cent extra by the time he arrived, ten seconds after my pizza, at half past ten.

He was North African, a businesslike family-man type who explained that he'd just spent more than an hour unblocking a woman's pipes. He said this with no double entendre at all, shaking his head and repeating 'coffee and hair, coffee and hair' as he shone a torch at my sani-broyeur.

'Blockage or leakage?' he asked.

'Leakage,' I said, not bothering to ask why I'd had to

explain this to the operator at thirty-four cents a minute if she hadn't passed on the information.

He grabbed a spanner from his toolbox and began work, with me holding the torch as his unpaid assistant.

'If you want my opinion, this whole country is blocked and leaking,' he said. 'The kids are blocked because they can't get jobs, and the money's leaking out because French companies are moving the jobs abroad. And even if you've got a job you can't make any money,' he went on, 'because they take it all away from you to pay for the politicians' mistresses and non-stop election campaigns. Do you have a job?'

'No, I'm looking,' I said.

'Be a plumber,' he told me. 'People will always shit, and they'll never want to put their own hands in it.'

'Me also, preferably,' I tried to explain.

'Then you'll stay living in this place. Better to get your hands covered in merde than to live in it, non?'

I shrugged non-committally.

'Voilà,' he announced a few minutes later, after apparently doing little more than fit a rubber condom around the leaking joint. 'That will be fifty euros, but give me thirty cash and I'll say you weren't at home. If they try to fix another rendez-vous, tell them you repaired it yourself.'

All my money was going down the pan, I thought as I handed over a ten and a twenty.

I would have slumped into an even deeper

unseasonable depression if my evening hadn't been rescued by a phone call from Marsha.

'What are you doing right now?' she asked me.

'Oh, spending some time at home, reading,' I told her. Actually it wasn't a lie, because I'd been perusing the list of ingredients on my little packet of spicy pizza oil, trying to work out if there was actually anything edible in it.

'That's great,' she said, 'people don't spend enough time reading. Want to come to a vernissage tomorrow night?'

This, I knew, was the opening of an art show, or rather the party to celebrate the opening. I'd been to a couple with Alexa.

'What's the exhibition?' I asked. Not that it mattered much. Most people just went along for the free booze.

'You'll see. Should be pretty sexy. Come on, it'll get you out of the house a bit. Reading's great, but you don't want to do it every night, do you?'

Looking round Jake's apartment, if you could actually call it that, I had to agree. The newly damp floor took the flat one notch further down from its previous atmosphere of cramped, but dry, squalor. Getting out of this particular house for good, or even for a few hours, was top of my list of priorities.

'Great,' I said. 'It sounds like fun.'

'See you tomorrow, then,' Marsha said. 'Looking

forward to it.' And even without the support of her sensual eyebrows, her voice was enough to feed a whole night of sultry dreams.

Trois

'Ce qu'on nomme culture consiste, pour une partie des intellectuels, à persécuter l'autre partie.'
What we call culture consists for some intellectuals of persecuting the others.

> Jean-François Revel, French intellectual, so he
> should know

I

THE FRENCH are very big on allegories. At school, they all study a seventeenth-century author called La Fontaine, who spent most of his life writing stories along the lines of Aesop's fables. Even today, La Fontaine's neat moral endings help the logical French brain to explain away almost any situation. Something untoward will happen, and a French person will say, 'Oh yes, it's just like the wolf and the shepherd, or the cow and the lobster,' and they'll tell you a story that has almost nothing to do with their problem, but makes them feel better because it has set the world back at right angles again.

When I woke up next morning, bent almost double on Jake's torture mattress, I was thinking about a story that Alexa once told me. It was one of La Fontaine's fables, she'd said, about a frog who agrees to give a scorpion a piggyback across a river, but only after the scorpion has promised faithfully not to sting the frog.

'Why would I do that?' the scorpion asks. 'If you drown, we both drown.' So froggie says, 'Hop on,' and sure enough, halfway across the river, the inevitable happens, and as the frog is sinking, it asks, 'Pourquoi?' and the scorpion says it couldn't help itself – stinging is what it does.

This was back when I was first considering going into business with Jean-Marie. He's a scorpion, Alexa warned me, and I was his frog. Except that he was a scorpion with an inflatable lifejacket. He'd sting me and save himself.

The analogy sounded a bit too neat for me, so I Googled it and found out it wasn't one of La Fontaine's fables at all – no one knows where it originated. I didn't dare confront Alexa about this, of course. And in any case, I didn't have much choice about going into business with Jean-Marie.

On this particular morning, as I lay on Jake's bed of nails, it occurred to me that the frog wasn't me, it was the tea room. While I was setting it up, I'd been constantly swatting at scorpions who were doing their utmost to sink it. First there was Jean-Marie, who'd had the original idea but didn't want to carry it through, then the architect who tried to overcharge me, and half a dozen more minor predators. So when My Tea Is Rich finally opened, it felt like a miracle.

And this was why I couldn't let Jean-Marie sink it now. What I needed was either to swat him off into the river (which I couldn't afford to do, because it would mean buying him out), or to procure some kind of antidote to his poison. But the most important thing was not to let him know that I was planning a coup, otherwise he'd sting the tea room straight away and start inflating his lifejacket.

So when he called me later that morning, I didn't bawl him out for acting behind my back. I pretended that I just needed some explanations.

'We must meet and talk,' he said, sounding like the Dalai Lama offering the world a chance to live in peace.

'Yes, and this time you've got to tell me *everything*,' I said in my firmest voice.

'Of course,' he agreed, far too easily.

'OK, let's meet near the Gare du Nord, I fancy a cup of Indian chai.' I hoped that the real Dalai Lama might be there to help me stay yogically calm.

'No, no. There's a place that I must show you.' Of course, there was no way he was going to bow to my demands. He told me I 'absolutely had to see' a garage out in the suburbs. A garage? Was he thinking of turning the tea room into a truck stop? Or starting up a pizza van?

But before I could ask for more details, he was gone.

So here I was, sitting on the Métro again, heading way out west, and wondering how to play things. The suburb Jean-Marie had summoned me to wasn't one of the northern riot zones, of course. Like most Parisians, he never ventured out into neighbourhoods where poor people divide their time between killing each other and trying to kill the police. No, this was a southwestern suburb, Boulogne, hardly even a suburb at all because chic western Paris spills right over into it. The only fights that go on in this part of town are for seats at the French Open tennis finals.

It was another warm day, and in the freebie newspaper I'd picked up at the Métro entrance a politician was moaning about the long weekends that were about to transform May and June in France into non-stop holiday months. This year, May Day, VE Day and the various religious happenings all fell on a Tuesday, giving the French several chances to take off their Mondays and spend four days basking in the sun. This clearly annoyed the bosses and the right-of-centre politicians, but probably explained why so many Parisians seemed to be in a spring-like mood.

I was on line 10, which snakes beneath Saint-Germain

and the rich south-west of Paris before hitting the posh suburbs. Opposite me, in the half-empty carriage, two relaxed-looking office guys were discussing one of the upcoming long weekends. I could tell from his accent that one of them was a well-integrated Brit. He was dressed exactly like his French colleague: smartish suit, crisp shirt open at the neck, slim briefcase on lap.

'Are you going away?' the French guy asked him.

'Yes, to the north of England.'

'By car?'

'No, train. We don't have a car.'

'You don't have a car? Not even a small one for weekends?'

'No, we don't need one,' the Brit answered, on the defensive. 'I wouldn't want one in France anyway, I can't imagine changing gear with my right hand.'

'Why not?' Now it was the Frenchman who was on the defensive, as if sitting to the left of the gear stick might be considered by the Brits as some kind of sexual perversion.

'Well, in England, we keep our strong hand on the wheel and change with our left hand.'

The Frenchman's head was shaking before the Brit had even finished speaking.

'But in France, we change with our more agile hand. You don't need your strong hand on the wheel – you never change gear when you're turning a corner, do you?'

'Au contraire,' the Brit retorted. 'In France, you need your strong hand on the wheel all the time – the roads are so bad.'

'Bad?' It was as if the *Anglais* had just insulted the Frenchman's mother's cooking. 'Your English roads are terrible. London is always being dug up. That's why your taxis are like tanks.'

I couldn't help thinking that they ought to shut up arguing and get an automatic. They had reminded me that I was still without news of my driving licence, so even if I'd wanted to go cruising along a *route nationale* (which, in my experience, were so well maintained that drivers were tempted to behave like suicidal jet pilots), I'd have had to go as a passenger.

'And what about French traffic lights?' the Brit said.

'What about them?' asked the French bloke.

'In France, they change straight from red to green. They don't go to amber first. There's an amber light in the middle, why don't you use it? French drivers are all just waiting to jam their foot on the accelerator.'

'Don't you know what green means? You need yellow to make it clearer?' the Frenchman accused.

'Well, some Parisians certainly don't know what *red* means,' the Brit countered.

'Bon weekend,' I wished them as I got off, but they were too busy arguing to look my way.

*

I came out of the Métro station, and turned off the main road into a street that was lined with small houses fronted by cobbled yards and tiny urban gardens. I walked by a waxy fig tree, bursting with green unripe fruit, and along a bank of tall purple irises, apparently queuing up for Van Gogh to paint them. There was even a grapevine sunbathing against a red-brick wall. I felt as if I'd stepped back at least fifty years in time, so it didn't feel at all incongruous to come upon a couple of classic English sports cars parked in the street: a racing-green MGB and a turquoise Triumph Spitfire, both of them open-top and ready for the road. I felt like leaping in and heading for the Riviera. Except that I didn't have a licence, of course.

The cars were standing outside the iron gates of a wide courtyard, which was surrounded on three sides by an old industrial building with frosted windows for walls. And covering almost every square centimetre of floor space, inside and out, were classic motors, most of them British or American. I'm not a car buff, but I recognised the rounded red nose of an Austin Healey and the torpedo lines of a Ford Mustang. There were also a couple of large American open-top saloons, anonymous but drenched in road-movie mystique.

'Ah, Pool, I see you are impressed.'

Jean-Marie had emerged from one of the workshops and was grinning at me. He was flanked by Amandine, looking as stylish as the cars in her dark business suit.

I shook hands with Jean-Marie but didn't know what to do about Amandine. Handshake or kiss on the cheek? Outside work, I'd have kissed her, but we'd only met once in a business meeting, so the done thing was to shake her hand. She was gripping her phone in her right hand, though, so for the time being, this was impossible.

Jean-Marie saw me hesitating and slapped me on the back.

'Kiss her, Pool. No one should ever miss the opportunity to kiss la belle Amandine.'

So we did *la bise*, and I would have told Amandine how good she looked if I hadn't guessed that her morning had already been overfilled with male comments about her attractiveness.

Instead I told Jean-Marie how attractive *he* was looking. His suit was even more spectacular than usual, a light grey tweedy-looking material with a Triumph Spitfire-blue lining. It was way over the top and yet somehow very subtle.

'You like it? It's English. You are a fan of Pool Smith, I think?' he said.

'You're wearing English suits now?' I was astonished. He'd always been a staunchly French dresser. Givenchy or die.

'Yes, it is very, how do you say, *stylé*? Like these cars, no?' I had to agree. 'Alors, Pool,' he went on. 'If I have

79

understood well, you agree that a diner is a good idea?'
So it was straight down to business.

'In principle, yes, but not in my tea room,' I said.

'*Our* tea room,' he corrected me.

'Yes,' I agreed. 'And it's a profitable business as it is, so
why don't we leave the tea room as a tea room and open
a diner somewhere else? I'm sure La Fontaine must have
a fable about not fixing a teapot unless it's broken.'

Jean-Marie looked baffled for a moment, and then set
his features in a mask of mute disagreement.

'It is profitable,' he conceded, 'but mainly as a lunch
place for office workers. In Paris now, diners are for
everyone, every time. Breakfast, lunch, weekdays,
Sundays: they are all good. And we have seen the other
day that it's so simple. For the food you only need four
ingredients: eggs, hamburgers, bacon, potatoes. And
when people finish, you just give them the bill. You tell
them: Go now, I want your table. And they love it
because it is part of the American experience.' He paused
for effect before getting in his sneaky rabbit punch. 'Of
course, what I can do is sell my part of the tea room to
some unknown businessman, and create some diners
myself.'

So that was his plan, I thought. But he should have
played his joker when I was at the diner, sluggish on
comfort food. I laughed.

'Maybe this businessman and I could go into

competition with you, Jean-Marie? And we'd sue you if you tried to use the name My Diner Is Rich.'

'But do you want to risk the extra cost?' he asked with fatherly concern for my welfare. 'You are not exactly rich. Will a bank trust you?' He looked at me with scorpion eyes. I glanced over at Amandine to see whether she was in on this sting, but she was looking as fascinated with Jean-Marie's back-stabbing negotiation tactics as I was.

'I'll have some funds soon,' I told him. 'I've started doing some consultancy work for the Ministry.' This was a partial lie, because all I'd done so far was call Marie-Dominique and agree to go back for a follow-up meeting, but what kind of idiot would tell Jean-Marie the whole truth in a business negotiation?

'Bon.' He waved a hand in the air as if to swat my objections away. 'I want you to see two things. First this.'

He pulled me inside the workshop, where two men in overalls were tinkering with one of the most beautiful cars I'd ever seen. It was a long, red, hardtop E-Type Jaguar. All the thrills of the 1960s rolled into one: the style of the Beatles, the curves of Brigitte Bardot and the sexiness of England winning the 1966 World Cup.

'Classe, non?' Jean-Marie lapsed into French to express his full admiration for the vehicle. 'And notice that it has been adapted for France.'

I bent down to look through the open window. Inside it smelled of leather, polish and honest old machinery. And the walnut steering wheel was on the left.

'Now come and look at this, both of you.' Jean-Marie put a hand on Amandine's shoulder to guide her into the courtyard. She sagged under its weight, and looked ready to bash him with her phone if the arm strayed any lower.

He shepherded us towards one of the big open-top American saloons, a Ford of some kind, painted a metallic brown. Not a very old model – 1990s, I thought – but its enormous front seats were wide enough to allow even the biggest doughnut addicts on the planet to park their butts comfortably, and the back seat could have accommodated an orgy. It was totally impractical for Paris, but begging to be loaded up with surfboards and driven down to Biarritz.

'Which car would you choose, Amandine, if you wanted to buy one?' Jean-Marie asked.

'To buy one?' Amandine gave it no more than a second's thought. 'Oh, the American car. It's much more fun.'

'You see?' Jean-Marie said. 'Amandine is a young, French working girl' – I was *almost* sure he didn't know the double meaning of the term – 'and she chooses the American dream before the English elegance, even if it is adapted for France. Sorry, Pool, but the diner wins.'

He held up two hands in the surrender position, the French way of saying that it wasn't his fault if he was so damn right about everything.

'Yes, but you wouldn't want to scrap the Jaguar, would you, Amandine?' I said. 'You wouldn't want to replace the tea room with a diner?'

'Well . . .'

'Do you think I should buy the American car?' Jean-Marie interrupted her musing. 'I will, if you agree to drive with me to Deauville for the long weekend.' He laughed as if to pretend that he might be joking, but I could see him watching for any sign of a positive reply.

Amandine's face hardened.

'I'm going to stay with my parents,' she said, no doubt to remind him of their yawning generation gap.

'Another time, then. There are lots of long weekends coming,' he said shamelessly.

'You're thinking of buying this car?' I asked him.

'Oh no,' Jean-Marie scoffed. 'I have bought the Jaguar. It is my style, and a much better investment. And I am sure you will like it too, my dear, when we drive back to the office,' he told Amandine. 'It is very, how do they say in English? Cosy.'

'If you're driving back to Paris, can I have a lift?' I asked. 'That way, we can keep on talking about the tea room.'

'Sorry, Pool,' Jean-Marie said, looking as unapologetic

as a kid who's just stolen your last chocolate biscuit, 'but there is space for only two people. Amandine will send you a document with my proposition for the dîner – or dîners.' And from the look in his eye, it wasn't the only proposition he had in mind.

II

That afternoon, I threaded my way through the forest of fossilised toothpaste in the Palais-Royal gardens and gave my name to the receptionist at the Ministry.

When I'd called Marie-Dominique, she'd told me to go straight to a meeting room, number 'zéro zéro sept', or 007. With the phone held as far away from my ear as possible, I'd listened to her explaining that everyone found this hilarious because French civil servants are known as *agents*, like James Bond. I agreed that it was hilarious and asked whether I was going to be an agent, too, if I took on the job. I thought perhaps it might speed up the process of getting a French driving licence.

'Oh no!' she boomed, as if I'd asked for a fast-track sainthood. 'You'd be a contractuel, a fournisseur.' I asked her what this was, and she told me the Ministry used lots of them. 'They are our security men, the people who provide our water fountains and toilet paper . . .'

Great, so I'd be on the same level as the loo-roll delivery men, I thought as I asked the receptionist, a man this time, to point me towards the James Bond suite, where I had a *groupe de travail* meeting.

'Which groupe de travail?' he asked.

'I don't know the name,' I apologised.

He shrugged. This had to be a common problem. 'Room 007 is behind the stairs,' he said.

'Which floor is it on?'

He was a thirty-something man who looked as grumpy as if he had been demoted to entrance-hall duties after managing an opera house in Saint-Tropez. He squinted at me and replied, 'Ground floor, of course. That's why it starts with a zero. Who are you?'

'I am, or will be, a contractuel.'

'You have a badge?'

'No.'

'If you're going to be a contractuel, you must get a badge.'

'Where can I get one?'

'Room 666.'

'Ah.' Sounded as though I was in for some more bureaucratic hell. Maybe I wouldn't bother with a badge just yet. I thanked the guy for the information and went to find 007, which turned out to be one of the rooms with barred windows, the scene of Alexa's attempt to break into the cultural establishment. So I'd made it before her.

Stupidly, I'd arrived on time, so there was no one else in the room, a bare, white-walled rectangle with an oval table, a dozen or so chairs and a whiteboard. Two of the walls were decorated with what had to be paintings daubed by a close friend of the Minister. I couldn't see why else anyone would choose to hang canvases depicting what looked like close-ups of accidents involving tablecloths and spaghetti bolognese.

I was just musing on the washing-up problems that these might cause when I heard voices, and people began to stream into the room, all deep in conversation – but not about the fact that they were fifteen minutes late.

'Can't we get a printout of the hierarchy?' Marie-Dominique boomed at a small guy in a grey suit, grey shirt and grey tie.

'Not until it's been approved,' he replied quietly, apparently used to her habit of shouting every word she said as if hailing a distant ship.

'When will it be approved?' asked a tall, thin guy with a swept-back shock of grey-white hair, like some nineteenth-century writer.

'As soon as we know who can approve it,' answered a small bald guy in a white polo shirt.

'Isn't it the Minister?' Marie-Dominique foghorned.

'Yes, but we won't know who can *pre*-approve it until the hierarchy has been decided,' concluded a slightly tubby guy in an unseasonable black rollneck sweater and black jacket.

'Well, have you brought a printout of the old hierarchy?' Marie-Dominique barked at the guy all in grey.

'I couldn't print it out because my secretary is printing out copies of the minutes from the meeting about the need to buy another printer.'

'OK,' Marie-Dominique shouted grimly, 'we'll just have to improvise. Ah, Pol!' She almost blew me off my feet, but I managed to walk towards the group and introduce myself.

The trouble with this was that they all spoke like the list of names and abbreviations I'd seen on the notice-board, reeling off introductions that I didn't have a hope of remembering, especially as some of them couldn't even decide who they were.

The tall thin one with long hair said he was something like Bernard Dupont, DG of the DEDADA, but that he might soon be SG of the DECACA. The all-grey guy and white polo man couldn't decide if they were from the BUDEC or the BEBOP.

'Anyway, the BEBOP is going to be merged soon,' white polo man told me helpfully.

'With the ALULA?' I tried to joke, but they just frowned. I saw now that the abbreviations weren't qualifications, they were all departments at the Ministry. Not that this helped me understand what they stood for.

We sat down around the table, everyone except me

behind a tricolour Ministry folder, and Marie-Dominique reminded us all why she'd called the meeting: to discuss the artists' residence.

'Are we allowed to call it that yet?' objected the tall thin guy.

'No, you're right,' she conceded. 'To discuss the Brittany Project.'

It really did sound like a James Bond meeting – to prepare an attack on a Communist sardine fishery, perhaps.

'More exactly,' she went on, 'to decide what we can decide. We already know what we *can't* decide. Our task is *not* to think of the public, that is a job for the SS.'

'The SS?' I couldn't help asking. I thought they moved out in 1944.

'Le Service des Spectacles,' she explained.

'But I'm with the S-DAP,' the black rollneck man seemed to say.

'Sous-direction des Arts Plastiques,' Marie-Dominique translated for me.

'Isn't the S-DAP part of the SS?' black rollneck went on. 'Should I be here?'

'We'd know if we had the printout of the new hier-archy, wouldn't we?' Marie-Dominique hooted. 'Why don't you stay here for now, but without taking any new notes?'

Everyone nodded their satisfaction, and Marie-

Dominique got back to her speech about decisions, the gist of which, if I understood correctly, was that they couldn't actually *do* anything. This was because they were a *groupe de travail* – a working party – rather than a *comité*, and hadn't received a specific *mission*. They'd only been given a *projet*. Their job was to report, not propose action.

I was beginning to get a tingling at the base of my skull, the first sign that my brain wanted to crawl out of the back of my head and escape.

'One question,' I managed to say before I suffered a self-induced lobotomy.

'Yes?' Marie-Dominique seemed surprised that it wasn't all crystal clear.

'What do you want me to do, exactly?'

'Didn't you read the file I gave you?'

'Yes, but . . .' How did you say it was just a collection of long, apparently meaningless sentences, like almost everything that had been said at this meeting?

'Read the file again,' Marie-Dominique interrupted me. 'We are a groupe de travail, so what we need is a consultative document offering us propositions.'

'What sort of propositions exactly?' I pleaded.

'Your propositions,' she said.

'Ah.' At last I understood. Their thinking was as woolly as a koala bear's ear. I could do what the hell I wanted.

'So it is clear now?' Marie-Dominique asked, and I

nodded decisively, earning myself a round of satisfied bureaucratic smiles.

We discussed deadlines (no stress) and payment (maybe, just maybe, enough to convince a bank to lend me the cash to get Jean-Marie off my back), and then Marie-Dominique declared that everything was 'parfait'.

'Now, which department is responsible for defining our theoretical objectives?' she asked everyone within a kilometre.

As a man, the four guys reached into their folders and whipped out sheets of paper. They held them up, staring at each other as if they'd all produced the ace of spades in a poker match. Only one could be genuine, and it was their own.

'You don't really need to be here for this part of the meeting, Paul,' Marie-Dominique told me, and I was out of there as fast as my grateful legs could carry me.

Perhaps I was still in shock, because as I passed the electronic numbers above the lift door, I thought: Why not go up to the sixth floor and get a badge? I'd already been through purgatory. I might as well go all the way.

I emerged from the lift in a very different part of the Ministry. No wide, airy corridors here. I was in the attic, in what had probably been the servants' quarters when this was a palace. There were no men in suits here, no chirpy young girls, just unsexy, unhappy people apparently padlocked to their computers, who watched me walk past as if I was an alien on a fact-finding tour of France. Not many visitors to this floor, I guessed.

Room 666 had a solid wooden door with a tiny hatch and a bell marked '*Sonnez*' – 'Ring', as if there was anything else you could do with a bell.

I obeyed the curt instruction, and after several seconds, the hatch opened and a large, closely shaven head appeared, still in conversation with someone else in the room. Finally, the guy laughed and turned to me as though I was part of the joke.

'Bonjour, I've come for a badge,' I said.

'No badges here,' he said and closed the hatch, only to open it a second later, laughing again. 'I'm joking,' he said. 'Have you got your contract?'

'No,' I confessed.

'Oh, pff,' he said, as if blowing a fly off my lapel. 'They rarely do.'

He opened the door to reveal a little security den stocked wall-to-ceiling with screens: a bank of CCTV monitors, two computers and an ordinary TV. A small man in a shiny blue suit was lounging in a high-backed office chair watching a dubbed American doctor series. A famous Hollywood actor was speaking perfect French in a strange voice, out of synch with his own lips.

'What's your name?' the big security man asked me as he sat down at a computer.

I told him and he laughed as though I'd told a ridiculous lie. Napoleon Bumface, for example, or Jean-Paul Merde.

'It's English,' I said, and spelt it out for him, very slowly.

'You're already in the system,' he eventually said, and both of us stared at the computer in astonishment at this miracle of efficiency. 'Contractuel – green badge, not blue. Dommage.'

'Pourquoi dommage?' I asked. Why was it such a shame?

'Blue, you get cheap coffee from the machines, and free cinema tickets.'

'Any film, any time,' the small guy said over his shoulder.

'Wow. And green?' I asked.

'Pff,' the big guy puffed. 'Rien.' Nothing.

'Dommage,' I agreed.

'You're just a contractuel?' he asked.

'Yes.'

'But do you come in for meetings?'

'Yes.'

'With different agents?'

'Yes, five today,' I said.

'Maybe you should have a blue badge. What do you think, Momo? Blue badge for the monsieur?'

'Yes, it's nearly the weekend,' the guy in front of the

TV said, and they both laughed. It was Wednesday.

So I posed for a camera, signed on a screen with a plastic pointer, and came out of there grinning like a koala who's just been winched to the top of a virgin eucalyptus tree. A blue plastic badge with my photo and signature on it. Cheap coffee and unlimited cinema tickets. What more could a Parisian worker ask for?

III

'Vernissage means varnishing,' Marsha told me when we met up that evening. 'It comes from the time when artists would put the finishing touches to their pictures at a preview.'

'I never knew varnish could be so noisy,' I said, battling against a shockwave of electronic music coming from inside the exhibition hall. We were half a street away and it was deafening.

The private views I'd been to before had all been refined gatherings where culture fans frowned knowingly at picture frames while keeping one eye on the drinks table. At most of them, the main source of noise was chatter. Now, though, my whole skeleton was vibrating in time to the pounding bass notes coming from the large stone building marked 'IZZ'.

It seemed to be the sole survivor of mass demolitions in the area. Every other building was a modern high-rise, most of them typical examples of French Stalinist architecture: grim towers like the barrel of a giant machine gun, or stark floodlit rectangles of concrete slicing into the night sky. We were high up in the 19th *arrondissement*, almost at the Périphérique, way beyond my usual Parisian stamping grounds.

'Why IZZ?' I asked as we walked past a group of black teenagers who were looking hungrily towards the bass rhythms.

'Why IZZ what?' Marsha said.

'What?' I tried again. 'Why is the place called IZZ?'

Marsha gave a laugh-scream that made the teenagers jump.

'It's not. Haven't you heard about it? It's called the One Two Two. It's the street number. A hundred and twenty-two.'

In my ignorance of all things artistic, I'd misread the writing on the wall. We stopped in front of the building so that she could explain.

It was all very 'serendipitous', she said. Back in the days when brothels were legal in France, this was where prostitutes were brought to get a medical certificate. It closed after the Second World War and was used as a truck depot before its roof started leaking too badly. Then it got forgotten until the city decided it needed an arts centre to liven up the neighbourhood, at which point they saw the serendipity. There had once been a posh brothel called the One Two Two (an English name to attract tourist toffs) at 122 rue de Provence near Pigalle, and this new arts centre was at 122 rue de Sousvilliers, so they called the new arts centre the One Two Two. Or IZZ, as I'd just renamed it.

'You're very well documented,' I told her.

'Yes, art and sex are two of my passions,' she said, swaying her jeans towards the entrance, with me following in their gravitational pull.

We joined the throng of trendies waiting to get through the entrance arch. Not one of them, I guessed, lived within five Métro stops of this 'local' arts centre. They weren't all young – some were grey-haired – but they all looked exactly the same. Impeccably 'un-styled' hairdos, white faces, the men unshaven, the women natural except for lipstick and eye shadow. And everyone's outfit was dominated by black. If one of them died, we'd be able to hold the funeral there and then. As long as jeans were acceptable dress code, no one would need to go home and change. Except me, that is. I was in one of my sunglasses-obligatory summer shirts, dressed to clash with any paintings.

Once you got through the crush at the entrance, the building opened out into a wide courtyard of scrubbed brick and narrow windows, a bit like a Victorian lunatic asylum.

The main exhibition space was a huge glass-roofed

hall framed with iron girders, presumably where the carriages used to park when the prostitutes were transported in. Now it was shaking to the beat of frantic techno as a mass of Parisians talked and boozed in a bath of pulsing fluorescent light.

'Let's try and find the art,' Marsha yelled into my ear.

'After we've found the drinks,' I suggested.

Armed with a plastic beaker each of red vinegar, we shoved our way to the wing of the building where Marsha said the studios were. At the top of a wide stone staircase, now blocked by sprawling legs, we reached a corridor of glass-fronted rooms.

'This was where they used to do the medicals on the street girls,' Marsha told me. 'Now the rooms are studios, attributed to the artists in residence. And some of them are even bigger intellectual whores than the working girls ever were.'

We were given a fold-out brochure by a smiling, slightly plump girl who was sporting a deep cleavage, tiny miniskirt and fishnet stockings. Her leaflet featured a black-and-white photo of a nineteenth-century female nude (long hair in a bun, plump thighs, blurred crotch) and was headed by two logos: 'IZZ' (or '122') and the Ministry of Culture's tricolour Marianne. Wow, I thought, if this was the kind of event my new employers put on, I was going to enjoy working for them.

I asked Marsha to explain the title of the show:

'*Ouverture des maisons closes*', or 'Opening of the Closed Houses'. It was, she told me, a French pun. What a surprise. *Maison close* was an old word for brothel, dating from the time when they had to keep their windows shuttered to protect public decency, and this exhibition was to celebrate the opening of the arts centre. Not only that, there was also a debate raging in France about whether to relegalise brothels, and the theme of the show was what would go on inside them. All that in one title. My head was aching before I saw any of the art.

The ache was cranked up to migraine level as soon as we stepped into the first studio. It was jammed with people, but not enough to hide the film being projected on to the far wall. This consisted of a loop, lasting about twenty seconds, of a woman in a dressing gown, a prostitute presumably, walking up a staircase followed by a man. Nothing else happened, apart from the man's feet going briefly out of focus. The two people appeared, walked upstairs, appeared, walked upstairs, over and over again, like some lift manufacturer's nightmare.

'It represents the dehumanising everyday existence of a prostitute,' Marsha translated from the brochure. I knew how the hooker felt, and I'd only experienced it for a minute.

The next room was even worse. Its walls were lined with dozens of small, square photos, each one of them of a penis in the process of ejaculating. They were all entitled '*Portrait de l'artiste*', and were being stared at by fascinated viewers, including a small, leather-clad dominatrix whom I recognised from somewhere. She saw me staring at her and turned away sharply.

'This proves what they say about French culture,' Marsha said.

'What's that?'

'That half of it is cul.'

Luckily, I was able to laugh at her linguistic joke. *Cul*, the French word for arse, is also a slang term for sex. It was a word I'd learnt early on, when someone explained to me that I was mispronouncing 'merci beaucoup' as 'merci beau cul'.

In one corner of the studio, an ugly man of about fifty, in a creased black shirt and white silk scarf, was holding court before a gaggle of admirers. The artist, I guessed. I just hoped he'd be keeping his trousers on for the evening.

'"The artist masturbated every day for a year and got a woman to take a photo of each orgasm. Fifty-two women, one per week of masturbation,"' Marsha read from her booklet. '"If a brothel had fifty-two prostitutes, servicing seven clients per day, each one would have to experience 2,555 orgasms per year, a total of 132,860 orgasms. The artist's aim during his residency at the One Two Two is to produce 2,555 photos."'

'Sorry,' I said, 'but what a wanker.'

'He won a prize,' Marsha said. 'The Prix Guy Étalon, a very respected art prize in France.'

Hang on, I thought, I know that name. Marie-Dominique had mentioned it. Yes, that was it. Her new artists' residence was going to be named after him. Who, I asked Marsha, was this Étalon guy?

'He was a French performance artist. Big in the nineteen seventies and eighties,' she explained. 'He disappeared for a while, then got himself arrested outside the American Embassy in Paris during the Iraq War for pulling a Stars and Stripes out of his butt. He'd stuffed it up there, a whole square metre of silk. He went to the Embassy gate, dropped his trousers and pulled it out. There was a big scandal in France. He died of a ruptured colon while he was under arrest inside the Embassy, and later he won a posthumous medal as if he'd fallen in battle. Légion d'Honneur or something. The Americans kicked up a fuss. They said giving him a medal proved that France regarded them as enemies at war. You seriously never heard about all that?'

I admitted I hadn't. People pulling things out of their backside isn't my kind of art. I tend to draw the line at sawn-in-half cows. He had given me an idea, though.

'If you want to create a buzz about your bookshop,' I said, 'maybe you ought to set up a book prize. Publish a shortlist and then have an awards ceremony. Could be great publicity.'

'Yeah,' Marsha agreed, her nose almost pressed against one of the hideous photos. 'Worth thinking about. Shall we get out of here before I decide I never want to see one of these things ever again?' She gestured towards a pink scrotum. 'God, it all reminds me too much of Jake's poems.'

I took her hand and steered her through the crush. We'd just escaped from the penis room when I was surprised to see Amandine walk up and grab Marsha. Marsha screamed with delight and they kissed each other madly on the cheeks.

They noticed me staring.

'Paul? You know—?' they said simultaneously, and started laughing.

Marsha explained that Amandine had done a *stage* – an internship – as her assistant when she was working for a magazine a few months earlier. In a previous life, Marsha had been a culture writer at an American fashion mag, apparently. I felt guilty about not finding this out before. It was only while they caught up on each other's news that I remembered I was angry with Amandine.

'Her boss wants to turn my tea room into an American diner,' I told Marsha. 'And you agree with him, don't you, Amandine?'

I stared at her accusingly, my glare tempered only slightly because she was looking even hotter than when

I'd seen her in her work outfit. Her hair was loose, her blouse tight, and her skirt would have made Jean-Marie faint.

'Don't you think a diner is a good idea?' she asked me.

Her question deflated me a little. I'd had time to think about it, and had come to the conclusion that, in fact, a diner was a bit of a brainwave – as long as it wasn't in my tea room.

'Diners are hip,' Amandine went on. 'Much hipper than ordinary, old-fashioned cafés.'

Unfortunately, I agreed with this, too. Traditional Parisian cafés all had the same furniture – those heavy marble-top tables and uncomfortable fake-wickerwork chairs that pick holes in your trouser seat. What made things worse was that a Coke was often twice the price of a glass of wine, and half the waiters were manic-depressives. Young Parisians were boycotting them in droves.

'There was a survey,' Amandine said, 'and people said they were bored with café au lait, wine and bad sandwiches.' With a click of her fingers, she dismissed everything that tourists have loved about Paris for the past century or more.

'But the tea room isn't boring. People love it,' I said. 'I love it, too. There's no way I'm going to let Jean-Marie close it. And anyway, he can't do anything without consulting me.'

Amandine laughed. 'You know him. He doesn't consult people when he wants to do something.' She gave us a look that made it all too clear she wasn't only talking about business.

'Hey, you two have obviously got lots to discuss,' Marsha said. 'Maybe I'll leave you to it?'

'No, I was just going,' Amandine said. 'To a party. You want to come?' She directed her question at Marsha, but I thought it diplomatic to answer.

'Let's stay here,' I said to Marsha. 'We can have a look at some more porn and then have a dance, if it is actually music and not just ear art.'

'OK.' Marsha looked pleased that I'd chosen to spend some exclusive time with her.

'You don't necessarily have to tell Jean-Marie what I said about the tea room,' I told Amandine.

'Don't worry. I've forgotten our conversation already,' she said. 'When I'm out of the office, I prefer to imagine that he doesn't even exist.'

Marsha and I spent less than ten seconds in the third artist's studio. One glimpse of a six-foot-square Expressionist close-up of a vagina was enough for both of us. We pushed our way downstairs, grabbed some more plastic beakers and sloshed them across the room towards the DJ, who was starting to pump out some danceable music instead of the fractured squeaks and heart-attack beats he'd been playing before. Marsha and I danced, drank, danced some more, then kissed and forgot everyone else in the whole heaving building. I noticed the dominatrix staring at me, and at one point I thought I saw Alexa out of the corner of my eye, but I decided not to pay them any attention. And in any case, Marsha was suggesting that it was time to get a taxi to her place.

IV

In my experience, it's never a good idea to confuse sex with sport. There are, for example, men who get more aroused by a football match than they do by their wives and girlfriends. A woman could leap naked into some guys' laps during a televised game, and they'd ask if she'd brought a can of beer. With Marsha, it was slightly different. She seemed to think that sex itself was a competitive sport, somewhere between rodeo and synchronised swimming. Every now and again, a leg would suddenly appear over my shoulder or her head would pop up in some improbable place. I almost wished I'd worn a helmet as well as a condom.

And all the time she was chanting yes, yes, yes (or rather yis, yis, yis because of her accent), like an Olympic coach ticking off pre-prepared manoeuvres. I was the team member who didn't know the routine.

I don't mean to be ungrateful, but it was all a bit depressing. It involved less love than a game of tennis. Rather than being the physical melding of two souls, it was a bout, and I was the one who was knocked out at the end of it.

Afterwards, as Marsha lay on her stomach, breathing heavily into a pillow, I wondered if she was going to ask me to check the stopwatch to see if we'd broken any endurance records. Instead, she smiled over at me and said, 'Six.'

So it *was* synchronised swimming, and she was giving me a mark out of ten. I wondered if it was for artistic impression or technical difficulty. Then I twigged. She was saying 'sex', presumably to remind herself that what we'd just done had been more than mere gymnastics.

'Sex,' she repeated, turning over to look me in the eye. 'It's what separates humans from animals, isn't it?'

Now, normally I am willing to agree with whatever a woman says after we've made love. But in this case there was no such harmonious afterglow.

'Animals have sex,' I objected. 'All of them. Even slugs have sex.'

'Not good sex.'

'Chimps have frequent sex with as many different chimps as possible,' I said, 'and some people think that's what good sex is.'

'OK, well argued, Paul, but you know what I mean. Animals don't make an art form of it.' (Or a medal-winning sport, I thought.) 'It doesn't inspire them to write novels and poems.'

'No, but apparently, if you gave an infinite number of chimps a typewriter, one of them would end up writing *Lady Chatterley's Lover*. After they'd all finished having sex with each other, of course, which could take a long time given that there's an infinite number of them.'

She laughed, and rolled over to kiss me and shut me up. The first time we'd kissed properly since diving on to her bed. This was more like it, I thought.

'I don't think there are any animals that kiss,' I said. (There are female insects that give fatal love bites, of course, but I wasn't going to raise that dangerous subject.) 'And as it happens, kissing is one of my favourite activities.' I moved in for a smooch.

'No time,' she said, speaking directly into my mouth.

'What?'

'My friend Philippa said she could get me into La Night, you know, that new club in the Ninth?'

'You want to go out to a club?'

'Yeah.' She had already leapt off the bed and was pulling on a glittery T-shirt.

'And you just thought of that now?'

'Yes. Don't you find that sex helps you think? It also occurred to me that that book prize you talked about ought to be a competition. You know, like, more of an event? A talent contest, maybe.'

'Oh right, so when you were saying, "Yes, yes, yes," you were just running through your to-do list?'

'No,' she laughed, wriggling now into a pair of tiny denim shorts. 'Thinking doesn't stop me enjoying the sex. Honestly, you guys are so sensitive. Come on, Paul, take me clubbing. You like these shorts?'

Using the plural seemed rather generous, but I nodded approvingly.

'OK, so get dressed, fill me with champagne and then we can come back and you can pull the shorts off.'

Which, on balance, didn't sound like too bad an offer.

Quatre

'J'ai libéré Paris une fois. Faudra-t-il que je le refasse?'
I liberated Paris once – do I have to do it again?

> Charles de Gaulle, on hearing that the first
> hamburger restaurant had opened in Paris

I

THE NEXT morning, when I woke up, my first impression was a mixed one. I was happy to be where I was (that is, not on Jake's too-short, creaky, possible health-risk sofa bed), but slightly worried about what would happen when I opened my eyes. Marsha was definitely one of the sexiest women I'd ever met, but I wondered about waking up with someone who thought the mating game was more about the game than the mating. To put it bluntly, I felt like one of Jake's conquests. I was afraid Marsha would be staring at me, trying to work out how to explain politely that she didn't want me to stay for breakfast.

So I was a bit nervous about turning over for that first morning-after eye contact. And then confused when I realised that, in fact, there were no eyes to make contact with.

On the pillow was a sheet of paper with a squiggled sketch of a naked female body and a large message: 'Call me NOW!'

I eventually found my phone in my jeans, which had ended up draped over a shelf of tall art books and battered volumes of classic French literature, and I'd just got back under the duvet to make the call when my phone began buzzing.

'Oh merde.' It wasn't Marsha, it was Jake. Against my better judgement, I answered.

'Bonjour, man. So did you do the deal with her?' he demanded.

'Bloody hell, Jake.' I shouldn't have been surprised. Jake is not one of life's natural romantics. I once heard him talking to a girl he was supposedly dating. She was fishing for compliments, as Parisian women often do, and she said, 'I'm so scared that you'll open your eyes and decide that I'm really not that good looking at all.' And Jake replied, 'No danger, the lighting in this place is so low I can hardly see you.'

'Alors, did you do the deal?' he repeated.

'You mean did we shag? Yes, if you must know. But if you mean am I going to stay in her rent-free apartment, then I'm not so sure.'

'No, I mean, will she publish my poems?'

'Oh. We didn't talk about that.'

'But you have promised me, man.'

I should have told him to bugger off and call back when I'd had some coffee, but suddenly I felt sorry for the guy. He sounded so desperate.

'Well, we did come up with one promising idea. She's thinking of holding a contest, a literary talent contest, with the winner getting a publishing contract. You could enter that.'

'Oui, formidable, man. Free expression. Tell her I'm a candidate.'

'OK,' I agreed, feeling a sudden sense of divided loyalties. Maybe I ought to warn Marsha not to run her competition, or even open a bookstore. Make it a flower shop or a *boulangerie*, I'd tell her. It might be safer.

Marsha was in fine form when I eventually phoned her. She was at the shop with Mitzi and Connie, and fired up about her opening party.

'You will be a judge, Paul, right?' she said. No argument possible. 'You, me and Amandine voting for our favourite Parisian poets. It's going to be a blast. Hey, you still in bed?'

'Yes,' I confessed.

'Naked?'

'Yes.'

'Can you wait there, like, an hour, hour and a half? I want to come and jump on you.'

'Oh no, I've got to go to the Ministry of Culture, dammit.'

'You sure? You don't know what you're missing. Well, yes you do. So why don't you tell the Ministry to fuck off and stay in bed so I can fuck you?'

'It's incredibly tempting, Marsha, but I can't. I really need this job.'

After we rang off, I had to go to the bathroom to stare in the mirror and make sure that it had actually been me talking. Truth was, I didn't have to go to the Ministry at all, not straight away, anyway. And it wasn't like me to lie my way out of sex, especially with someone so beautiful. I didn't understand it.

II

After a long, hot shower at Marsha's place – I could definitely relate to one or two aspects of Jake's 'find a girl and move in with her' policy – I headed back up to the 18th. I found the front door of his building wedged open, and a note taped to the wall saying that the digicode was broken. It wasn't surprising. The keypad was ancient, and the five plastic buttons that made up the code had been used so often that you had to jab at each number with your thumb as if you were trying to punch a hole in the wall.

It was symptomatic of the run-down state of the building, which had seen much better days. It was an elegantly designed six-storey apartment house built, according to an inscription carved into the façade beside the main door, by a certain '*P. Couderc, architecte*', in 1886, at a time when both Monsieur Couderc and the land-owner probably thought that the whole of Paris would become a stylish network of boulevards populated by men doffing their top hats to ladies with parasols. No one could have dreamt that some of those boulevards would one day become semi-permanent traffic jams of honking delivery vans, and that the ground-floor boutiques would be taken over by phone shops with booths rented out by the minute to poor people trying to stay in touch with their families halfway across the world.

In Paris, you often see a posh apartment house in the most surprising neighbourhood – a sudden outbreak of Art Nouveau in a street of plain concrete, brick and plaster. Jake's building had never been quite that stylish, but the entrance hall had some nice nineteenth-century touches: a chessboard marble floor (much battered now, with broken tiles replaced by grossly mismatching colours); an arched ceiling with the remains of a heavy brass light fitting that had probably supported a chandelier before it was replaced by a stainless-steel lamp; and a flirtatiously curved wooden banister rail leading to the upper floors. The concierge's *loge* had long ago been turned into the dustbin cupboard, which some of the tenants treated as one big landfill. The concierge herself had been exchanged for a cleaning company, whose overalled employees came in once a week to hose down the hall and landings with a nostril-searing solution of bleach and lavender oil. Once a month they also turned the wooden stairs into miniature ice rinks, so that on polishing days you had to clamber upstairs with both hands on the banisters, your feet shooting about in all directions like a cow trying to stand up on a frozen pond.

Anyway, at some point, the owners must have voted to upgrade one part of the building: the letterboxes. Painted red and cream, they stood out in the dingy entrance hall like a Monet oil painting hanging in a bus shelter. And they were veritable wall safes. The only way to steal a letter would have been to chisel out the whole block and take it away to dynamite it open. The effect was spoiled slightly by the layers of paper labels stuck over the name tabs, as tenants came and went, but it felt good to know that, if ever I did ski down six flights of stairs and fracture my skull on the broken tiles, at least the refund for my medical expenses would sit safely in my letterbox until I was well enough to collect it.

Jake had given me the key to his box, and this morning, in amongst a nearby supermarket's offer of twelve litres of sterilised milk for the price of six, and an estate agent's note saying that he would help me to sell an apartment I didn't own, were three important envelopes.

The first one I opened contained my contract with the Ministry, offering me a very generous per diem and the chance to bill them for all *interventions*, a pleasantly vague word that sounded as if it could generate lots of expenses. The only condition was that all my work needed to be pre-approved by Marie-Dominique, which probably meant more brain-frazzling meetings with her and her colleagues.

This Ministry envelope also contained a memo addressed to all blue-badge holders. I could collect my free cinema pass whenever I wanted, it said, and I would be receiving an information pack about my pension rights. Which was weird – I was just starting work and they wanted me to retire already?

The second letter was a little note from the préfecture saying they had my driving licence. I knew this already, but it was kind of them to admit it, and I was not overly anxious when I saw that the handwritten name in the space on the photocopied letter was semi-legible and misspelt – it seemed to call me Paul Vessie, *vessie* being one of the few medical words I knew, and meaning bladder. Paul Bladder. My only real worry was that the letter said my application would be dealt with before a date which had been left blank. But at least there was a printed '20 . . .' at the end of the date box, so I knew it was going to be sometime this century.

The third letter was less personal but much more frightening. It had obviously been sent out to everyone on the Ministry of Culture's list of *agents* and *contractuels*. It was a communiqué from all the unions I'd seen represented on the Ministry's noticeboards, and seemed to be a version of the leaflet I'd been handed on my way out. The 'Non!' was smaller but more clearly explained. Apparently, the unions were all agreed on one thing: no money for elitist projects like a new artists' residence.

The Résidence Guy Étalon was, I read, 'a confirmation of government discrimination between the needs and rights of ordinary workers and the desires of an already-favoured elite'. They were calling for all employees (including, apparently, people like me whose job was to get the project moving) to protest when the Minister returned to Paris after his two weeks representing French culture in the cocktail parties and luxury hotels of Cannes. Rendez-vous outside the Palais-Royal a few days later. It looked as though my contract was about to be terminated before I'd even signed it.

'Bonjour,' Marie-Dominique said, quite softly for once (I had taken the precaution of turning down the volume on my phone and wearing earplugs, of which my local pharmacy stocked a surprisingly large range). 'Don't worry,' she replied when I told her why I was calling, 'it's as I said before, they are just saying "non" to everything.'

'But this letter is très spécifique,' I argued. 'They are against the new artists' residence.'

'Not really. They are just trying to annoy the Minister because of all the restructuring in the Ministry. They say that it is an *astuce*.'

'Astuce?' I didn't know the word.

'Oui, un trick, as you say in English. Our new administrative structure will be very stimulating.' She sighed with pleasure, like someone who has spent her whole career since the *baccalauréat* studying different ways of administering French bureaucracies. 'The new Minister is creating new departments and sub-departments, n'est-ce pas? And the unions do not agree with this. Because you get automatic promotion if you have years of seniority in a department. But if the department is new, there is no seniority for ordinary agents. In some cases, this might mean a reduction in future promotions or bonuses or holidays. You see?'

'Not really,' I confessed. 'What has this got to do with the residence?'

'It is being created by my new department, and the directors of new departments have been parachuted to the top, if anyone can be parachuted to the top of something' – she guffawed at her bureaucratic joke – 'thereby getting instant promotion above the former heads of the old departments.'

'Now I understand,' I said. I'd always heard that the French civil service was a sort of giant filing cabinet, with people moving slowly up, drawer by drawer, and then bailing out when they reached retirement age to land on the plump mattress of their pension. In fact, though, what Marie-Dominique was describing sounded more like a French queue, with people getting marooned at the back because others were allowed to push in and join their chums nearer the front. The never-changing lives of these *fonctionnaires* seemed to be changing at last. No wonder the folks up in the Ministry's narrower corridors looked so depressed. And this also had to be why Marie-Dominique, the head of a new department, was so boomingly happy.

'The Minister will calm the unions,' she assured me. 'It's not really about our project at all. It's a negotiating tactic. In the fonction publique it happens every time we want to change a lightbulb.'

'So I can start my work for you?' I asked.

'Yes, of course. Just send me a brief description of what you intend to do so that I can approve it.'

'We don't need a meeting?'

'No.'

I tried to stop myself giving a whoop of relief.

'There's only one thing you should be aware of,' Marie-Dominique added. 'To coincide with the Minister's return from Cannes, there is going to be a transport strike. I think they want to see him get stuck in a few traffic jams. I hope that won't disrupt your trip to Brittany.'

'Oh no,' I assured her. A transport strike, stop *moi*? Surely it couldn't be that hard to drive a train.

III

It was time for a think. And not in Jake's apartment, where at any moment, thinking could be interrupted by the plumbing, the yelling neighbours, amorous pigeons flapping about on the roof, or the arrival of Jake himself wanting to try out a new poem.

So I made for the café closest to Jake's garret. When he first moved into his apartment, the *bistrot* on the corner of the street was a dump. It was a dark room furnished with old, unmatching tables, and populated by wrinkled men in dirty shirts who would prop up the bar and spend hours peering at the racing pages. The landlady looked like a retired wrestler and the coffee tasted as though it had been filtered through her sweat-stained nylon pullover. Jake, of course, loved it. He said it was 'real Paris', as though decent lighting and a drinkable espresso weren't Parisian.

Since then, however, the café had been sold and refurbished, and now it was unashamedly boutiquey: velvet armchairs, pink-and-red wallpaper, black panelling, globular light fittings. The same crinkly old guys were still at the bar, but now they looked like life-size sculptures put there so that arty types could get an odour-free look at the area's low life. There was a new barman, too, a smart guy in a spotless white shirt, who spent much of his time with his arms folded, waiting for the neighbourhood to get gentrified.

The makeover was starting to have an effect, though. A few of the area's dyed-blonde mums would chat and smoke the afternoon away in the new movie-director chairs that now lined the pavement outside. And at lunchtimes, some of the black lacquer tables attracted office workers, who were slowly being lured away from older, more established cafés to this formerly grungy street corner. Lunchtime is the key to success for any restaurant outside touristy areas. Tempt the local office workers in two or three times a week and you'll make a living. Lunching is one of a Parisian's favourite pastimes. When done properly, it can feel like a miniature holiday, or a short romantic encounter that ends before emotional complications set in, simply because everyone has to get back to work. And part of the enjoyment is the guilty pleasure – every minute after 2 p.m. is a forbidden fruit plucked from the tree of life. Anything beyond two thirty is a mortal sin, and all the sweeter for it.

What, I wondered, was attracting the office workers to Jake's corner café?

Quatre

I had a peek at one of the plastic-covered menus standing on a terrace table. It featured most of the café standards like onion soup, smoked herring with warm potatoes, boiled egg with mayonnaise, several kinds of steak – rump, *entrecôte*, *faux filet*, *tartare* – but had a few novel additions – *rillettes de maquereau* (mackerel pâté), a *salade asiatique* with spicy chicken and warm noodles, even a *far breton*, a sort of prune flan that you don't usually get outside Brittany. All this as well as the *menu du jour*, with the option of having the *entrée/plat* or *plat/dessert* at a reduced price.

There was also, I noticed, a whole section of the menu given over to *Nos Hamburgers*. They now did a straight *hamburger classique*, as well as a bacon burger, something called *un hamburger spécial cheese*, and a chicken burger, presumably for the many people in the neighbourhood on a pork-free diet. 'All our homemade burgers are served with a mixed salad and a glass of fries,' it said – '*un verre de frites*'. They were offering an upmarket version of the fast-food restaurant's carton of French fries. A Parisian café imitating McDonald's? It was the world turned upside down, or rather flipped over and grilled on both sides.

When the barman came out to the terrace to take my order, I asked him who the new chef was.

'It's the owner's husband,' the guy said helpfully.

'Where did he work before?'

'I don't know.'

'Is he Breton?' I asked.

'I don't think so. Why?'

'Far breton,' I said, pointing to the tart in the menu. 'I've never seen it outside Brittany.'

'Are you Breton?' he asked me.

'No, I'm Britannique,' I said, hoping this would qualify as a pun.

'OK,' he said with crushing indifference. No pun, then. 'So what can I get you?'

I ordered a coffee and a slice of the *far breton*. I'd had it once during a weekend in Brittany with Alexa. I remembered that I'd bitten into a date stone – Breton recipes apparently didn't include a line about removing pips from dried fruit – and Alexa had found it highly amusing to see an Englishman holding his jaw after being assaulted by a French pastry.

I'd loved its creamy stodginess, though. Given my current lack of cash, it would count as early lunch. And it would also get me in the mood for wading through the report that Marie-Dominique had given me, which at first sight was as impenetrable as a bed of Breton seaweed at low tide.

Later, aided by chewy mouthfuls of very fresh *far* washed down with hot, tasty coffee, I actually began to see through the verbiage in the report. Behind the endless sentences of long Latin words (at least three *-ations* per line, I reckoned), were some very simple concepts.

All they really wanted was for me to explain how the 'sourcalisation of the ingredientation of the restauration at the residencialisation' or something similar, could be 'of local and preferably organic origination'.

This begged a very obvious questionalisation, of course: how did they expect a Breton artists' residence to source local coffee, sugar, rice and olive oil?

It was, basically, well-meaning bollocks. And expensive bollocks, too. The budget per meal was more than the price of the three-course menu at Jake's corner café. I'd always thought that the concept of the French artist included a bit of starvation – wasn't it a cocktail of hunger pangs and absinthe that had inspired Van Gogh, Picasso, Matisse and co. to push back the boundaries of art in the hope of inventing something new and expensive to sell to collectors? These overfed artists in Brittany would be spending most of their time sleeping off their massive meals. Hardly surprising that the civil servants were saying that the project was too elitist.

Still, I reasoned, that wasn't my problem. I was all for getting my hands on some of the French State's cash if it would pay for a decent place to live. My only worry was getting to Brittany before the train drivers went on strike. Well, no, that was far from being my only worry, but it had just become the most urgent one – the wilting slice of industrial *fromage* atop my *hamburger spécial* of problems.

*

IV

Obviously harbouring no hard feelings about my refusal to have sex with her, Marsha called to invite me to play *pétanque*. The old men's game from Marseille was, she explained, back in fashion. Throwing their *boules* about had become young Parisians' favourite sport. So she suggested we have a picnic that evening, in the hottest hotbed of this new activity up in the 19th, not far from the One Two Two arts centre, on the gravelly bank of the Canal de l'Ourcq. The *right* bank, Marsha stressed, not the left, which was where the untrendy locals played. She'd also invited Amandine and the handbag twins, Connie and Mitzi.

We met at the canalside at seven o'clock when the sun was still strong and the first picnickers had already claimed their pitches along the tree-lined bank. Marsha was looking as wonderful as ever, in a loose but sexy flowery blouse and another of her pairs of microscopic shorts. Her lips were painted scarlet, but she didn't seem to mind smudging them with a long hello kiss.

As I wiped lipstick off my mouth, chin and cheeks, we walked along the canal and I checked out the other picnickers. Marsha was right – this part of town was getting seriously trendy. There were still a couple of old-school student picnics – a six-pack of Kronenbourg and a packet of cigarettes – but most of them were of a sophisticated new breed. One group of arty twenty-somethings had spread out a rug and were arranging formal place settings with paper plates and plastic cutlery. They had brought a leg of ham with a vicious-looking bone-handled clasp knife embedded in it, and a large tub of homemade potato salad. They even had serving spoons. Another bunch were sitting around a big *tarte Tatin* with a pot of *crème fraîche* – they looked like a cross between that Manet picnic painting and an advert for the Normandy tourist board.

Marsha was carrying a couple of bottles of chilled champagne, so I was glad that I'd come amply supplied. I'd convinced myself that the promise of Ministry money gave me an excuse to splurge, and my Monoprix plastic bags were bulging with apéritif nibbles, a couple of baguettes, a Camembert, a log of goat's cheese, *taboulé à l'orientale*, slices of smoked swordfish, a fresh lime, four punnets of long French Gariguette strawberries (exactly the colour of Marsha's lipstick) and – get this – some little finger-wipes in sachets like the ones they give you in seafood restaurants. French civilisation in a packet.

Marsha and I laid out her blanket at the edge of the canal. The water looked soupy brown and unappetising, but the view was spectacular.

On the opposite bank, a couple of barges had been converted into waterside bars, and people were lounging on the decks, chatting to each other's sunglasses. To our right were the twin buildings at either end of an old canal bridge. One was a cubic stone warehouse that had been converted into student rooms, the other a hotel that had been enmeshed in metal grapevines. To our left, a neon-lit cinema was bathed in blue light like a spaceship about to blast off. It would all have been much too industrial for Paris, except that the scene was set against the constant clack of *pétanque* balls, as the new converts behind us tested their skills.

We'd just finished setting out the food when Amandine arrived. Marsha declared that this was the perfect time to open the champagne and celebrate the first meeting of her new poetry-judging panel.

'Let's have a quick chat before Jake gets here,' I suggested as we clinked glasses.

'You invited him?' Marsha asked curtly.

'Well, he kind of invited himself,' I said. 'And he is letting me live rent-free in his apartment, so I couldn't really say no. He's not so bad when you get to know him.'

Amandine laughed.

'You've met him?' I asked her.

'No, but Marsha told me about his poem.'

The two women shared a grimace as though they'd just spotted a dead rat floating in the canal.

'He called me,' Marsha said. 'He wanted to know how many poems he could perform.'

The girls did the dead-rat look again.

'You can't blame him for being keen,' I said. 'It's his dream to get his poems published in Paris.'

'He will get published, online, like all the other contestants,' Marsha said. 'And maybe in an e-book compilation.'

'No, he wants a book,' I told her. 'He's strictly old school. He wants a little volume he can carry around in his pocket and show people, like Baudelaire or Rimbaud. When he was living in Louisiana, he was going to change his name to Rimbaud until he realised that they thought he just couldn't spell Sylvester Stallone's screen name.'

'Well, we can't show any favouritism,' Marsha said, and Amandine nodded. 'His poems scared the shit out of me. And this isn't going to be a French-style competition, Paul. The winner isn't going to be our best friend.'

'He wouldn't want that anyway,' I assured her. 'He's got to think he's won on merit.'

Marsha laughed, rather cruelly, I thought.

Right on cue the man himself turned up, his shirt as rumpled as a used tissue and his feet clad in the first pair I'd ever seen of mismatching training shoes – one a high red Nike, the other a low striped Adidas. What else could he be but a punk poet?

I had to ask. 'What happened to your shoes, Jake?'

'Oh, a woman has threwed all my other shoes out the window,' he said. 'You know how it is.'

'And don't tell me, she threw your jeans out, too, and a car ran over them?'

'No,' Jake protested. 'It was a bus.'

He kissed Marsha hello and hummed his admiration for Amandine.

'French name, n'est-ce pas? You Parisian?' he asked.

'Yes,' Amandine said, smiling despite herself at this stray-spaniel apparition.

'Oh,' Jake groaned. These days, straightforwardly French girls were off his wishlist of nationalities. 'You don't inhabit in the rue Beaubourg, do you?'

'No,' Amandine said.

'You look like a voisine I had there. She was très belle, but just as French as you.'

'Thanks for the compliment, I think,' Amandine said.

'Yes, she lived in the apartment on the other side of a cour. And she always looked at me when I did the repassing.'

'The what?' I asked.

'Repassing.' He moved a closed fist from side to side.

'Ironing?' Amandine guessed.

'Yeah, merci,' Jake said.

'You do *ironing*?' Marsha asked, raising an eyebrow at his rumpled appearance.

'Yeah,' he protested. 'It's not my fault if a woman throws my things out the window. Anyway, when I repass the iron, I sometimes do it naked. And, well, I didn't have any ree-doh, you know?'

'Curtains,' Marsha prompted him.

'Yeah, those, so the girl used to regard me naked. And then one day I'm repassing next to the window and she's looking, and then she disappears. Two minutes later, she arrives at my door and she has, like, some clothes or something in her arms. And I asked her, "You have come to join me for some naked repassing?" and you know what she said?'

We all shook our heads.

'She said, "No, I brought you some ree-doh." Curtains.'

We all laughed, including Jake, though maybe not for the same reasons.

'You Parisiennes are crazy,' he said to Amandine as she took a therapeutic guzzle of champagne. 'Here, I brought this.' He dipped into a carrier bag and produced two bottles of wine.

'Wow, this is good stuff,' Marsha said, reading the wine labels.

'Yeah, well, you know, we're celebrating *le printemps*,' Jake said bashfully. 'And they were just lying there in my ex-girlfriend's kitchen.'

Connie and Mitzi were coming along later, so we decided to have a game of *pétanque* while we waited.

We found ourselves a stretch of unoccupied gravel

and Jake threw the little *cochonnet* for us to aim at. Marsha went first – a strong, sporty throw – and then Jake. Their *boules* landed at almost exactly the same distance from the target, on opposite sides of the *cochonnet*.

While they were measuring out whose ball was winning, I took the opportunity to ask Amandine if she had any more news on the tea room/diner front.

'No,' she said, but sighed as if she was thinking exactly the opposite. I asked her what was up.

'I shouldn't tell you this,' she said. 'You know, Jean-Marie is my employer. I am supposed to keep his secrets. But . . .' She shook her head and took the plunge. 'He told me something,' she whispered.

'About the tea room?'

'No, about you.'

'Me?'

'Yes, he told me why he calls you Pool.'

'It's because he's French and can't pronounce my name. No one can.'

'I can, Paul,' she said, though I didn't like to tell her that it was more of a 'Pole'.

'Why does he say Pool then?'

'It's because of the French sense of the word. You know, poule.' And she imitated the wings of a clucking hen.

'You mean like a poulet? A cop?' I asked.

'No, poule is the feminine. In French we say poule

mouillée, wet chicken, for someone who has no courage. He is mocking you. Every time he says your name he is calling you a wet chicken. And now he even tells *me* this. You must be very careful of him. We must both be careful of him.'

All of which naturally put me off my aim, and I sent my *boule* bouncing way beyond our *cochonnet* and perilously close to the unprotected feet of a girl playing further along. She yelped as the heavy metal ball thudded next to her bare little toe, and I had to go and apologise, even though I thought that these new-generation female *pétanque* players might do better to wear something more protective than open sandals.

Connie and Mitzi's footwear was just as impractical when they arrived about an hour later, wobbling across the cobbled canal path on absurdly high heels that made them limp and sway like tightrope walkers with one leg shorter than the other. Jake saw them coming and dashed to grasp each of them by an elbow and guide them the last fifty metres or so. He looked as though he was carrying two identical dummies for a trendy children's clothes shop. The girls were doing their usual double act, both wearing pink fake-fur jackets and short skirts in one of their flashy tartans. As the trio progressed – Jake the laundry mishap and his two designer mannequins – every picnicker and *pétanque* player stopped to watch the procession, and it felt only natural for Marsha, Amandine and myself to give them a round of applause when they finally made it to our pitch.

We all stooped to give the twins a *bise* on the cheeks, and they placed their offering ceremonially on the picnic blanket: a gift box from Paris's poshest macaroon shop.

It seemed almost inappropriate for them to squat on the edge of the blanket rather than pull out some portable thrones, but they sat down and began chatting excitedly about their new premises. They'd seen France's First Lady walking past their door, and had already dropped a free handbag off at the Élysée Palace, with a card inviting Madame to their opening. They were clearly a pair of saleswomen with killer ambition.

The conversation moved on to the exhibition at the One Two Two. All the girls had seen it, and Amandine even went so far as to say that the vagina Expressionist painter had something to say about something, and not just 'hey, look at this!' She knew how the painter felt, she said, thanks to the ogling eyes of her lecherous boss. Connie and Mitzi laughed in unison and began to complain about macho handbag manufacturers, which was a concept I'd never thought about.

While they talked art in rapid-fire French, I whispered a key question in Jake's ear.

'Sorry, but which one is which again?'

'Connie's from Bolivia and Mitzi's from Krishgishtish,' he seemed to say.

'From where?'

'Kyrgyzstan,' he said. 'You know, between Kazakhstan and Tajikistan, just west of China.'

Trust him to know the location of every former Soviet Republic.

'She's hot, don't you think?' Jake said.

'She's cute, yes,' I agreed. She had a Central-Asian glow about her – rosy cheeks and glinting, almond-shaped eastern eyes. 'Though I hope you don't just like the colour of her passport. If you mess her around, there'll be hell to pay with Marsha. She'll kill both of us.'

'Allez, man, you think I'd do that?' he asked, but I didn't have time to reply honestly because Marsha had decided it was time for us to do some work.

'Come on, guys. We're not going to play sexy French maids for you. Get serving.'

So Jake and I morphed into butlers and distributed platefuls of picnic fare, and Jake remembered that he'd brought some mood lighting. He got a thick white candle out of his carrier bag and melted the base so that it stood upright in the dip between four cobblestones.

'Et voilà,' he said, lighting the wick.

The girls applauded him.

'Tu es très poétique,' Mitzi said.

'There are some people who inspire me,' he told her,

and then ruined it all by offering to read her one of his poems.

'After the picnic, please,' I begged, and we all tucked in.

Despite the mildly stagnant odours wafting off the canal and the constant tramp of feet passing just inches from our plates, it was one of the best picnics I've ever had. The lights from the barges opposite and the cinema further along the bank were glowing brightly now, colouring the whole surface of the canal basin. The soundtrack was laughter, conversation, the thud of *pétanque* balls and the melodic strumming from an invisible picnicker who'd decided, in typical Parisian fashion, to play his way through the entire Bob Marley songbook, fortunately without murdering the words in a French accent. And Jake's gallantry had made Marsha forget that he'd invited himself. The mood was one of harmony and what the French call *gourmandise*. This is not, as some people say, gluttony, because *gourmandise* is a positive thing. It implies hearty enjoyment, even to excess, and the French approve of that. So even after we'd finished the champagne, and were opening our second bottle of Jake's red, none of us were feeling the slightest bit guilty about over-indulging. We were paying homage to the gods of good living, who are the only deities to slip through the net of France's official state atheism.

Mitzi opened the gift pack of macaroons to reveal what looked like a pop-artist's paintbox.

'OK, let me tell you the flavours,' she said, reading from a list in the lid. 'Pineapple-lime, melon-rum, strawberry-lychee, clementine-pomegranate . . .'

I didn't like to seem ungrateful – they'd probably cost a fortune – but I find macaroons a bit textureless at the best of times, and these flavours were going to be like eating solid marmalade. When it was my turn to dip into the box, the twins saw me hesitating.

'It's la sélection fantaisie tropicale,' Connie said. 'I hope you don't prefer simple chocolate or coffee?'

'No,' I assured her, selecting the most exotic one – kumquat-mango – and taking a violently sweet mouthful.

'They look like Andy Warhol hamburgers,' I said, once my gums were clear of goo.

'Oh, blasphemy!' Connie shrieked.

'You don't like hamburgers?' I asked, and Connie poked her tongue out in disgust. I gave Amandine a meaningful smile.

'No, it's the sense of chic that makes Paris Paris,' Mitzi said. 'Hamburgers aren't chic.'

'That's so veritable,' Jake said, as if he knew something about chic.

But I saw Amandine shooting me an impatient, you-think-you're-clever look, so I changed the subject, giving everyone a rundown of my food-related job for the Ministry.

'If you're thinking of going to Brittany by train, you'd better go soon,' Marsha said.

'I'm planning a quick trip before the transport strike kicks in,' I said. 'The only difficulty will be travelling around to see the food suppliers.' I told them about the police arresting my driving licence.

'No problem,' Jake piped up. 'I will drive you.'

'You will?' I asked.

'Yes. You get me a train ticket, I will drive you in Brittany.'

'Don't you have to work?'

'Work? Pff,' he said, sounding alarmingly like a French civil servant.

'Have you actually driven since you got your French licence?'

'No, but driving in France will be just like in the US, except with smaller cars and more drunks. Pas de problème, Paul. Have confidence. Trust moi.'

I was trapped. Trusting Jake was not always advisable, but helpfulness was his main redeeming quality. If I told him I was moving my tea room across Paris to a new *arrondissement*, and that every teabag had to be carried individually, on foot, from the Champs-Élysées to a new shop in the Marais, he would happily spend the next forty-eight hours doing the carrying. He would probably lose 10 per cent of the bags after stopping for a smoke or a coffee and leaving them in a *tabac*, and give another 10 per cent away to a Tajikistani girl in exchange for the promise of a date, but the original intention would be all good. Jake was always there for you, even when you would have preferred him not to be.

'Thanks,' I said. 'Let me look into trains and stuff.'

The macaroons disappeared, and only Jake and I seemed to think they were anything less than a divine invention. But Jake hid his scepticism well, and began devouring Mitzi with his hungry blue eyes. His charm offensive was officially under way, although I had my doubts about his chances. The two women were so alike, and sitting so close, it was almost as if they were sharing a kidney. They were a unit. Shit, I thought, maybe they were a couple? But Jake was crooning away at them, expressing his undying love for kumquats, pomegranates and (less credibly) fashion, all the while piling on the flattery in true *séducteur parisien* style.

'So, what did you think of that note I left on your pillow?' Marsha asked me.

'It was a great present to wake up to,' I said. 'Very life-like drawing. Really sexy.'

Amandine tactfully strolled away to make a phone call.

'Well, for the time being at least, I'm afraid a drawing is about as sexy as it's going to get,' Marsha said. I must have looked surprised, because she laughed, and mouthed, 'Time of the month.'

'Oh, right. But that doesn't stop us sleeping together,' I said. 'I mean, just sleeping. Could be cosy.'

'Aah,' she cooed, ruffling my hair. 'You're cute. No, I get these bloody awful cramps and I need the space to fling my arms about and swear into the pillow. Best if I sleep alone for the next few days.'

Like I said, she wasn't the most romantic of women. Refreshingly honest, though.

So after we'd cleaned up our empties and folded the blanket, we all said very civilised goodbyes. It was *bises* all round, except for a long, tongue-entwining kiss from Marsha. And then Jake carried the wobbling twins across the cobblestones, while Marsha and Amandine strode away together, deep in conversation. I set off in the other direction, picking my way between the splayed legs of late picnickers and wondering how to organise a fact-finding tour of Brittany hampered by a looming transport strike and Jake's offer to act as chauffeur in a country where he'd almost never driven. A warm, damp wind began to gust along the canal, like a warning of stormy mishaps being blown in from the west.

Cinq

'Nous les Français, nous sommes très proches de la nature – nous devons toujours soit la recouvrir d'une autoroute, soit lui consacrer un poème, soit la manger'.

We French have a very close relationship with Nature – we always want to lay a motorway across it, write a poem about it, or eat it.

Pierre Vertefesses, former French Minister of the Environment, who was accidentally shot by a boar hunter in 1997 while out collecting snails

I

THE TRIP to Brittany started out perfectly, in the first-class carriage of a TGV. Officially, it was a strike day, but most of the TGVs were running. The strikers obviously didn't want to provoke public outrage by disrupting people's weekends. I'd accepted the French railways' kind online offer of an upgrade for a few euros extra, and now I was lounging in a soft, wide armchair-style seat equipped with an electric socket that actually worked, ensuring that I would never run out of musical protection against any sudden outbursts of poetry from the seat opposite. Yes, against my better judgement, I'd accepted Jake's offer. Luckily, he wasn't in reading-aloud mood. He was writing a new entry for the poetry competition. Or trying to.

He'd rolled up pieces of a napkin from the buffet and stuffed them in his ears to block out the conversation from across the aisle. Two women with hooped blue-and-white Breton T-shirts and identical haircuts – neck-length bobs held back by velvet headbands – were discussing whether either of them should have a fourth child. Not a good idea, they agreed, because it would mean moving outside Paris into the *banlieue*. Although *pourquoi pas*, because so far one of the mothers had had three boys, and a girl would be nice. But then again no – the nanny moaned enough about three children, so a fourth might make her leave. And with four, would there be too big an age gap between the youngest and a new baby? Perhaps. Or perhaps not. And so on. And on. And on. The bizarre thing was that the two husbands, floppy-fringed French exec types with polo shirts, hairy arms and large watches, were sitting there, one of them reading *Le Figaro*, the other a yachting magazine, completely oblivious to their domestic fate.

Meanwhile, nearby, a huddle of six kids aged from

about ten down to three, were sharing games consoles, colouring or silently reading. Not one of them was munching snacks, fighting or texting. Wow, I thought, these French middle classes can be scary.

'It's going to be a trilogy!' Jake suddenly shouted, apparently trying for Marie-Dominique decibel levels.

'Take your earplugs out,' I told him.

'A love trilogy,' he told me, more quietly.

'A *ménage à trois* of poems? Cool,' I said, hoping that would be the end of the conversation.

'Yeah, I'm calling it "Fuck Fuck Fuck".'

'Jake . . .' All French people know that word, and one of the kids had turned round to see where the English swearing was coming from. As usual, Jake didn't seem to understand what was going on in the world around him, namely that the women were nudging their husbands and wondering aloud whether this loud American looked like a first-class passenger.

'The poem's just getting hot,' he said. 'Chaud,' he translated for his new French audience, before bunging up his ears again.

Smiling apologetically at our fellow passengers, I took refuge inside my headphones.

We spent the next three hours or so gliding through the green-and-gold French countryside, a seemingly infinite expanse of cornfields and woodland. I saw a few flashes of the wide, silky River Loire and its golden sandbanks, and then, just after the urban intrusion of Nantes, I caught sight of the curly bridge that meant we were almost at the coast. The Pont de Saint-Nazaire is a soaringly high suspension bridge that takes an odd, meandering S-route across the Loire. Apparently, it was originally meant to cross the river diagonally, but at the last minute the engineers realised that this wouldn't leave enough room for a central river channel, so they had to twist the central span straight and build curving ramps up to it. I've also been told that it dips slightly in the middle and suffers from chronic cement erosion. Reassuring proof that French engineers don't get it right every time.

As soon as the regulars saw the bridge's S-bend, they began to gather up their magazines, newspapers, bags and children, and a few minutes later we pulled into La Baule – by my reckoning, two minutes early. These TGVs are amazing, I thought. Their arrival time is calculated as the moment your feet actually touch the platform.

So I was in an optimistic frame of mind as we walked into the station hall with the small horde of weekenders, and I didn't much care when we found a note taped to the glass door of the car-hire booth saying that all cars picked up after 7 p.m. had to be fetched from the main office, on the edge of town, even though it was only 7.10 p.m., and it seemed to me to be totally insane to close your office ten minutes before a Paris train arrived in town. For once, though, I took the insanity in my stride. Well, almost.

'Didn't they tell you where to pick up the car when you reserved?' I asked Jake.

'Yes. No. Well, yes,' he replied worryingly. I'd got him to hire the car because the rental people wouldn't let me book in his name using my credit card. That was absurd, I argued. After all, at worst, I was just being stupidly generous. But they replied that it was policy – the name on the driving licence had to be the same as the one on the credit card. I tried to ask whether there was a gang of perverted criminals that went around paying for people's car hire against their will, and forcing their generosity on unwilling renters, but my French let me down and the irony fell flat on its face. Anyway, the upshot was that Jake had hired the car.

'I believed we would get it at the station,' he said, 'but maybe that was an *erreur*.'

Maybe wasn't the word.

Luckily, all the weekenders were either getting picked up by family or walking to their seaside second homes, so we hopped unchallenged into the lone taxi waiting outside the station.

The driver asked us if we'd had a *bon voyage*, and where we'd be staying, and Jake began to interrogate him about the most common nationalities of female tourists visiting this part of France, while I sat back to enjoy the start of my first mission for the Ministère. With a few phone calls, I'd set up a tasting tour of local food producers and a meeting with a local Chamber of Commerce lady – what could possibly go wrong?

We drove for ten minutes or so through silent tree-lined streets of nineteenth-century houses, and then into a typical French edge-of-town zone with a furniture warehouse, car showroom, two chain restaurants and a DIY-garden store, the kind of place that blights even the cutest French seaside resort or historic town. The car-hire office was out here, and open, so I hung on to some of my store of optimism, even when the taxi driver jammed a receipt into my hand and accelerated away with an unnecessary squeal of his tyres. He was obviously still in shock at Jake's over-detailed answer to the question 'what do you do in Paris?'

'Just because this is France, it doesn't mean you can talk non-stop about sex,' I told him.

'The provinciaux are so coincés,' Jake moaned, meaning hung-up.

'No, the problem is that these conversations of yours aren't consensual. You rape their ears.'

'Hey, good one, man. Can I use that line?' He began digging around for his notebook.

'Be my guest,' I told him. 'But please don't credit me for it. Now maybe we should get our car?'

'Uh?' Jake looked up from his notebook and seemed to

notice for the first time that we were standing beneath a huge sign saying '*Location de voitures*'.

Inside a prefabricated hut, the car-hire guy was like car-hire guys the world over: white shirt, tie decorated with company logo and coffee stains, and the expression of someone who can't wait to go home. But he smiled, wished us *bonsoir* and asked for a reservation number.

For a moment, Jake paled. He began tapping an empty back pocket in his crumpled jeans, and I feared the worst. But then he tried another pocket, smiled, and pulled out a folded sheet of paper.

'Voilà,' he announced, just as my phone began ringing. I wouldn't have taken the call, but it was Marie-Dominique, no doubt checking that I'd managed to find Brittany. Not wanting to deafen the car-hire guy or shatter his windows, I went outside to take her call. It was beginning to drizzle.

'Bonsoir,' she yelled, and I held the phone at arm's length.

'Bonsoir, je suis en Bretagne,' I shouted back, and a loud gust of rain confirmed the fact.

'Très bien,' she bellowed, and went on to broadcast to the whole of western France that she had set up a meeting the following morning with the director of the artists' residence.

'Excellent, so there is no problem with the unions?'

'Pah,' she roared. 'Have you got a pen and paper? I will give you the director's mobile number.'

'Can't you text it to me?' I pleaded. The rain was picking up, and I was keen to get back indoors, not least because Jake seemed to be having some kind of disagreement with the car-hire man.

'No, you write it down,' Marie-Dominique ordered, and I had to rummage around in my jacket pockets for a pen and the printout of my train e-ticket. As I did so, I saw Jake performing a worrying French gesture: both arms held out, elbows bent and palms held upward as if to catch two coconuts. I'd seen it before, and it usually meant 'what the hell do you expect me to do?' Not a good sign.

'Go ahead,' I told Marie-Dominique. Luckily she was speaking so loudly that I could put my phone on the ground and use both hands to write.

She dictated the number, and as I read it back I was relieved to see Jake give me a double thumbs-up and follow the car-hire guy through a doorway at the back of the office.

I went indoors to finish talking to Marie-Dominique in the dry. The clouds had turned from evening grey to stormy gunmetal, and the rain was now bulleting down.

As I put away my phone, I heard an engine growl to life somewhere outdoors. Bloody hell, I thought, he's got us an upgrade to a sports car.

There was a crunch of tyres on gravel, and the engine sound began to move down the side of the prefab towards the front forecourt.

'It's all I had left,' a voice behind me said. It was the car-hire guy, coming back into the hut through the other door. 'It's a bit more expensive, too,' he added.

I opened the front door expectantly, heard a racing gear change, and saw Jake swing into view, struggling to control the large, powerful engine and wide tyres of a Ferrari-yellow . . . dumper.

A dumper. Yes, a skip on wheels, the kind of vehicle that builders use to transport mounds of earth or broken bricks, a chugging, windowless, roofless, industrial tractor. A one-seater, too. Jake was perched on a sort of saddle, the lone rider of a vehicle built for one.

'What the fuck?' My question was in English, but the car-hire guy understood it and gave a shoulder-raising shrug of indifference and helplessness. This was my *merde*, not his.

'It's all I had left,' he repeated.

'But we hired a car,' I protested, in French.

'Not chez nous,' he said, shrugging again.

Jake juddered to a halt in front of the open door and called to me to throw the bags into the skip.

I turned to the car-hire guy.

'Monsieur had reserved with our competitors, not us,' he said. 'I called them for you, but their office is closed now. All I can give you for tonight is this brouette.'

'Allez, Paul, it's raining. Let's get to the hotel,' came a wet plea from outside. 'You have remembered to reserve a hotel, n'est-ce pas?'

There were, of course, several courses of action open to me. I could, for example, have asked the car-hire guy to phone the taxi driver and apologise on my behalf for the obscenities he'd had to put up with during our previous trip. Or simply get us any other taxi in town. I could also have begged for a lift from the car-hire guy. More satisfyingly, I could have asked to borrow a piece of car-maintenance equipment and used it on Jake's skull.

Instead, I grabbed our bags, threw them into the skip, and climbed in after them. I think I even waved goodbye to the car-hire guy as Jake rattled us away towards the street. The rain lashing in my face, the puddle forming in the bottom of the skip and slowly drenching my backside, the spine-wrenching jolts as the little suspension-free dumper bounced into town: they were all punishments that I fully deserved for entrusting my fate to Jake. Here was a guy who couldn't even put together a pair of matching shoes, and I'd let him hire a car.

'Follow the signs to the harbour,' I shouted over the farting engine and the howling gale. 'It's the Hôtel du

Port. But you can just dump me in the water. I'll sleep with the fishes tonight.'

II

It was breakfast time at the hotel. At least I'd got that right. We were sitting in a sunlit room, feasting on a *petit déjeuner* of strong black coffee, six-inch lengths of crusty baguette and unlimited little foil packs of unsalted Breton butter. My only gripe would have been that there were no miniature tubs of orange marmalade in the jam basket. Don't the French understand the need for something tangier in the morning than bland apricot or strawberry?

Actually, that wasn't my only gripe – I was also pretty unhappy with Jake's conversation.

'I vote we keep it, man, it's fun.'

'No, Jake, we're getting something with at least two seats.' I rubbed my back as I remembered the crunching sound my coccyx had made every time it was slammed against the bare, rusty metal of the skip on the way to the hotel. Against all expectations, my body had actually come in contact with something less comfortable than Jake's sofa bed.

'But it's *amusant*. It's got a flashing light, and an alarm. You can make it go beep beep beep beep.'

A dream – or was it a dream? – flashed into my mind.

'Didn't I hear it beeping in the night?' I asked him.

'Yes, it was moi. I took it for a promenade.'

'You went out driving in the middle of the night?' My screech of disbelief caused the other guests – all of them middle-aged French couples here for a weekend of screech-free fresh air, no doubt – to stop in mid-gulp and stare at our table.

'Yeah,' Jake said. 'It stopped to rain, so I sortied for a moment. I hoped that maybe I could pick up a girl. It's an original line: Bonsoir, you want to ride in my brouette?'

Despite myself, I had to laugh.

'But I thought you had the hots for Mitzi?' I asked.

'Oui, but so far, she isn't hot for me. So, you know, I decided to try . . .'

'And did it work?'

'No. I only saw one person, an old lady who was taking her dog to shit in the jardin public. So I experimented with the lights and the beeper. It's très amusant, this brouette.'

'Well, we're taking it back. Or rather, you're taking it back, while I phone to try and get us the car you actually hired.'

'It's a dommage, though. I bet no one has ever wroten a poem about having sex in a brouette.'

'No, and I know why,' I said, feeling my spine twinge in sympathy.

*

An hour later we were cruising along the Breton lanes in a growling Peugeot. Admittedly it was only growling because it had a knackered engine, but to me, the ride couldn't have felt smoother. I wound down my window (no electric luxuries in this old model) and stuck my nose out to enjoy the wafting perfumes of sun-warmed pine needles and breeze-borne salt.

Driving along the dramatically named 'savage coast', we passed granite cottages where generations of fishermen must have arrived home at dawn carrying freshly caught mackerel for breakfast. Now many of the houses were shuttered up, waiting for their new urban owners to arrive with their packets of smoked Norwegian salmon. All along the winding clifftop road, patios and gardens surrounding white, tile-roofed houses spoke of loungers and barbecues that would soon be pulled out of the garage for the summer to come.

We crossed the headland and hit the salt marshes, some of them flooded, some of them dry. In the pools, long-legged water birds stuck their backsides in the air as they prodded for food. The drained areas were dotted with piles of salt that looked like the stashes of reckless cocaine dealers.

The only problem with the place was that it looked so good I wished I'd come here with Marsha rather than a hairy poet. Which in turn reminded me of the last time I'd been in Brittany – with Alexa. A disastrous trip. We'd ended up having a huge row about, if I remembered rightly, the ethics of fish farming. The things French intellectual women find to argue with their boyfriends about . . .

But I had no time for distractions from the past, least of all from Alexa. Jake and I were on our way to meet the lady from the Chamber of Commerce, who was to fill me in on the kinds of local produce I could buy for the artists' residence. She had a very Breton name – something like Gwendolen Kergueneguenec. I'd forgotten to print it out, so as Jake drove, or rather meandered across the whole of the available road surface while mumbling to himself, I hunted my phone for the email she'd sent me. This wasn't easy, because ever since arriving in Brittany I'd been getting about one message per minute sending me maps, restaurant phone numbers and weather reports, and offering me extra holiday minutes so I could call my friends and say what a great time I was having trying to use my phone while being interrupted every few seconds.

Before I'd had time to find the relevant email, Jake suddenly slammed on the brakes to avoid sending a woman flying over the sea wall and on to the deck of a fishing boat moored below. She'd been standing opposite the café where we were due to meet, hugging a plastic folder to her chest. She was about forty, with short, straight hair that seemed to have been styled by two warring hairdressers: one wanted her to be bright auburn, while the other was determined to turn her into a blonde, so that her head now looked as though it belonged to an albino tiger.

Apart from the unconventional hairdo, she was very formally turned out, in a long blue linen jacket and matching trousers, and was apparently delighted about this visit from the Parisian Englishman, despite Jake's attempt to run her over. She was smiling broadly as I got out to say hello. Jake stayed in his driver's seat and began scribbling in his notebook. That explained the mumbling – he was in writing mode again.

'Bonjour, Paul West,' I introduced myself.

'Bonjour, Guenkerguenerguekerec,' she said, or something like that. 'Guelkerm.' Great, I thought, she has a pet name that will be much easier to pronounce.

If only.

'Guelkerm to Bretagne,' she went on. 'You 'ave bin ear biff ore?'

It's always a tricky situation. You can't tell someone, 'Sorry, your English is too comic for us to have a serious conversation, why don't we speak French?', because when a French person comes straight out with English, it means they're longing for a chance to speak it. Denying them their pleasure would be as cruel as spitting on a slice of *far breton*.

Anyway, my French is a joke at the best of times, so I soldiered on with Gwen's English.

'This is my second time here,' I told her, as slowly as if the realisation was just dawning on me. 'It's very beautiful.' And it was – a traditional Breton waterfront overlooking a glittering bay that tapered out into a horizon of rich green woodland.

'Lovely weather, too,' I said, looking up at the clear sky.

'Yes, in zis bay we 'ave ze – 'ow you say? – meek rock lemur.'

'What's that?' I asked. A timid local mammal, it seemed.

'A Mick Rock lay mate?'

'Sorry?'

'Macro climb eight?'

'Ah, a *microclimate*.' I nodded. Every French person I'd ever met had told me that their area was just that little bit warmer and drier than anywhere else around.

''Ere is never snow,' she added.

'No.' Probably rains too much for that, I thought, although it was a gloriously refreshing spring day. No doubt just as gloriously refreshing as everywhere else along this coast, but who cared?

'You know about zis Ray John?' she asked.

'Who?'

'Zis Ray John? Zis aria.'

'Oh, the *region*. No, not much,' I confessed.

'Aaah.' She smiled and raised her eyebrows, as if I was

missing out on some major secrets. She pointed towards an island at the mouth of the bay, where gulls were circling above the frothing surf.

'Long time ago,' she said, touching my arm as if to prepare me for a shock, 'on zis isle were living parrots.'

'Parrots? Attracted here by the microclimate?'

'Yes, many of zem.'

'Very exotic.'

'No, very dangerous. Zey kill some fishers.'

'They killed fishermen? Surely not.'

'Yes, yes, zey kill zem.' She touched my arm again to press home her point. 'And', she continued, 'zey were English.'

'Man-hunting English parrots? Sorry, but ... Oh, I see.' The penny, or rather the doubloon, had finally dropped. 'You mean *pirates?*'

'Yes, English parrots, zey make camping on ze beach, and when zey want food, or drink or sex, zey come to ze village. Some of the people 'ere, zey descend from parrots.'

'And do you?' I asked.

'No, my family come from ze interior. We are far mares.'

'Farmers?'

'Yes.' She tapped the plastic file that she was still hugging in one arm. 'You want to 'ave coffee, talk about ze far mares in zis Ray John?'

'With pleasure.'

"'E come, your, er . . . ?' Gwen gazed into the car at Jake, and I understood why she was having trouble defining him. He was talking to himself while apparently trying to roll his long hair into cigarettes.

'My friend will join us if he wants a coffee,' I said, gesturing to Jake where we were going.

Inside, there were no crusty fishermen rinsing the salt out of their gullets, just a few French tourists enjoying a coffee. Even so, the café was fully equipped to set sail for the open sea. Its walls were decorated with enough lifebelts for a crew of twenty, there was a collection of oars hanging above the bar, and the ceiling was covered in an immense piece of sail canvas. Add to this the brass compass that was mounted in an alcove and the framed charts everywhere, and the place had everything it needed to navigate its way across the Atlantic.

Even so, the staff obviously planned on staying at least until lunchtime, because someone had written some tasty-sounding dishes up on the blackboard outside, most of them involving creatures that had very recently been swimming just offshore: *bar de ligne* (line-caught sea bass), *sardines entières grillées* (whole grilled sardines), *tourteau mayonnaise* (boiled crab salad) and *brochettes de Saint-Jacques* (scallop skewers). Every time I saw this kind of menu, it brought home to me how close to nature the French still live, even if they are doing their best to cram it all in their mouths.

Which, of course, was why I was there.

We sat at a table not yet laid for lunch, ordered a couple of *crèmes*, and Gwen opened her folder.

'It is good zat you are interested by ze local production,' she said. 'Ze big surfaces, you know, ze supermarket, zey sell too much ze imported production. Ze jambon from Dan Mark, ze sall-mon from Ireland, ze melon from Espagne. But really Bretagne can supply any sing you want. Saucisson!' she trumpeted, thrusting a catalogue under my nose. It featured a free-range pig that was too busy snuffling about in the grass to realise that its days were numbered. 'Very many pig in zis Ray John. 'E give you good price.' I noticed that the producer's name bore a strong resemblance to Gwen's. Though it was hard to be sure – with their Guers, Kers and Ecs, all these Breton names looked the same to me.

'You want B.O. or not?' Gwen asked me.

'They can deodorise pigs?'

'Uh?' She looked confused, but only as much as I was.

'B.O.?' I repeated.

'For veggie tables and froo-its,' she said. 'B.O. You know, wiz no chemicals?'

'Oh, yes. Bee-o, organic.' Gwen's accent was making me forget stuff I already knew. She meant *bio*, short for *biologique*. I'd laughed when I first heard this French word for organic – all food is biological, isn't it? Except some fast food, of course, which is made of flavoured Lycra. 'I definitely want B.O. vegetables,' I said. 'The people eating this food will be artists, very delicate souls, we can't poison them with chemical fertilisers.'

'Zis is ze best B.O. producer.' Gwen pulled out a leaflet dotted with grinning potatoes and dancing leeks – veggies raised on strictly organic hallucinogenics. 'Good, but expensive, off course,' she said. 'B.O. is expensive.'

'Right.' Budget was the least of my problems. I took the leaflet and asked for more information on organic meats.

'You want we visit some of zem?' she offered.

'Yes, let's set up some meetings for this afternoon or tomorrow. First I have an appointment with the director of the artists' residence.'

'Ze what?' Gwen was frowning at me as though she didn't realise artists could actually reside anywhere.

'The artists' residence. You know, the Ministry of Culture building? Just along the seafront here?' She was still looking lost. 'Le building du Ministère de la Culture?'

'Ah, oui, you mean Sainte-Vierge-des-Algues. Ze monastère.'

'The *ex*-monastery,' I corrected her. The building formerly known as the Holy Virgin of the Seaweed had been sold off by a religious community who had apparently had enough of the Atlantic wind whistling up their cassocks.

'I 'ave meet ze director.' Gwen fiddled uncomfortably with one of her blonde streaks. ''E is . . .' She groped for the right word, as she had done when trying to describe Jake. 'Parisien,' she finally said, making it sound as if it was a mental illness. Which it can sometimes be – a sort of paranoia that makes you think everyone's trying to be more snobbish than you. ''E play music in ze night. Opéra. Very strong. And 'e sing.' She let out a piercing squawk that was obviously meant to be an imitation of the director's taste in serenades, but sounded more like a killer parrot on the hunt for human flesh.

Just then Jake walked in. There was a sense of urgency about him. Oh God, I groaned to myself, he's left the handbrake off and let the car roll into the sea.

'Paul,' he called, before he'd even reached our table.

'What is it?'

He came over, grimacing, apparently in pain. Shit, I thought, the car must have squashed a fisherman on its way down.

'Can you . . .?' he asked.

'Can I what?'

'Can you think of a rhyme for anal?'

I was so relieved that there had been no loss of life or vehicle that all I could think was: Thank Christ he asked it in English. And the even crazier thing was that I actually gave his question a few seconds' thought.

Gwen was smiling patiently, which Jake obviously

interpreted as an interest in his poetic problem. He introduced himself and seemed about to ask her for some obscene rhymes, so I leapt in and told Gwen we had to rush if we were going to be on time to see the director.

'I'll phone you later,' I promised her as I dragged Jake towards the door.

III

'Correct me if I'm wrong, Paul, but I'm sensing un peu de stress from you.'

Jake and I were sitting on a seat overlooking the bay. The concrete bench was set beside a rusted cannon pointing at the island where Gwen's parrot pirates had nested.

The tide was rushing out, revealing gleaming beds of smelly seaweed on the rocks below us and golden sandbanks beyond. Already, a small army of people were foraging for seafood with spades, nets, picks and rakes. There was a noticeboard on a nearby wall informing them that they could harvest 'only' five kilos of mussels each, five kilos of whelks, and three dozen oysters. It was enough to set yourself up as a fishmonger, and all free. Who needed a massive catering budget?

I wished I could go out there and vent my frustrations on some poor unsuspecting mollusc. I also wondered about burying Jake up to his neck in the sand to wait for the rising tide.

'You want to parley about it?' he asked, and I felt my irritation with him drift away on the fishy breeze. It wasn't his fault if he kept inflicting his poetry on me, after all. I was the one who'd dragged him out here as my driver.

'Yeah, you're right,' I told Jake. 'Thanks for asking. I feel as if I—'

But I didn't get any further with my attempt at a heart-to-heart.

'Or perhaps we both need to be alone for a moment,' he went on. 'I mean, I'm very content to be here to aid you, Paul, but I have work to do, you know.' He held up his notebook. 'And this is an inspiring place. Do you know the second meaning of the French word for mussel?'

Not wanting to guess, I decided to have a closer look at the ex-monastery, which was a short stroll away along the sea wall. It was a sober whitewashed stone building, four storeys high and overlooking a lawn that ran down to the beach. On the roof was a blackened wooden spire with a clock that had stopped, presumably when the monks stopped winding it up. It all looked very abandoned.

When it was time for the meeting, I returned to tell Jake he didn't have to come along. He could stay and finish his poem.

'Oh, non, man, I've finished it. And I want to meet le

directeur. The residence might have some space for artists of the written word, right?'

'Like obscene American poets, you mean?'

'Not obscene, man, just honest. And the French appreciate honest art. You see that art expo at the One Two Two? A bit tame, but très honest.'

I led the way to the monastery, a sense of impending doom settling on me like the pungent odour of rotting seaweed.

IV

There was a time, or so the legend goes, when the directors of France's museums, theatres, artists' residences and similar temples of culture used to roam the country like King Arthur's knights. They would arrive in a town, unhitch their cultural baggage, slay or tame the local dragons, 'save' a few damsels, and then move on after a couple of years, with tales of their grandeur echoing in their wake.

That was in the old days, though, before France began to realise that its coffers weren't bottomless. Now, it seemed, some of these directors were more like beached whales – lost and stranded, with no hope of returning to the Parisian feeding grounds.

Gérard Macabé was one of these. He wasn't exactly stranded – he was living only a ten-minute walk from a railway station. But I'd rarely seen anyone more washed up. Judging from the empty bottles decorating his office, he was probably on a full-time liquid diet.

He was about fifty, bald on top, with a crown of long grey-black hair and whitish whiskers that looked like the result of a week not shaving rather than an attempt at a real beard. His clothes, also off-white, were loose and flowing: a collarless shirt and a beaten-up suit. He was trying to project a bohemian image, but, I wondered, who to? He wasn't wearing a wedding ring. Divorced, I guessed, no doubt messily so.

His office was dominated by a Gothic wooden desk and ancient bookshelves that probably used to sag under the weight of leather-bound volumes, but were now a combination of filing cabinet and bottle bank. Even so, it was an enviable place to work from. The open bay window looked out at a sublime Breton coastal landscape: a white-sand beach, tidal rock pools, and, to the right, the graceful arc of the stone harbour wall dividing the calm turquoise of the bay from the choppy cobalt ocean beyond.

Apparently giving her blessing to the whole scene was a plaster statue of the Virgin Mary standing in one corner of the room. She appeared to be floating on a bed of seaweed while deep in conversation with a fish, and Gérard had heightened the surreal mood by hanging a chain of pierced bottle tops around Mary's neck and balancing a cigarette between her fingers. Not very respectful to the previous owners of the building, I thought, but presumably the Virgin was living on borrowed time, anyway – ripping out the religious symbols was going to be part of the atheist French State's conversion of the monastery into an artists' residence.

If the conversion ever happened, that is . . .

'Résidence?' Gérard's monastic-looking throne creaked as he turned to stare out of his bay window at the sea. He seemed to be looking for inspiration as to what a *résidence* might be. 'Is that what it's going to be now?' he asked me.

'Yes. And I am here to discuss the food budget.'

'Really?' He sighed philosophically and, noticing that his glass was empty, began to look around for a bottle. There was one right where I was sitting, on the other side of his immense desk, but it was hidden from his view by a pile of papers, and I wasn't going to help him find it.

'Voici!' Helpful as ever, Jake reached across from his seat, next to mine, and lifted up the bottle.

'Holy Virgin be praised!' Gérard blew a kiss at her statue and twisted off the cap. 'Get some glasses, have a drink.'

'No thanks, we'd better—' I began my standard no-drinking-this-early speech, but Jake beat me to it.

'Merci,' he said, and headed off towards a stretch of bookshelf that held some glass tumblers.

'Surely Marie-Dominique Maintenon-Dechérizy told

you about my visit?' I said, proud not only of my French sentence but also of remembering her full name.

'Probably,' Gérard said, more interested in Jake's progress than my question about his job. 'The name rings a bell. I've been here six months, and at the last count I had received twenty-seven mission statements from as many different departments about what I'm supposed to be doing here. That's one every . . .'

He trailed off, and both of us set about trying to calculate.

Jake saved me from mathematical embarrassment by coming back with two dusty glasses.

Gérard poured out three over-generous measures of clear amber liquid. I hadn't looked at the label but I guessed it was some kind of French hooch, like Calvados, the Norman apple-based alcohol that can sear a hole in your palate and do similar things to your brain.

'Allez!' Gérard motioned to Jake to take the other two glasses, and drained his own in one, as if it was mineral water.

'Chin,' I said, the French word for cheers, and took a sip of an oily liquid that instantly numbed the tip of my tongue.

'Chin!' Jake called out heartily, and, still on his feet, leant over to clink glasses with Gérard.

'Merci,' Gérard said, taking Jake's glass and draining that, too.

'So you've had twenty-seven mission statements,' I said. 'But Marie-Dominique's, about the résidence d'artiste, that was the last?'

'Yes,' Gérard agreed. 'Probably. Though there will probably be more mission statements, from the Ministry of Culture or elsewhere. Holiday camp, museum, research institute. If you ask me, it'll end up as a dogs' home for the pets of train drivers.'

'But they will all need catering, n'est-ce pas?' I ventured.

'Who, the dogs?' Gérard spluttered a laugh into his empty glass.

'Could it be a résidence de poètes?' Jake butted in.

'Why not?' Gérard said, giving a poetic sweep of his arm and accidentally throwing his glass out of the open window. I was relieved to hear it land with a tinkle of broken glass rather than a shout of pain from some innocent passer-by.

'For foreign poets, too?' Jake added.

'Mais oui! Qu'est-ce qu'un poète, si ce n'est un traducteur?' Gérard was obviously quoting something about a poet being a translator.

'Baudelaire!' Jake trumpeted, grabbing my full glass and holding it up in a toast. This time he made sure it was out of Gérard's reach.

Gérard filled his remaining glass and joined in the toast.

'You know Baudelaire?' he asked.

'Of course,' Jake said, and put on a poetic frown that made it obvious he was about to do some quoting of his own. 'Je plongerai ma tête amoureuse d'ivresse dans ce noir océan . . .' he intoned, meaning, if I understood correctly, that he was going to plunge his love-drunk head into a black ocean. Which, so I've heard, was the kind of thing French poets used to do.

'Perhaps we could visit the kitchens?' I said.

'Bien sûr,' Gérard agreed, glugging back the rest of his glass of hooch. 'I need another bottle, anyway.'

He led us down a magnificent wooden staircase, past dark patches on the white walls where picture frames had once hung. It was a slow process, because Gérard seemed to have taken enough tumbles to learn that stairs could be deceptively mobile things, apt to duck out of the way of his feet. It took five full minutes for him to edge his way down to the ground floor clinging on to the banister.

At the foot of the stairs, in a wide, wood-panelled hall, he let go of the banister and launched himself in the direction of a double door. After only one or two adjustments of his trajectory, he gripped the door handle and opened up, almost falling to his knees as the door swung away from him.

'Voilà le réfectoire,' he announced, his voice echoing in a long, empty room that must once have held a table for fifteen or twenty people. It had excellent potential. It opened out on to the lawns, where there was room for a large patio beneath some mature, leaning pine trees. If I were an artist being entertained at France's pleasure, I wouldn't say no to having dinner here – in summer, at least. In winter, the long French windows probably rattled like Gérard's glass as his trembling hand poured out the first shot of the day.

'Et par ici, la cuisine,' he said, pointing in one direction and walking in another. Those three full glasses of high-octane alcohol were beginning to take serious effect.

Jake and I beat Gérard to the door at the end of the refectory and opened it, guiding the director into a musty room lined with vintage, and much-used, kitchen equipment: a range of six gas rings, a pair of deep metal sinks, fitted cold cabinets, and a long stainless-steel preparation surface. All of it would probably get torn out and replaced when the building was renovated, but there was certainly enough room for a decent catering kitchen, or for artists to prepare their own food if they felt creative at mealtimes.

'Et par ici, la cave à vin,' Gérard slurred, his last dregs of consciousness sending him towards a metal door in a corner of the room. He slammed nose-first against it and clung on. 'They left some bottles,' he added. 'Very Christian of them, n'est-ce pas?' His knees gave out and he began to sink slowly towards the floor.

'Don't let him get through there,' I ordered Jake, and started dialling Gwen.

'Qu'est-ce tu fais, Baudelaire?' Gérard asked Jake, who was trying to steer him back towards the refectory.

'Allô?' Gwen answered.

I told her about Gérard's semi-consciousness, in English out of courtesy.

'Drink?' she asked me.

'Drunk,' I said, more clearly.

'Dronk?'

'Il est ivre mort,' I told her. 'Il faut appeler un médecin.'

As if to make my French even clearer, Gérard began to roar his opposition to being ushered away from the wine cellar.

'We need to get you some coffee,' Jake told him.

'Bad for the heart!' Gérard objected. 'Too much adrenalin!'

'I'll send a doctor,' Gwen told me, in French. 'But you see what I meant – he has a very strong voice, n'est-ce pas?'

'Yes,' I agreed, 'he should be an opera singer.'

'Opera singer, moi?' Gérard had overheard me. 'No, I'm the director of a future car park. The director of a wasteland. The director of nothing.'

Here, at last, he was talking sense. And I was going to have to break the news to Marie-Dominique.

*

V

First, though, I went through the motions of visiting some food producers with Gwen.

I admired a field of swaying potato leaves, comforted by the knowledge that only organic poop had been dumped on them. I visited some goats that smelled worse than the homeless men who sleep in Saint-Michel Métro station, but whose cheese melted so deliciously on the tongue that I bought half a dozen pats to bring home with me.

But even as I was picturing the hot goat's cheese salads I was going to make myself, I couldn't help thinking that all this might be a waste of time. If half of what Gérard had said was accurate, there was no point in my writing a report.

Still, consolation for these negative thoughts was provided by the sausage-making machine. We were at a pig farm, watching a hair-netted butcher do his party trick. He slipped a length of transparent pig entrail over the nozzle of the machine, held the condom-like sheath in place, pressed a button, and *boing*, the machine whipped out an instant ten-inch stiffy that would have made the best-hung porn actor blush with envy. The sausage-maker did this a few times, and then started to play to his audience, producing misshapen benders in all directions, like a catalogue of erectile dysfunctions.

Gwen was screeching with laughter, while Jake got his pad out and started making notes, although I for one couldn't think of a rhyme for sausage.

Despite the comedy, Gwen kept enough of her Chamber of Commerce wits about her to inform me, as Jake drove us out of the pig farm, that all this fun was being had with minimal damage to the environment.

'Only five microgram of nitrate per litre,' she announced proudly.

'What does that mean?' I asked.

'No merde in ze reever,' she said. 'So no merde in ze sea, and no toxic seaweed. Well, almost.'

'Hey, let's go for a swim,' Jake piped up, inappropriately as ever. 'There's a nudist beach, n'est-ce pas?' he asked Gwen. 'Une plage nudiste?'

She rather nervously admitted that there was, and I had to agree that a swim sounded a great idea. I told her we'd drop her off at her office first, and she accepted with a heart-warming show of gratitude.

So, after thanking Gwen for her help, promising to read the reams of literature she'd printed off from websites I could have consulted myself, and begging her to keep a protective eye on Gérard the dipso director, I let Jake swerve me through the salt marshes. And despite four or five attempts to nose-dive the car into a pond, he soon had us zipping along a fragrant-smelling coast road, behind a dune crested with rustling pine trees.

'Every time when I go to the ocean, I visit the nudist beaches,' he told me.

'Why do I find that so easy to believe?' I answered.

He was a little disappointed by this Breton beach, though, because it was almost empty of nudes. In the space of a couple of hundred metres there were only three or four stripy canvas windbreaks up, with pairs of bronzed legs protruding from behind them, and a male couple were splashing each other playfully in the waves. Personally I was delighted. It was the long, white curve of sand that we'd seen from Gérard's window, and looked even better close up than it had from a distance.

'Allez!' Jake said, throwing his jacket on to the sand and tugging at his belt.

Now, I was literally sleeping in his bed at the time, but we'd never seen each other naked. So I hesitated. I don't know if girls have the same problem, but for best mates to strip off together outside the hearty male atmosphere of the sports changing room is always awkward.

Jake, though, obviously had no reservations about getting his clothes off under any circumstances. Within seconds, he was already down to his socks.

And, despite my doubts, I followed suit. The combination of sun, crashing surf and the need to forget that Gérard, the incapacitated director of the non-existent artists' residence, might be getting sozzled yet again as he looked out of his window towards us, had me ripping off my clothes and sprinting for the sea. The shock of the cold water stung me all over, and no doubt had a certain area of my body shrinking like a sausage machine filmed in reverse. Though even this shrinkage didn't protect me as I bodysurfed in on one of the waves and skidded to a halt in the shallows, giving myself a sand-burn that was going to have Marsha asking some probing questions about what I'd been up to in Brittany.

Ah yes, Marsha. I had to call her, and soon. During the goat farm and sausage factory visits, she'd kept trying to phone me. Her first voicemail asked whether I was definitely going to be a judge in her competition, so I quickly texted back that of course I was. She replied almost immediately, asking whether I was 100 per cent sure, because she'd be 'up *merde* creek' otherwise. Again, I answered yes. But she'd called three or four times more, and I hadn't answered. I was beginning to suspect that she might be one of those people who have to share all their organisational worries with you. The slightest thing goes wrong and they bombard you with angst. And meanwhile, I had a few of my own things to organise.

Now, though, the thrill of the clear, cool ocean on my skin was flushing all the angst out of my system. As I crouched down and let the waves crash into my face, I even began to think that I should adopt a stance of total denial as far as Marie-Dominique and the Ministry were concerned. *Problèmes? Quels problèmes?* If I gave a full and frank account of the trip to Brittany, my contract might be out of the window as fast as Gérard's empty glass. Perhaps I should just ride it all out and keep quiet? After all, I didn't care if there was an artists' residence or not. My job was to submit a report about potential food sourcing. I didn't care if it was ever actually sourced. The wisest course of action was a discreet cover-up.

Which, as it happened, was exactly what I wished Jake would do. He was out beyond the breakers, swimming on his back, having perfected a stroke that lifted his pelvis, and all its attachments, out of the water every time he kicked his legs. Lucky for him, I thought, that Gwen's man-eating parrots were no more than a translation mistake.

I hated to spoil his fun, but it was time to cover ourselves up again and get back to the city.

VI

On the train back to Paris, I typed up my notes and cobbled together a cut-and-paste catalogue of the food producers I'd visited. All it needed was a little padding out with more suppliers from the internet, a few sample locavore menus, a linguistic going-over by a native French speaker, and I'd be able to send in my report and claim my prize money.

I called Marie-Dominique and told her I'd like to

arrange a meeting in the next couple of days. OK, she said, set one up with my secretary. Which would have been fine if the secretary ever deigned to answer her phone. So I had to content myself with leaving voice-mails telling her 'c'est très urgent'.

My day was rounded off with a reassuringly normal reunion with Marsha that evening. Well, as near to normal as she could manage.

She said we should meet at La Pagode, a Chinese building in the middle of the posh, and ultra-French, 7th *arrondissement*. It was, she told me, more than a hundred years old, and had originally been built as a gift for the wife of a Paris department-store owner. But the lady obviously wasn't a fan of all things oriental because she ran away with her husband's business partner, and soon after that the pagoda was sold off and turned into one of Paris's first cinemas.

When I arrived there, I got a bit of a shock. There aren't many buildings in central Paris with an impenetrable bamboo plantation in the courtyard or bright red wooden monkeys grinning down at you from the rafters. It all boded very well for our night out, I thought. I was just in the mood for a comedy kung fu movie.

Sadly, though, as soon as Marsha arrived, she dispelled my illusions. There was nothing Chinese about the films being shown here – there was an art movie festival on. So I had to sit through a French epic in which, as far as I could tell, two sophisticated French couples couldn't decide which combination to shag each other in: husband-wife, husband-wife-mistress, husband-wife-other husband, husband-mistress-other husband, two wives, two husbands, or all together. Which wouldn't have bothered me too much if the characters hadn't blathered on for hours about their needs and desires and what to have for dinner.

Even so, once we were free of the cinema, I was all for getting a bite to eat, but first Marsha wanted to show me how things were progressing at her new shop, so we cabbed across town to the Marais. As we drove, she told me how she had badgered and charmed workmen into putting up shelves in all the right places. She'd batted her eyelashes at the telecom people to get an internet account open, and she'd hooked up some kind of e-book download station so customers who were allergic to paper could get their books in digital format. She'd even snapped up the stock of a more traditional bookshop that was closing down. More amazingly yet, she'd also found time to create a buzz about the poetry competition.

'Fufty intrants all-riddy!' she gushed, her accent veering out of control with the excitement.

We were now standing in her upstairs events space, a long, wooden-beamed room with a podium by the window, and several stacks of folding chairs leaning against one wall.

'But I'm worried about Amandine,' she told me. 'She's been saying she wants out.'

'Why? She was totally up for it when she talked to me.'

'It's her boyfriend. He's a possessive prick by the sound of it. Doesn't want her on stage in the limelight. He's been trying to get her to give up her job with your old lech of a boss, too. Sounds like a cliché on legs.'

'Yes,' I said, distractedly. I was still stuck on 'boyfriend'. I hadn't imagined Amandine with a bloke, even though she was more than beautiful enough to have all of Paris chasing after her, and not just her sex-mad boss. 'Jean-Marie is a health risk,' I said. 'But she seems to be handling him very well. She's not going to drop out of the jury, is she?'

'No, I talked her round,' Marsha said. 'But we're going to have to put a curtain up at the front of the table so her boyfriend doesn't think anyone's staring up her skirt. Honestly, the French say they're against the veil, but give them a public vote and half of the guys would say yes to long skirts and baggy blouses for their own wives and girlfriends. You're not like that, are you, Paul?'

I didn't need to be a genius to work out the correct answer to that one, so I kissed her and said that, on the contrary, right now I was thinking how nice it would be if she was even less hidden by clothing.

'My thoughts exactly,' she said, grabbing my shirt and pulling me towards her. 'I was wondering,' she went on as she undid the buttons, 'has none of your other girlfriends ever asked you to wax?'

'Wax what, exactly?' I asked.

'Just your chest, silly,' she said.

'No, no one's ever mentioned it, and no one is going to be pouring hot wax anywhere near my nipples if I can help it.'

'Oh.' She sounded disappointed in my former girlfriends' lack of firmness on the issue of chest hair. 'Hey, that reminds me. I saw that ex of yours yesterday, here outside the shop again.'

'What? Alexa?'

'The one who was here the other day. The photographer. Bitch was taking photos of the poster in the window.'

'What poster?' I asked, deciding that it was not the time to argue about whether Alexa was a bitch or not.

'The one advertising the poetry competition. I was indoors with the workmen. I noticed someone getting a shot of the shopfront, and thought, great, I'll go and ask what it's for. But when she saw me coming, she buggered off. She was halfway to the rue de Bretagne by the time I got out into the street. What's she doing hanging around here? And what's she got to be so furtive about?'

'I don't know,' I said. It was all completely baffling.

'Yeah, well, can you call and tell her to lay off?'

'Well . . .' I hadn't talked to Alexa since we split up.

'Unless you still feel some loyalty to her, of course?' There was an edge to Marsha's voice.

'No, I don't feel any loyalty to her at all,' I said, wondering how true that was. 'I'll call her and ask what she's up to.'

'Thanks.' Marsha showed her gratitude by resuming the undoing of my shirt buttons. 'Bet she never asked you to wax, did she?' she asked. 'Too much of a hippie, by the look of her. Tell her I'll wax her if she comes back here again.' Which was not something I wanted to see, mainly because it reminded me too much of the film we'd just watched at La Pagode.

Any remaining eroticism in the air went out of the window a few seconds later when my phone began buzzing in my pocket.

'You're going to *answer* it? *Now?*' Marsha said.

'Sorry, but it might be Marie-Dominique's secretary.'

'Is she that much of a hottie?'

'It's Amandine,' I said, looking at the screen.

'Oh, another hottie.' Marsha turned away in protest.

'Paul? Are you anywhere near the Champs-Élysées?' Amandine asked. It sounded urgent.

'No, I'm with Marsha, at her shop,' I said. 'Is there a problem?'

'Yes, but I wanted to tell you in person, not on the phone.'

'Can it wait till tomorrow?' I asked.

'Not really,' Amandine said. There was a short silence, and then she began speaking softly and quickly. 'I heard Jean-Marie talking to a low-yah.' Like many French people, she couldn't pronounce lawyer. 'He was discussing whether he could force you to sell your share of the tea room. Non-respect of contract, inability to pay expenses, things like that. He wants to take over so that he can install his diner. And he told the low-yah he needs a result inside a week. I am in favour of the idea of a diner, but this isn't *fair*. You've got to do something, Paul.'

'I hope it was very urgent,' Marsha said when I rang off.

'Yes,' I said. 'Very. I'm in the *merde*.'

And for once it sounded like an understatement.

Six

'Ceux qu'on aime, on ne les juge pas.'
You don't judge the people you love.

> Jean-Paul Sartre, who famously tried to love as
> many of his students as possible

I

YOU'D THINK that French lawyers would be cheap. The law they practise is all based on Napoleon's 200-year-old *code civil*. Obviously it's been updated a little bit to include recent innovations like the internet and equality for women, but basically it's unchanged since l'Empereur sat down and decided how he wanted France to be managed. So surely, I thought, all a French lawyer needs to do is look up the relevant clause in the index? That must be cheaper than British law, which gets rewritten every time some loony magistrate delivers a judgment.

Yet French lawyers seemed to be just as keen on making money as their British counterparts. When I called the guy who had helped me with the legalities of starting up the tea room, I could almost hear the timer ticking in the brisk tone of his voice.

He was only a little older than me, and we'd been on friendly terms, but it had been a good year or more since I'd spoken to him, and in the interim his career had obviously moved into higher financial echelons.

'I can look again at your contract,' he said in the transatlantic accent he'd picked up doing a year at some absurdly expensive American university.

'How much will it cost me?' I didn't feel I had the time to ask in a politer, roundabout way.

'I will give it an hour or two,' he said, and then told me his current hourly rate, which made me catch my breath and wish he could deal with my problem in, say, three minutes.

'But do you think Jean-Marie can do this to me?' I asked.

'I can't say without looking at the contract. Do you know the name of his lawyer? I could talk to him.'

'No, I don't,' I said quickly. I could just imagine the two of them comparing notes, the clock between them, like two chess players in reverse, gleeful that the minutes were mounting up.

'I'm sure we can find a way to block him,' my lawyer said dubiously. 'Leave it with me. I'll call you in a couple of days.'

I hung up, unsure whether this had been a reassuring conversation or not. It was a bit like a woman at an airline counter telling you not to worry because she was sure she'd be able to get you on another flight home. If the worst came to the worst, she'd sell you a seat in first class. My problem wasn't so much could I stop Jean-Marie shafting me? It was more a question of could I *afford* to stop him?

II

Next up, problem number two on my long list.

'Bonjour, vous êtes bien sur le répondeur d'Alexa. Hi, this is Alexa's answerphone.'

It was spooky hearing her voice again after so long – a year or more. It was the same voicemail message, too. Hadn't she moved on in life?

I hung up. I had so much to say that I was bound to break the sixty-second barrier. I always find that any voicemail more than a minute long starts to feel weird.

I was sitting in Jake's garret, and the morning sun was heating the zinc roof about three centimetres above my head so that it felt as if I was in a space shuttle burning its way back into Earth's atmosphere. I moved the sofa bed closer to the open window, and stuck my feet out into the fresh air.

Keeping one eye out for any pigeons that might decide

to use my toes as a perch, I looked Alexa up online, and found that she'd been very busy since we split up. She'd held several photo exhibitions, won a magazine's travel picture prize, got herself a fancy new website (which included, I was flattered to see, a few of her old portraits of me), and popped up as a credit in several books. Things were going well, and I was genuinely pleased for her.

I clicked on the contact link at her website and wrote her an email. After the usual 'long time no see' and 'how are things?' pleasantries, I asked her why she'd been taking photos of the tea room and 'the new English bookshop in the Marais'. Was there something I should know about?

To my surprise, she answered immediately, with a text message.

'Yes, but it would take a long time.'

I wondered if this was an invitation to phone her, but decided to stick to texting for the minute.

'Best not to hang around the bookshop again,' I told her. 'Owner's not happy.'

'Pity,' she replied. 'I was thinking of going to the poetry contest.'

I knew I had to talk her out of this.

'We definitely need to talk. Can I phone in five minutes?' I asked. I could go down into the street, or find a peaceful spot on the staircase where she wouldn't hear any stray *enculés*.

She didn't reply. Which presumably meant no.

I was just swearing to myself when Jake walked in.

'Bonjour, man,' he said, plonking himself down on the sofa bed beside me and staring at my computer screen. 'Hey, is that Alexa? I brought letters. Have you got a poon-aze?'

In all the years I've known him, I've never quite got used to Jake's surreal mind, so I answered the only bit I understood.

'Yes, it's her website,' I said.

'Cool, but you're not bezzing her any more, right?'

Baiser meant screwing. I didn't bother to reply. Instead I asked what he'd meant by 'letters'.

'Ah yeah, I opened the boîte downstairs.' He handed over two envelopes. 'You got a poon-aze?'

'A what?'

'Oh merde, what do we call them?' He held up a thumb. 'You know . . . poon-aze?'

While he wrestled with his linguistic problem, I looked at my letters. The first was an electricity bill. It was in Jake's name, but I was the one using the electricity, so as long as it wasn't a demand for a year's arrears, it was only fair for me to pay up.

The second was from the Ministry. I opened it and got a pleasant surprise. A very friendly note informed me that my free cinema pass was ready and that I could go and collect it any time. I just hoped it didn't stipulate that it was to be used exclusively for French art movies.

'Maybe I'll use one of the old poon-azes,' Jake said. He was standing by the large map of Paris hanging on the back of the door. 'Each poon-aze', he told me, pointing at a drawing pin, 'marks a place where I have had a femme – you know, baisé.'

I'd looked at the map several times since I moved in, and the obvious Jakesque reason for the pins hadn't occurred to me. There was one marking the apartment, logically enough. Others were dotted at random across the city, including one in the middle of the river. What, I asked him, was that?

'Bateau mouche, man,' he said.

'And is that one in Notre-Dame cathedral?' I asked.

'Oh yeah, man, Christmas Day, everyone chanting and shit, and I cached myself in the confessional with this atheist Cuban chick.'

'You're on the highway to hell, Jake. You're going to need some heat-resistant drawing pins.'

'Is that what you call them in England?'

'And now you need a new one?' I prompted.

'Well, no, at least not yet.'

'So you plan these things in advance, like some general with his map of the battlefields?'

'No.' He looked almost embarrassed, which had to be a first. 'I'm just . . .' He didn't seem able to think of the right word, but his finger was tapping on the 8th arrondissement. I looked more closely and saw that he was aiming just west of La Concorde, a chic zone as yet empty of conquests for him.

'Hey, that's the rue du Faubourg Saint-Honoré,' I said. 'Where Mitzi has her new boutique. You're fantasising about her, aren't you?'

His silence was just as telling as a lawyer's. It counted as much as any words he could say. I laughed and clapped him on the back.

'Welcome to the world of normality, Jake. You've met a girl and you haven't leapt in for the instant shag. And now you're fantasising about her, you're imagining what it might be like, hoping it will happen. And you feel unsure of yourself, excited about how things might turn out, nervous that it could all go wrong. It's fun, isn't it?'

'I don't know,' he said. 'Not bezzing, just looking. I feel like a voyeur. And you call that normality?'

III

There's a stock character in every film about the FBI: he or she is permanently at their computer, hooked up to a phone, collecting and redistributing information like some kind of digital chess grandmaster.

A call comes in from a field operative: 'All we know

about the suspect is that he visited Miami sometime between 2001 and 2009 and hired a grey Ford. Or it might have been a black Honda.'

The geek gets to work on the keyboard and ten seconds later he or she replies: 'Subject's name is Jack Smith, age forty-five years, six months and three days, weight 128 pounds, and he's now walking along Santa Monica Boulevard wearing a powder-blue shirt and size nine Timberlands. No, hang on, nine and a half. He's a left-handed Gemini. Need to know his favourite ice-cream flavour?'

Well, Marie-Dominique's secretary was exactly *unlike* that character.

Her name, I knew, was Monique, and I'd been introduced to her very briefly on my first visit to the Ministry. She'd shaken my hand as though she was afraid I might give her bird flu, her nervousness no doubt the long-term effect of the decibels aimed at her by Marie-Dominique.

She worked in the cubicle next to Marie-Dominique's, and had her back to me when I arrived at her workspace. I was just about to cough politely when she turned around. She'd heard me coming. Or rather seen me – she had a small round mirror propped up by the side of her computer. And if I wasn't mistaken, the coloured pattern I'd seen on her screen just before she turned round was a game of solitaire.

'Bonjour,' I said, and introduced myself again.

'Bonjour.' She rattled the large beads of a wooden necklace that was hanging down over a beige T-shirt.

'Marie-Dominique n'est pas ici,' I said. Stating the obvious seemed like a safe opener.

'Elle est en congé,' Monique said, pointing at the wall by my head.

It was the holiday chart, showing everyone in the department's *congés* right up till the end of August, with blue days clearly meaning holidays. There were as many blue lines as Napoleon's army. And the next two days were coloured in for Marie-Dominique.

Having answered my question, Monique was now looking anxious for me to piss off and leave her to her solitaire.

'I need to make a rendez-vous with her for when she returns. Is that possible?' I asked in my best French.

'I don't know,' she said.

'Don't you have her diary?' I asked.

'Yes, of course.' She nodded towards her computer's blank screen.

'And are there any spaces in the coming days?'

She turned back to her computer and clicked around for a full minute. Her card game appeared and disappeared. A Word file opened and closed.

'Merde,' she muttered.

'Is her diary on holiday, too?' I asked, giving a little laugh to show that I was joking. But she just kept clicking.

Finally she turned back again. 'There are possibilities,' she said, reluctantly.

'So can I make a rendez-vous?'

She sucked air through her teeth to show that this was as difficult as, say, borrowing France's presidential palace for a hen night.

'You can see when she's free, n'est-ce pas?' I asked.

'No.' She rattled her beads again.

'Why not?'

'She makes some of her appointments herself, and sends me an email to write them into her diary. We will have a phone call to discuss her upcoming appointments.'

'Ah, when's that?'

'I don't know. She hasn't sent me an email about it yet.'

At which point, I experienced the feeling that you often get when dealing with French bureaucracy: an urgent need to slam your head repeatedly against the corner of the nearest desk to stop yourself reaching out to strangle the person opposite you.

'I have an idea,' I said. 'Can you write me down for ten o'clock on the day after tomorrow . . .' Monique began to rattle her beads in alarm, but I held up my hand to placate her. 'And if Marie-Dominique says no, she or you can call me to tell me the new time.'

Monique stared at me, clearly weighing up the relative advantages of humouring me and arguing her case. In the end, I guessed that it was the desire to get back to her computer game that won the day for me.

'OK,' she said, 'dix heures?'

I didn't need to be Sherlock Holmes to detect that she wasn't typing this into Marie-Dominique's diary, but I thanked her for her infinite kindness and asked whether she had my cinema pass.

'Dans votre casier,' she said, pointing at the wall opposite the holiday chart. Hanging here was a square, wooden case of twenty or so pigeon holes.

'Right at the bottom,' Monique said.

And there, miraculously spelt with no mistakes, was my name, and nestling above it, a crisp white envelope.

I turned to go, wishing Monique a *bonne journée*. But she wasn't finished with me yet.

'As a contractuel, I'm not sure you should have a cinema pass. Normally, they're only for full-time staff.'

'Ah,' I said, giving her the Parisian shrug of ignorance about why the universe lets some people win the lottery and others fall headfirst in a cowpat.

'Maybe I should ask Marie-Dominique about the pass when I discuss your rendez-vous with her?' she said.

So victory was hers. Which was inevitable, really. This was her world.

'If you think that's necessary,' I said. 'It's your decision.' I pocketed the pass, gave her another friendly *bonne journée* and left.

Or tried to, anyway. Outside the lift, a guy of about

fifty with grey hair cut (or rather uncut) like a 1970s pop singer was hovering.

'Monsieur Wess?' he asked, scrutinising me above half-moon reading glasses.

'Oui.'

He held out his hand and crushed mine while saying a name that I was in too much pain to hear. I did gather, though, that he was the rep for one of the unions.

'We're going to have an Asthma meeting,' he said.

'Oh, I don't suffer, luckily.'

'Uh? I'm not sure you understand. Ass-Ma,' he repeated more clearly. 'L'Assemblée sociale des ministères et administrations.'

'Très bien. Formidable. Well, have a good meeting,' I said. *Bonne réunion.* You always have to wish French people good something or other if you want them to bugger off, and my phone had begun buzzing with an incoming call from Marsha.

'We know what you're doing,' he said, narrowing his eyes at me.

'You do?' I replied. 'Perhaps you will explain it to me.'

This threw the Frenchman for a second, as English deadpan always does.

'Well, I've informed you.' He wished me a good 'end of the afternoon' and marched down the corridor towards Monique's office.

*

Marsha was calling to ask me if I could come to the Marais. It was the night of her first poetry competition, and she wanted me to help get things ready.

'Bien sûr,' I told her. 'Tout de suite.' The ministry was turning me French.

Some people rave about Parisian buses and the wonders of gazing out at the street life, people-watching from on high. But these ravers are either tourists or insane. On an average day in central Paris, even outside rush hours, it would be quicker to walk backwards on all fours to wherever you're going than to take a bus. That's why, when given the choice, I opt for the Métro. Who needs street life when you're zipping along several metres below the traffic jams, ten times faster than the bus?

Recently, I'd also noticed something new about the buses. Maybe it was the downturn in the economy, but Parisian bus passengers had lost their inherent ability to be politely rude to each other. In the past, I'd witnessed some surreal arguments:

'Are you going to sit in that seat, monsieur?'

'Are you perhaps accusing me of being impolite, madame?'

'Oh, no, monsieur, just a little lacking in gallantry.'

But these days, with everyone's nerves apparently on edge, it was more often a case of:

'Hey, don't you let old ladies sit down?'

'Shut up, you wrinkly old cow.'

The economy had a lot to answer for.

Today, though, I wanted to call Alexa on my way to the shop, and although there is decent phone reception on the Métro, you naturally spend a lot of time saying, 'I'm about to go into a tunnel.' So I hopped on a number 29 bound for the Marais. Miraculously someone stood up just as I got on, and, after a look round to check for more worthy tenants, I parked my grateful backside on the furry green seat. However, from my new low viewpoint, I noticed the bulge of a pregnant tummy further down the aisle. Until that moment, it had obviously been covered in some kind of invisibility maternity smock, because the two teenagers in the priority seats hadn't spotted it, so I got up and offered the almost spherical woman my newly acquired trophy. This meant I had to go and stand in the area near the bus exit doors, which was already pretty full because of two pushchairs.

At the next stop, I was still trying to manoeuvre myself into a position where I could get my phone out of my pocket without elbowing a harassed young mother in the boobs when yet another pushchair-wielding woman tried to enter through the exit door, provoking a polite but vicious row with the people trying to get off, followed by several attempts to shove me through the bodywork of the bus as everyone shifted about to accommodate the new buggy.

I gave up, started chanting the essential mantra of *pardon, pardon, pardon*, and wrestled my way with polite violence towards the exit.

Fresh air at last, even if I was still a brisk fifteen minutes on foot away from the Marais. No problem, it was a couple of hours before Marsha's big night got under way.

Alexa was still on voicemail, so I concentrated on enjoying my walk, and especially on keeping pace with the bus, which overtook me and dropped behind several times en route. I was soon on waving terms with the pregnant lady I'd given my seat to.

At every stop, I watched the same battle to get on and off, as though one lot of people were convinced there was a deadly flu virus on the bus, and the other lot had heard that in ten seconds every passenger on Parisian public transport would be given a million euros. Meanwhile, I strolled along the pushchair-free pavement, feeling detached and superior, until the bus turned towards the Pompidou Centre and I carried on into the northern Marais.

Marsha was understandably in a flutter when I got to the shop. Her fluttering was paying off, though, because the main window was a checkerboard of posters. 'Has Paris Got Literary Talent?' their loud red lettering demanded, a question likely to get up the locals' noses and generate a bit of publicity.

The ground floor had been turned into a cool, cosy place where you'd want to hang out and browse: a multi-colour tartan reading room with trendily reupholstered armchairs and a sign promising more of the same upstairs.

That was where I found Marsha, setting out red wine bottles on a trestle table while simultaneously talking on the phone and miming something to a tall, pale-skinned guy with no shirt on.

She saw me, kissed me briskly on the mouth and finished her phone call.

'Oui, là, là,' she shouted over to the shirtless guy, who was moving a loudspeaker into place. 'Gregory's the sound man,' she told me. 'He does all of Connie and Mitzi's shows.'

'Does he really need to show off so much chest?' I asked. The guy was scarily smooth-bodied, like some hybrid between a human and a handbag.

'Ah, poor Paul's jealous,' she said. 'And talking of jealousy, did you call your ex and tell her to piss off?'

Leaving aside the question of whether Alexa was jealous, which I didn't think she was, the true answer to the question was no. But sometimes the whole truth just gets in the way.

'I told her not to bother you at the bookshop,' I said, which had been the gist of my text message.

'How did she take it?'

'Philosophically.' Which could mean anything, I told myself, including not bothering to reply.

'OK, thanks, Paul.' Marsha seemed satisfied. 'Now I need you to do some sound testing.'

She got me to sit in each of the three chairs on a podium that had been set up on one side of a low stage. We tried out the judges' microphones, while Gregory, or perhaps Grégorie, taped cables to the floor.

Marsha stood at the back of the room listening to me talking nonsense into the mics: 'Testing testing, one two three, has he got smoother legs than me?', which Gregory didn't seem to understand, luckily. Then she got me to move to the mic stand at the front of the stage, where the poets would be. Recite some poetry at me, she said, to see if I can hear you.

'The boy stood on the burning deck, spouting a load of rhyming dreck,' I began. 'To be or not to be, doesn't sound very suicidal to me. If Shakespeare had made Hamlet rhyme, actors could learn it in half the time.'

'Very good, Paul,' she called from the back of the room. 'If none of our contestants turn up, we'll see how long you can keep going.'

'No, Jake will be here, never you fear,' I said, suddenly incapable of saying anything that didn't rhyme.

'Don't depress me, please,' Marsha said quite seriously.

'Come on, Marsha, you're being too harsh.'

'On Jake? That's like being too harsh on a pitbull.'

When we'd finished testing mics, I slipped out into the street to make a quick phone call. This time, I let Alexa finish her voicemail greeting, then left her a simple, to-the-point message.

'Alexa, please don't come to the bookshop tonight. You'll only drop me in the merde with my new girlfriend. And I've got enough problems without this. Our old friend Jean-Marie is trying to cheat me out of my share of the tea room. I need to work out a defence strategy, so I'd really appreciate a little peace of mind. Anyway, so we'll talk soon, right? Though not tonight, perhaps. Well, definitely not tonight, OK? Thanks, bye, see you. Though not tonight. Right, bye then.'

Like I said, simple and to the point, with only a shade of panic when I got close to the sixty-second mark.

After another half-hour or so of chair-moving, glass-unpacking and duct-taping, various other helpers started to arrive. Connie and Mitzi turned up, clad in tastefully clashing tartan jackets. Mitzi took me aside to whisper that she'd heard Jake's poem, and hoped it wasn't autobiographical. I told her that it was definitely a product of his imagination. Reassured, she and Connie began fine-tuning the decor, moving their plaids and chairs about and taking photos.

A couple of Marsha's journalist friends also came along and she went off to record an interview, so I was left with Gregory, who'd finished taping things and was enjoying a glass of wine out on the pavement. I joined him, and was about to ask him whether he actually owned any shirts when I saw Amandine marching towards the shop from the rue de Bretagne. She was in silhouette against the bright evening sunlight, but she seemed to be trying to shake off something that was stuck to her hand.

Then I noticed that there was someone behind her. A guy, also in silhouette, who now reached forward to grab her.

I set off towards her at a sprint. As I got closer, I realised she was arguing with the guy in French.

'You OK?' I asked her.

'Ah, salut,' she said.

'C'est qui, ce mec?' the guy hissed, so that it came out as 'skissmeck'. I'd heard the question before. It's what French men say when guys like me talk to their girl-friends – who is this bloke?

'Bonsoir, je suis Paul,' I said, holding out my hand in greeting.

'Bonsoir. Thomas,' he said, more cordially, but still with a touch of skissmeck in his eyes. Apart from this, he seemed a decent enough guy: cool-looking, neatly unshaven, chic designer clothes.

Amandine explained that I was one of the other judges and Thomas was her boyfriend.

'I just need to have a conversation with Thomas, then I'll come in to the shop,' she told me.

'OK.' I turned around and walked straight into Gregory's bare chest. He'd obviously followed me. 'And this is Gregory,' I said.

Amandine and Thomas nodded, the skissmeck melting visibly from Thomas's eyes. He'd decided that this was my boyfriend and that I was no longer a rival. I didn't bother to put him right.

On the short walk back to the shop, I explained to Gregory about Amandine's boyfriend not wanting her to be a judge.

'You not like zat wiz Marsha?' Gregory said with a fierce French accent.

'No,' I said, 'maybe I'm weird, but I quite like beautiful women to be beautiful in public.'

'And booty-full men to be booty-full?' he asked, and laughed when I couldn't think of a reply. 'Come, let us find some bad wine,' he said.

By the time Amandine finally arrived at the shop – alone – I was on the doorstep with Greg, who was telling me funny stories about the hysteria behind the scenes at the fashion shows he'd worked on.

Amandine kissed me hello and I introduced the still shirtless Gregory.

'You dumped the other guy?' he asked her in French. 'If you're single again, you don't need to worry about being alone. You're beautiful. Every guy in Paris will be after you.'

'I'm not worried about being alone,' she snapped. 'I'm much more worried about being with a dickhead.'

She used just about the worst French insult possible – not just *con* (the word for vagina, but also a male idiot), but *petit con*. There was something about being an undersized vagina that was horrifically insulting to a Frenchman.

'Oh, please don't think I'm trying it on with you,' Gregory said. 'Your boyfriend's more my type. Want me to take him off your hands?'

Amandine laughed and demanded wine, so I took her upstairs to the drinks table.

There, she poured it all out. She'd met her boyfriend at business school. It had been great when they were students, then he had become moody when she went off to New York for her internship, got even worse when she'd confided in him about Jean-Marie's antics at work, and had lost the plot completely now that she was going to be on stage in front of an audience, especially in this trendy, English-speaking context that he felt excluded from.

'Sorry to bore you with this, Paul,' she said. 'You probably want to know what's going on with Jean-Marie.'

Instinctively, I looked around to see if he was eavesdropping.

'So what exactly did you overhear?' I asked her.

She took a couple of seconds to get it straight in her mind.

'I heard him on the phone. He didn't know I was in the next office. Like I told you, I think diners are a cool idea, but he was getting really personal about you. He was saying you'd always been an "emmerdeur", a pain in the butt, opposing him in everything. He said he wasn't going to let a "petit con d'Anglais" frustrate his strategy to expand the restaurant side of his business. So he told his low-yah to screw you at all costs.'

Holy *merde*, I thought. It was even worse than I'd feared.

'I've contacted my lawyer,' I told her. 'He reckons we can stop Jean-Marie somehow.'

Alarmingly, Amandine laughed.

'I wouldn't bet on it,' she said. 'There's nothing he hates more than opposition to his little plans. We both know that.'

'Hey!' Suddenly there was a gust of perfume and Marsha's arm was draped across my shoulder. She kissed Amandine hello, and gave me one of her ironic eyebrow lifts. 'Sorry, you two having a private huddle?'

I felt stupidly guilty. 'Just discussing business,' I told her.

'No problem, Paul,' Marsha said. 'How's about we look at the running order for tonight?'

She talked us through the programme. It was simple stuff. She would introduce the evening, talk about the launch, and then the poets would do their thing. After vetting out the wackos, she had signed up sixteen contestants. They each had five minutes to perform, and, unlike TV talent shows, we couldn't buzz to shut a performer up. That, she said, was dictatorial and rude, and I had to agree. After each poem, we'd vote, and in this, the first round of three, a poet needed only one vote to go through to round two.

Only one vote? I breathed what I hoped was an invisible sigh of relief.

'But I want you to promise me that you won't show any favouritism, OK, Paul?' Marsha said.

'If Jake's crap, I'll vote against him. Promise.'

'Promise accepted. And, to add a bit of audience participation, we'll have a vote at the end, and they get to kick one person out.'

Bloody hell, I thought, she's worried about me being biased towards my friend, and here she is stacking as many odds as possible against him.

'But that's even more dictatorial and rude,' I objected. 'Someone gets voted through, then their hopes are dashed when they get humiliated by a public vote of disapproval? It's awful.'

She had no time to reply, because the sound of angry shouting suddenly burst in the window from below. We looked down to see a huge, open-topped car parked outside the shop, and a furious van driver yelling that he couldn't get past. The owner of the convertible, meanwhile, was simply shrugging as if to say: What do you expect me to do, widen the street?

I leant out and added my own contribution to the scene.

'Bonsoir, Jean-Marie,' I said cheerily, as though I had no idea he was trying to stab me in the back.

He looked up and saw me. Ignoring the van driver's insults, which were now being accompanied by frantic hoots, he returned my greeting with equal hypocrisy, and asked why we hadn't asked the police to block off the street for our event.

'Block off the street?'

He shook his head in despair and reached inside his jacket pocket for his phone, no doubt to have a word in a highly placed ear. Typical Jean-Marie. He'd only been there ten seconds, and already he'd taken over.

'I thought you'd bought the Jag,' I said when I got down into the street. He was sitting in the driver's seat of the American convertible we'd seen at the garage in Boulogne. He'd got rid of the van driver somehow, and was now looking smug, though classily so, in another of his trendy English suits.

'Yes, I have bought the Jaguar. I have rented this

car for a short time. It is, let's say, a subliminal campaign.'

'Subliminal?'

'Yes, people see this in the streets of Paris, and they think: Hmm, America, I want to go to a diner.'

I forced a laugh. He was clearly a man on a mission. But at the same time I saw the unpleasant logic of the idea. To Parisians, used to their cramped streets and endless traffic lights, this car did represent a kind of freedom, and a similar one to the release they'd get from picking up a hamburger in both hands and jamming it into their mouths rather than fiddling about with a knife and fork, trying to eat asparagus without looking obscene.

'That doesn't mean to say they don't want a tea room,' I told him. 'People like the London taxi experience, too. A fun English lunch then back to their computers.'

Jean-Marie shook his head. 'We will have a meeting,' he said, as he did when he wanted to avoid any subject. 'Is Amandine here?'

'Yes, and I've just met her boyfriend. He's the insanely jealous kind.'

Jean-Marie beamed.

'Jealous boyfriends are signposts on the road to success, my dear Pool,' he said.

'Why is that?' I asked.

'If a boyfriend is jealous, it means that the girl, or woman, is already . . . conquise?'

'Conquered?'

'Yes. It is just like in business. When your rivals realise they must counter-attack you, it is too late. They have already lost.' He gave his smuggest smile yet.

'But what if the rival smashes a bottle of wine over your head?' I asked, longing to do just that. 'And I'm not sure that Amandine is conquered anyway.'

'Ah?' Jean-Marie stopped grinning and looked me up and down. 'So there is a second jealous rival?'

'No, just because I say *you* haven't conquered her doesn't mean *I'm* trying to do so. I honestly think she just wants a job, Jean-Mary.' I pronounced it as two women's names – making Jean rhyme with bean – and he did a double-take. 'It's tough in France at the moment,' I went on, 'even for business-school graduates like Amandine. She just wants to work, not to get chased around Paris by her boss in a vintage car.'

Voilà. I'd gone a bit further than I'd meant to, but at least I'd said it. Jean-Marie was eyeing me coolly, deciding how to react.

'I think, Pool, that you are confusing business and pleasure,' he finally said, which was a classic case of pot and kettle if ever I heard one. 'Perhaps it is better if I choose a different person to work with you for our joint project? Have you met my new assistant? She is perhaps less . . . distracting than Amandine?'

This had to be the gorgon I'd spoken to on the phone, the one chosen by his wife to discourage any thoughts of 'working late at the office' or 'dinner with a client'.

'Whatever helps us both to focus on business, Jean-Mary. I just want to work, too,' I told him. 'Doing this Ministry report has really focused my mind on the food business again. I think that with a little updating of its menu, the tea room could do even better than it is now.'

I saw Jean-Marie struggling to keep the carefree expression on his face. I was sure he would have loved to demolish my idea there and then, but he had to resist the temptation if he wanted to keep his machinations secret.

'Très bien,' he finally said. 'Now can you ask Amandine to come here? You may not know it, but I gave her permission to leave the office early today. And now I need to talk to her.'

'She's upstairs,' I said, and turning to look up at the window, I saw Amandine leaning out, staring straight down at us.

Sept

'La poésie doit réfléchir, par les couleurs, les sons et
les rythmes, toutes les beautés de l'univers.'
*In its colours, sounds and rhythms, poetry must reflect all the
beauty of the universe.*

Madame de Staël, 18th-century French writer,
who'd obviously never heard any of Jake's poems

I

THE ROOM was loud and getting sweaty. All the
chairs were taken, and people were leaning against
every square centimetre of wall space. But, unlike the bus
crowds, the mood amongst Marsha's audience was
friendly. The roar of chatter was deafening but happy.

Jean-Marie had had his confab with Amandine and
was now sitting by the stairs, looking chilled in his cool
suit despite being about twenty years older than almost
everyone else in the room. He was obviously unaware
that Amandine's boyfriend, Thomas, was glowering at
him from a few rows back, in between shooting shy,

apparently apologetic glances at Amandine herself.

She was with me, sitting close to the open window, on the judges' stage.

'Thanks for defending me against Jean-Marie,' she said. 'You know, you are worrying him. He wanted to ask me why you called him Jean-Mary.'

'What did you say?'

'That you probably couldn't pronounce French names very well.'

'Did he accuse you of telling me about his Pool thing?'

She was going to answer, but Marsha, who was standing at the poets' mic, called for hush.

'This evening is all about words, and the love of words,' she announced. 'Someone once said that a picture paints a thousand words. But a few words can paint a million pictures. Any one word can mean a million different things to a million different people. That's why we have psychiatrists to analyse the hell out of every-thing we say. And tonight, the word we're interested in is talent. Literary talent. I want to know if you lot have got it. I bloody hope so. So let's see. The rules are simple. One poem per person, five minutes maximum, and if one of the judges likes you, you're through. All you need is one vote. And first up, all the way from San Francisco, is a guy called Laurie Shoreman!'

While the mercifully white-shirted Gregory played a blast of the old 'flowers in your hair' song over the sound system, Marsha came to sit at the central microphone on the judges' table, and a tubby guy with curly black hair and baggy I'm-not-fat-really clothes picked his way between the chairs.

Acknowledging the applause, Laurie said hi to everyone and launched straight into a polished spiel.

'A friend wrote to me recently that tweeting is just pithing in the wind.' He paused for laughter, and got it. 'But I think he was wrong. I'm pretty sure that soon, there will be no written works over 140 characters long. That's all our attention spans will take. We'll express everything in short, sharp bursts. Haikus will be epics. Even a sonnet will feel like Wagner's Ring cycle, which, in case you didn't already know, consists of four operas lasting a total of fifteen hours. That's fifteen hours with your phones turned off, people.' He got the jeers and oohs he probably wanted. 'Which is why,' he continued, 'I've written a new, short version of the Ring cycle. It's all about everyday objects that will soon be things of the past. I call it my Thing cycle.'

He held up a printout and the room fell silent.

'Phoning without Skype,' he intoned. 'It's a ring of the past.' He got a laugh.

'Paying for music – it's a sing of the past . . .' More laughter and a few groans.

'Paying for absolutely anything on the internet – it's a sting of the past.'

I thought I detected a pattern emerging.

'Genuine low-cost flights – they're a wing of the past.'

'Oh come on,' I said, more loudly than I'd intended, into my microphone.

On stage, Laurie froze in disbelief, his mouth open.

'Paul, you're not allowed to interrupt, remember?' Marsha said into her mic.

'I'm sorry, but come on, Laurie.' This provoked an ironic cheer and I saw what I'd done. 'Pardon the accidental poem, but what are you going to say next? Doorbells, they're a ding of the past?'

This earned me a mixture of laughs and howls from the crowd, and a scornful puff from Laurie.

'No one says doorbells are going to disappear,' he scoffed.

'But I wish you would, mate, sorry,' I told him, this time getting more cheers than disapproval, the two of them joining in an eruption of noise. And suddenly I understood. Oh, the feeling of power. Pouring scorn on someone's work without having to do better yourself. This judging lark was positively orgasmic. I knew what it was like to be a dictator and, believe me, it felt *good*.

Marsha wasn't happy, though.

'We're not on TV, Paul. You have to let them finish. Sorry, Laurie. Did you have any more?'

'Unprotected sex – it's a fling of the past?' he said, but the spell was gone, and everyone groaned.

And suddenly I felt like a total shit. The poor bloke had had the balls to get up on stage and I'd ruined it all. How did those TV judges sleep at night?

'Well, Laurie' – Marsha cut through the hubbub of audience chatter – 'despite what Paul says and his feeble attempt to imitate you, I liked it, so you get my vote. What about you, Amandine?'

'Yes, very modern, very spirituel – witty. I vote yes,' Amandine said.

'You're the first one through!' Marsha roared. People cheered, Laurie flipped me a playful finger, and I shrugged my acceptance of defeat, relieved that I didn't have to feel like a shit any more.

Second up was a punky woman called Suzie, a gap-year student whose face was pinched and aggressive but whose poem was anything but a rant. It was a melancholic series of Parisian sketches that had everyone listening in respectful silence. She described a poor African cashier working in a posh Latin Quarter supermarket. Back home in her shitty suburb, her five kids can't do their homework because . . .

'Their two-room apartment doesn't have enough chairs,
    For them all to sit down and learn Baudelaire.'

The eldest daughter dreams of becoming a lawyer, but . . .

'The teachers tell her don't be so dumb,
This is a school for what the president calls scum,
The best you can hope for is the same job as your
    mum.'

It was delivered deadpan, in a composed, quiet voice, and earned a huge cheer and three yes votes.

The third candidate was just plain weird. A tall gangly English bloke, an ugly version of the young Hugh Grant, who nervously introduced himself as Richard from Bristol, and then launched into the sort of poem that only an Englishman could write after having too many cucumber sandwiches at teatime. He recited from memory, his eyes closed and his large white Adam's apple bobbing:

'Richard is a name that doesn't rhyme,
Richard thinks about this all the time,
How he's afflicted with a poetic curse,
He can never star at the end of a verse.'

This wackiness got wackier, accompanied by titters from the audience, but I have to admit that I drifted off to the sound of his Sunday-afternoon, tea-on-the-lawn voice, and only returned to consciousness when he got a big final laugh and a round of applause.

Guiltily, I voted for him. Marsha and Amandine didn't agree. They thought he was too old-school and irrelevant, but Richard didn't care, and from the way he bunched his fists in victory, it looked like the first thing he'd won since getting an algebra prize at primary school.

The fourth candidate was, in my opinion, a cheat, but everyone adored him. A hunky Californian with dread-locks and biceps who plays slap bass guitar is going to win *any* competition in Paris. He was the American Dream personified. Jean-Marie ought to ride him around Paris, I thought, instead of that old car of his. The guy would get young Parisians drooling.

This said, I didn't understand a word of his actual poem. I wasn't even sure what language it was in, but it didn't matter. Amandine, Marsha, all the women in the room and a good proportion of the guys looked as though they would have voted for him if he'd done nothing but sweat.

Marsha broke with her tradition and got up to con-gratulate the guy – whose name was something like Rock or Rod – with a kiss, but I didn't mind at all. I could see why he'd have that effect on a woman. Amandine, though, was getting the evil eye from Thomas about her gushing 'yes' vote, and I watched the poor girl replying to him with a 'what do you expect me to do?' shrug.

After this, things understandably got a little anticlimactic. A Canadian woman recited a tasteful poem about love in a *chambre de bonne*, but I couldn't vote for it because all through, I kept hearing voices in my head yelling 'enculé!' and feeling the lumpy skeleton of Jake's sofa bed digging into my kidneys.

There were a few totally disposable entrants, including one awful rap by a New York rich kid who imagined himself pelting gendarmes with Parisian cobblestones during the May 1968 riots, and who lost my vote when he rhymed 'Sorbonne' with 'petrol bomb'.

And then Jake was at the mic.

He was last on our list. Whether he'd asked to be top of the bill, or Marsha had stuck him there so that she might be able to claim that all the places in the second round were already taken, I didn't know. Either way, I could see as he stood on the stage and looked out into the crowd that he felt his big moment had come. He looked slightly nervous, although he knew, surely, that he could count on me for the necessary vote. He flicked his long hair out of his eyes and began to speak.

'The French for dildo is godmichet,' he began. 'But the French normally, you know, abréger?'

As *godmichet* and *abréger* had rhymed, no one seemed certain whether he'd begun his poem or not, and people frowned at his sudden silence. Oh shit, I thought, he's screwing it up.

'Shorten,' he finally said. 'The French usually shorten their word for dildo. From godmichet to god. So God save the queen means something très sexy to the French, no?'

Everyone laughed except me.

'And that is the subject of my poem,' Jake said. 'It is titled "Waiting for God".'

I looked across and saw Marsha shaking her head at me as Jake began to recite in his strange Franco-American accent:

> 'The girl walked in the bedroom door,
> I seen what she carried, and said merde alors.
> It was long, pink, ribbed and clammy,
> Vibrating at me like a drunk salami . . .'

Trying to tune out Jake's lurid, approximate rhymes, I looked into the audience and saw Jean-Marie staring at me. Still wondering how much I knew, perhaps, and who'd told me? As if to confirm this, he switched his attention to Amandine, and then back to me, like a turret slowly aiming its cannons.

Abruptly, though, my trance was broken by an unexpected sound. People were actually laughing. A few women had their hands to their faces in shock, but the guys were spluttering with mirth. I couldn't help hearing Jake's last two lines:

'Ma moralité is, don't use this dildo for anal,
Or you will enter a world of pain, y'all.'

It was possibly the worst rhyme in the history of poetry, but the audience erupted in a multi-layered mixture of gasps, groans and whoops. The last thing you could accuse Jake of was causing indifference.

'Well,' Marsha asked when the noise died down, 'what do we think?' She, from the look of her, was thinking 'never again'.

'Sorry, it's too disgusting,' Amandine breathed into her microphone, 'non merci.'

About half of the audience cheered agreement, including her boyfriend, but a good proportion booed her.

Marsha called for quiet and then told Jake that listening to him was 'like being forced to watch a surgical operation – on myself. What about you, Paul?'

I could feel her trying to hypnotise me into kicking him out. The look in her eyes seemed to be saying: Vote yes and the sexiest thing you'll be doing tonight is reading one of Jake's poems.

I grasped for words that wouldn't hurt my friend too much.

'Unforgettable,' I said. This, sadly, was true of all of Jake's poems.

'So how do you vote, Paul?'

Marsha's eyes were drilling holes in my skull. People

in the audience were shouting out suggestions, with 'yes' and 'no' getting an equal share. I shook my head in resignation. Anal, pain y'all? Who could possibly vote in favour of that?

Then I caught Jean-Marie's eye again, and saw him smirking at me, obviously relishing my discomfort. And it struck me that for all Jake's faults, there was one thing about him that you had to admire. He was honest. Often horrifically, unwisely so, but at least there was no hidden dark side to him. With Jean-Marie, you could have a map, Satnav and a native guide and you still couldn't be certain where you stood with him.

'I have to . . . give you my vote,' I told Jake.

The audience erupted with howls of disapproval and cheers of laughter. Jake punched the air, while Marsha glowered at me and Amandine grimaced as if she'd just bitten into a rotten orange.

I was watching Jake pick his way through the crowd, getting high fives and wry grins in equal measure, when I noticed a camera pointing at me.

People had been holding up phones throughout the whole evening, of course. But this was different. It was a large black camera, pressed to an eye rather than being held at arm's length. And the partially hidden face behind it was one that I recognised. She must have seen me staring straight into her lens, because she pulled the camera away and gave me an embarrassed smile.

Alexa, damn her. I looked across at Marsha, who, luckily, was too engrossed in a conversation with Gregory the sound guy to have noticed. I was on the point of getting up and going to ask Alexa what she thought she was doing here, when I saw Jean-Marie weaving his way to the poets' stage.

'Excuse me,' he said into the mic. 'Excusez-moi.'

Everyone looked up at the middle-aged chic guy smiling at them from the front of the room. Another poet, they seemed to think.

Marsha said something to Gregory, who went to try and disarm Jean-Marie.

Jean-Marie was a politician, though, and no one grabs a microphone from a politician without shooting him first.

'I have an objection,' Jean-Marie said.

'An objection?' Marsha asked into her own mic.

'Yes. The poets were all Anglophone. This is France. Do we have no French poets in Paris?'

Marsha tutted. 'We decided to have only English poems, because you can't really compare poetry in two languages. It would be like having beer and wine in the same competition.'

'Excuse me, but you can't have a poetry competition in the city of Verlaine, Rimbaud and Baudelaire without French poets.'

By now, I could see that Marsha was in a bit of a panic.

She was itching to tell the interfering bastard to let her get on with *her* competition, in *her* shop, but there were too many people watching, and – more to the point – filming with their all-seeing phones.

Jean-Marie must have seen her weakening, because he got in a low punch.

'And frankly,' he said, 'the poems we have heard this evening were less like wine and beer than some other fluids that it would not be gallant to mention.' He shook his head at Jake, and then at me.

It was something about that shake of his smooth, arrogant head that made me snap.

'So you're against the invasion of what you call *Anglo-Saxon* culture?' I asked, making sure that my microphone picked up every syllable. 'Does that include food?' I saw Jean-Marie's expression morphing from suave self-assurance to something far more murderous, but it was too late to stop now. 'Because this, ladies and gentlemen, messieurs, mesdames, is a man who wants to open a chain of American diners in Paris, and whose American car is currently blocking the street outside.'

Any support that Jean-Marie had earned had just dematerialised into French mist, and I couldn't resist going for his throbbing jugular.

'And he's only disrupting this competition because he knows that I'm going out with Marsha, whose bookshop this is, and he wants to piss me off. He's also trying to screw me out of the café that he and I own. An *English* tea room, by the way, which proves how big an opponent of Anglo culture he is . . .'

The jeers and laughter were almost drowning me out by now, but I'd come to the end of my speech anyway, mainly because I realised that, for the second time that evening, I'd gone too far.

Jean-Marie's look of hatred was pretty satisfying, but Amandine's mask of pure shock much less so. Oh shit, I thought, I've really dropped her in it now. First the revelation that I knew about the Paul-*poule* business, and now this.

Jean-Marie took a deep breath and handed the microphone to Gregory.

'That was not a good idea, Pool,' he told me. He turned to Amandine. 'Not a good idea at all,' he repeated, in French.

With this, he made his way slowly to the door. It was actually a pretty dignified exit. Unlike Amandine's – she stumbled out of her judge's chair, tripped over her microphone lead and practically bounced from audience member to audience member in an attempt to catch up with Jean-Marie.

I felt I ought to follow.

I got out into the street just as Jean-Marie was starting his car engine. Amandine was clutching a door handle, talking to Jean-Marie in urgent French.

I went over to interrupt. 'I got a call from my lawyer today warning me that someone wanted to revoke our contract together,' I told him. 'It didn't take me long to guess who that was.' Not very convincing, but I hoped it might take some of the spotlight off Amandine.

Jean-Marie took no notice.

'You want to keep your job?' he asked Amandine.

Before she could answer, there was a loud shout from the other side of the car.

'Casse-toi, vieux con!' It was Amandine's boyfriend, Thomas.

'Not now, Thomas,' Amandine begged, but he repeated his catchphrase and looked as though he was wondering which to damage first, the car or its driver.

Jean-Marie swivelled his head slowly towards Thomas like some kind of Terminator.

'Non, c'est toi qui va te casser, petit con,' he told Thomas.

Thomas tried to throw a punch, but someone came and grabbed his arms from behind. It was Gregory.

'Don't. The vieux con will only have you arrested,' he told Thomas.

'So, are you getting in?' Jean-Marie asked Amandine.

'No, I am,' came a female voice from behind me.

I turned to see Alexa standing at my shoulder. Everyone looked at her in astonishment as she slipped past me and gripped the door handle.

'May I?' she asked Jean-Marie.

He did a quick double-take before replying, 'Bien sûr.'

The smugness had returned to Jean-Marie's face as he put the car in gear and began to edge forwards, his new passenger busy doing up her seatbelt.

'A très bientôt, Pool,' he told me, and drove slowly, victoriously away, watched by a silently shell-shocked Amandine, a vocal Thomas and a straining Gregory, who was using all his roadie's upper body strength to hang on to his loudly struggling prisoner.

As for me, I wasn't sure how to feel, except that something about the poetry evening had gone very, very wrong.

'Hey, guys, coming to celebrate?' Jake tumbled into the street, wedged as usual between his miniature twins. 'Great soirée, huh? Brilliant result!'

He didn't seem to understand why no one shared his enthusiasm.

Huit

'Qui s'excuse s'accuse.'
He who apologises, accuses himself.
Stendhal, 19th-century French writer, who sounds
as though he never warned anyone he was suffering
from syphilis

I

WOMEN WITH forceful characters are fun as long as they're not using their force against you. With them, I usually find that the safest thing to do is say sorry and let them decide exactly what I should be apologising for. They always have a few ideas, and are at least partly satisfied to see a bit of grovelling. With Marsha, though, saying sorry didn't quite go to plan.

'What for?' she asked, which stumped me for a second. There was so much to choose from. 'For voting through your obscene friend Jake?'

'Yes,' I said, though that hadn't been on my list.

'Or for letting your business partner screw up my whole poetry evening?'

'Yes,' though I couldn't claim any credit for that, either. Jean-Marie was his own man, and probably wouldn't be my business partner for much longer.

'Or for not telling your ex to stay away from my bloody shop?'

I wasn't going to confess to that one. I'd begged Alexa to stay away, and for some reason she'd ignored me. I intended to find out why, and to ask her what she thought she was doing by going off with Jean-Marie in his car. I couldn't believe there was anything sexual in it (not from her point of view, anyway), but there was clearly something going on between them. Why else would she be lurking around the tea room and Marsha's shop at exactly the same time Jean-Marie was plotting to deprive me of the first and screw things up for me at the second?

But in my experience, with a strong-minded woman like Marsha, there's little point defending yourself – it only makes them madder. So all I could do was opt for some minor plea bargaining.

'I told her to stay away,' I said, 'but obviously not persuasively enough.'

'Yeah, well, you tell her from me that I have ways of persuading people to do things. Men and women.'

'Right.'

'Now sorry, Paul, but I need to be alone to work out a damage-limitation plan.'

We said goodbye and hung up. Yes, the conversation wasn't taking place over a nightcap in her apartment. It was the morning after the competition, and I'd spent the night at Jake's place. When I'd tried to apologise the night before, she hadn't even wanted to listen – which quite frankly had come as a relief. I wasn't too bothered about spending the night alone. It had been an intense day, cluttered with voices. My brain needed some quality time with itself. Now, though, sitting on Jake's cranky sofa bed and listening to the sounds of the street below, it was time to get down to business.

So I took a deep breath and put in the inevitable call to Alexa. It wasn't going to be an easy conversation.

Once you got to know her really well, you realised that she had four distinct phone voices.

The first was a no-nonsense business tone that said, 'Yes, I may sound like a sexy young woman but that doesn't mean you can pull any merde on me.' Perfect for calling the electricity people or her building managers.

The second she used when she was being cool and trendy, like when she was dealing with someone in the photography business. It was chummy yet aloof, and while using it she usually called the person *tu* rather than *vous*. She would also add syllables to words – 'oui-er, c'est vrai-er' – and laugh a lot. It meant: 'We're all in business together, so we're all equally trendy and worldly-wise,' while at the same time reminding them: 'Don't get any silly ideas, mon ami.' You can never be too careful.

The third voice was for when she was talking to her friends. It was much more relaxed and warm – a purr that could sound almost motherly. While we were an item, she used this voice to talk to me, with a few pet names and terms of endearment thrown in on top.

The fourth voice, though, seemed to be entirely dedicated to being mad at me, and it was scary. It was cold and clipped, and punctuated with long silences. 'Oui?' she would say when she took my call, pretending she didn't know who was on the line. And if I asked whether everything was OK, she'd reply, 'Oui, oui,' distractedly, as if she was simultaneously checking her nails for chipped varnish. This was the voice I was expecting now. Even though I was the one who had every right to be mad at *her*, I knew that getting mad at her would only make her mad at me.

Surely, I thought, after last night, she would actually pick up the phone? She had some serious explaining to do.

The answer was no.

'We *really* need to talk,' I told her inbox. 'I'm assuming that you and Jean-Marie weren't only comparing notes on models of camera and vintage car?'

It had to be a record. I was pretty sure I'd got in under the ten-second barrier.

By now, Jake's garret was starting to do its microwave-oven act, so I had a quick shower and went down to the corner café, where I grabbed the last free table on the terrace and hooked up to their Wi-Fi.

Getting a Ministry of Culture badge had clearly put me on some kind of mailing list, because I had received a crop of circulars, ranging from the plain irrelevant – the third-floor water fountain in the Montparnasse annexe was for the use of third-floor offices only, unless those on the fourth floor were also willing to change the bottle when it ran out – to the totally wacky. A man in the Ministry's Palais-Royal HQ had found a woman's skirt under his desk and was wondering whose it was because, he said, 'My backside is too big for it.' Almost immediately someone at government email central had posted a terse reminder that personal communications were not to be sent on this network and, according to regulation B1998.3, finding 'non-work clothing' in the workplace was a personal incident. Humour was also forbidden, this time according to an amendment of rule C4423.5 that banned any criticism of the State.

In short, anyone in the French civil service who actually read all this bumf hardly had a spare minute for a cigarette break before it was time to knock off for lunch.

I was browsing through the list of ministerial emails when I noticed that Amandine had sent me something. It was from her personal address, and the subject field was bare. Oh *merde*, I thought, here was another woman I owed an apology to. I'd tried to say sorry the night before, but she'd dashed off immediately after Jean-Marie and Alexa had left, waving everyone, including her boyfriend Thomas, away. I opened up her message, hoping it wasn't going to be a 'you dropped me in it you bastard' rant.

'Lmook at thjis, I saqw it on JM's screeb,' it said, and ended with a link.

It led to a website called '*Non à l'anglais*' – 'No to English'. Under the title on the home page was a quotation in French from King Louis XV, which translated something like: 'The English have corrupted the mind of my kingdom. We must not expose a new generation to the risk of being perverted by their language.' And beneath this was a promise to do 'everything in our power to boot all Anglo-Saxon culture out of France'. Overseeing the whole thing was an angelic portrait of Saint Joan of Arc, in full armour, holding a sword in one hand and a crumpled Union Jack in the other, as if she was about to use it to blow her nose.

It was extreme stuff, but not lacking in humour. They had a competition, the '*Shit de la Semaine*' (which could, I suppose, be translated as 'Merde of the Week'), in which they awarded a Union Jack- or Stars and Stripes-patterned turd to a person who had used gratuitous English in the French media. This week's winner was a politician who had referred to 'le credit crunch' in a press conference. The week before, some washed-out French singer had tried to create a buzz by lighting up a joint during a live TV interview and, when asked by the presenter to put it out, had responded with, 'I yam too rrrock and rrroll for ze French taylayvision.'

More worrying, and less humorous, was the section called '*L'Occupation Linguistique*', and its list of *collaborateurs* – people and places promoting the use of English in France. Collaborators? I mean, the French may still have a hang-up about what many of them did during the Second World War, but it was a bit much equating English-language magazines with Nazi occupiers.

The bad news was that there were links to My Tea Is Rich and to Marsha's bookshop. The tea room was apparently 'promoting the usurpation of French cuisine, which has, after all, been added to the UNESCO World Heritage list of cultural treasures, and in its place serving Anglo-American *merde*'. Which wasn't a very friendly way of describing our tasty salads and sandwiches. And my menu naturally came under attack for being 'a veritable Anglo-American pizza of English words and tasteless ingredients, many of them not translated into French'. Which was untrue – these days, there were

French translations cluttering up half the menu, even when they were pointless. What kind of idiot needed to be told that 'soup' meant 'soupe'?

And there, at the top of the list of bookshops 'attacking the rightful domination of the French language in its own homeland', was Marsha's new store with its 'foreign poetry' competition. The website said that the contest 'excluded Francophone creators from gaining public recognition in the very city that was home to Verlaine, Rimbaud and Baudelaire'.

I read that sentence again. Wasn't it almost word for word what Jean-Marie had said when he grabbed the microphone?

Bloody hell, I thought, or should it have been *enfer en sang*. It looked as though Jean-Marie was in bed with these ethnic cleansers. He was working for the enemy, for the same people who were attacking the tea room he co-owned. Undermining My Tea Is Rich had to be part of his plan to buy me out on the cheap. Who was the *collaborateur* now?

Incredibly, though, this wasn't the worst thing about the website. Because there was another collaborator in there. Or *collaboratrice*. All the photos in the '*Occupation Linguistique*' section were quite obviously by Alexa. They weren't as arty as her usual stuff, but the little vignettes of, for example, my menu lying on a table alongside a plate of half-eaten fruit cake, or the poster in Marsha's window reflecting a couple of trendy girls passing by and apparently smiling at the idea of the poetry competition – they were pure Alexa. It was just sad that such classy pictures were set alongside racist rants about supposed linguistic genocide.

She was still not taking my calls, but I left a rant of my own on her voicemail, and this time I didn't care about going over the minute mark.

'How can you do this to me, Alexa? You're actually working for these loonies who want to get the tea room and the bookshop closed down? And collaborating with Jean-Marie? Are you also doing photo shoots for the Front National? Putting together a nice Facebook page for them – illegal immigrant of the month, with his name and address so the loonies can go and firebomb his apartment? Fucking hell, Alexa.'

OK, that last allegation was over the top, but she deserved it. I was tempted to go round to her apartment – she was almost certainly still living at her dad's place near Bastille – for a showdown.

As I hung up, I noticed that the other people on the café terrace were staring at me. A pair of the dyed-blonde ladies had lifted their glitzy sunglasses on to their foreheads to get a better view of the crazy *Anglais*. We were a long way from the Latin Quarter, so they probably didn't hear long, loud outbursts of English very often.

'Désolé,' I told them. 'C'est la merde.'

They nodded sympathetically. You can't go wrong with *merde*.

II

I was standing in the main hall of the One Two Two, the arts centre where I'd seen the pornographic exhibition with Marsha. The show was still running, but I was all alone, because the public was obviously staying away in droves. With the sound stage dismantled and the *vernissage* crowd gone, the arts centre was a vast, empty, glass-roofed hangar that was being used by the prevailing wind as a shortcut across the neighbourhood.

I was there to see Marie-Dominique, who had summoned me to a 'réunion très urgente'.

'We have some meeting rooms at the One Two Two,' she bawled down the phone at me. 'We have to use them because the Minister wants his new Parisian arts centre to be an integral part of daily cultural life. It's really very inconvenient. We will come from Palais-Royal by taxi, so we might be a little late.' As if she had been on time at our last meeting.

Here I was, then, waiting underneath a huge close-up portrait of a naked woman, in a neighbourhood where half of the female population walked about in headscarves for religious reasons. So much for bringing art to the people.

I decided to give Amandine a call to thank her for passing on the link to the loony website, and maybe do a bit more apologising.

To my surprise, she didn't sound angry at all, and even asked me if I was free for lunch.

'Have you spoken to Jean-Marie this morning?' I asked her.

'Not really, but I can't talk for long on the phone.' We arranged to meet in the Marais and said a hurried goodbye.

A few minutes later Marie-Dominique was marching towards me, two strides ahead of a small flock of her colleagues. I shook hands with her and her three disciples, and realised that I'd forgotten all of their names.

There was the tall thin guy with the shock of white hair, looking slightly sporty in a polo shirt tucked into smart trousers; the small guy all in grey, his suit today combined with a matching grey shirt; and the small tubby guy who'd worn a black rollneck, and was now in a black jacket.

'Voilà a building that the Ministry has converted into something very special,' Marie-Dominique boomed, causing the arts centre's metal beams to shudder. 'Not many visitors . . .' She looked about in a vain search for any sign of human life. 'But important work is being done here.' She raised her head towards the giant female nude.

Her male colleagues all cowered, as I'd done.

She led us up a staircase into a gleamingly new corridor of offices: a double row of eight coloured doors, pale blue, milky orange, pistachio and more, on either side of a wood-panelled floor that looked as though no one had ever set foot on it. We trod along it tentatively, as though we were visiting a deserted spaceship.

'Here,' Marie-Dominique said, opening the pale blue door and releasing a puff of stale, enclosed air. Someone flicked a wall switch and the overhead lighting pinged on, reflecting starkly off two rows of high-backed office chairs and a long, cigar-shaped meeting table made out of a single length of wood. On one wall there hung a large white screen, connected to a projector waiting for a computer to bring it to life. It looked like a fiendishly expensive meeting room that had never been used.

'Hm,' Marie-Dominique grunted. 'No coffee.'

The next five minutes were given over to deciding whether we should find someone in charge and enquire about state-funded coffee provisions for meetings, or go and buy some from the café hidden away somewhere in the public area of the building. Once it had been established that Marie-Dominique was managing the budget for meetings on this project, and that coffees could be billed to it, all that remained to be done was for her to borrow some cash from the tubby guy, make a note of who wanted what with how many sugars, and decree that the tubby guy should go and fetch the drinks because it still hadn't been established beyond all doubt that he was actually meant to be attending these meetings.

A mere twenty minutes or so later, we started to talk about the artists' residence.

'The reason I called this exceptional meeting,' Marie-Dominique roared at me, 'is so that you can give us a short verbal briefing before submitting your written report.'

'I've brought along a short *rapport préliminaire*,' I said. I'd found the term in an online dictionary.

I pulled a small sheaf of papers out of a folder, and all their hands went up as though I'd produced a gun.

'No, no, it's much too early for a written report, even a preliminary one,' Marie-Dominique foghorned. 'Why don't you just tell us everything now, informally, verbally?'

This sounded fishy, like an excuse to put off paying me for a written report, but I didn't dare say so.

'OK,' I said. 'So I went to look at Projet Bretagne,' I began, but I was cut off immediately by the tall thin guy.

'Sorry but it's Projet Bretagne *Deux*.'

'Deux?'

'Ah oui,' Marie-Dominique mooed. 'There's another project in Brittany now, and we don't want any confusion, so you must refer to this as Bretagne Deux.'

'What's Bretagne Une?' I asked.

'Bretagne *Un*,' the all-grey guy corrected me. 'The un refers to le projet, which is masculine, not to la Bretagne, which is feminine.'

I thanked him and asked what *le projet un* was.

'It's an orchestral concert hall,' the tubby guy said.

'Brittany lacks concert halls,' Marie-Dominique told me.

'Two thousand seats,' tubby guy said.

'Brittany is a very large region.'

'In the village nearest to the Minister's holiday home.'

'I thought you weren't meant to be speaking at these meetings,' Marie-Dominique snapped at him. 'Now, Paul, please continue. You saw our good friend Gérard Macabé, I presume? Was he dead or just dead drunk?'

They all laughed, as if this was a great private joke.

'You know about him?' I asked.

'Oh yes, how was the poor man?' Marie-Dominique asked, an indulgent smile on her face.

I used my DIY French to paint them as clear a picture as I could of Gérard Macabé's talent for bumping into walls and throwing glasses out of windows. I also mentioned the amount of contradictory mission statements piled on his desk.

'Look, Paul,' Marie-Dominique sighed, reducing the volume of her voice to almost normal for once. 'What you have to understand is that the director of a project like this never lasts more than a year. They are put in charge of an empty building while various departments fight about what is to be done with it, or until there is an election and a new Minister scraps all on-going projects. This is why someone like poor Gérard gets the job. It is his life. You mustn't worry about him. We just need to go ahead and prepare everything so that the artists' – er, Projet Bretagne—'

'Deux,' the tall thin guy chipped in.

'—can go ahead as planned,' Marie-Dominique concluded. 'Now, how soon could you start serving meals there?'

'Me?' I said. 'I thought I was just—'

Marie-Dominique held up her hands to cut me off. 'Someone, anyone?'

'Tomorrow,' I said. 'There's a kitchen. It's old, but—'

'And have you prepared some local food menus?' the all-grey guy asked.

But this was one step too far. They wanted me to give away everything? Next they'd be telling me I didn't have to write my report, and the payment I was expecting would be out of the window as fast as one of Gérard Macabé's glasses.

'I am in the process of writing the menus,' I said. 'I'll send them.'

'Yes, send those to me before the rest of your report,' Marie-Dominique said, back to full volume again. 'As soon as you can. Tomorrow?'

'OK,' I said. 'Can I also send you my expenses bill for

the trip to Brittany?' I'd looked up that key French phrase, too – *note de frais*, pronounced 'fray', not 'frays'. *Fraises* were strawberries.

'Yes, and you can include our meetings, of course. Including this one.'

'Excellent, merci.' I could almost feel the euros flowing towards me like the incoming Breton tide.

'Send the expenses to my assistant Monique,' Marie-Dominique said, and I felt the tide rushing out again. 'By the way,' she went on, 'I hear that you are involved in French culture yourself?'

I frowned incomprehension.

'Yes, our mutual friend Jean-Marie told me that you were judging a poetry competition?'

'Yes,' I admitted cautiously, wondering why he would have told Marie-Dominique this.

'When is the next round? I would love to attend. I adore poetry.'

So that was it, I thought. Obviously, Jean-Marie's main goal in life at the moment was to cause me *merde*, so why not send this *emmerdeuse* along to the shop so that the Ministère de la Culture would find out about Marsha's Anglo-only poetry competition and ban it? Anything to distract me from trying to save my tea room.

'I'll email you the date and place,' I promised, deciding that I might just forget.

*

III

Walking from République Métro to the Marais, I tried yet again to get through to Alexa. Still no reply. If she didn't answer soon, I was definitely going to show up at her apartment. It was only a ten-minute stroll from where I was due to meet Amandine.

The neighbourhood just north of the rue de Bretagne is very laid-back, but today, for some reason, I couldn't help thinking about the gruesome things that went on there during the Revolution. Alexa (yes, her *again*) had told me the story. Temple was the site of the prison where Louis XVI and Marie-Antoinette were held before their execution, and where their ten-year-old son, also inevitably called Louis, died of tuberculosis. And, apparently, in September 1792, a rioting mob had paraded the head of one of Marie-Antoinette's ladies around on a pike for several hours, having previously raped and hacked the poor woman to death, before trying to break into Temple prison so that they could commit similar outrages on the royal captives there.

Not that I saw myself as another Louis XVI, with Jean-Marie's Parisian rabble trying to slice my head off. Well, not exactly. Not yet.

Entering the rue Dupetit-Thouars, I saw that I was in a high-density lunching spot, with a wide, south-facing pavement that was perfect for café terraces.

On the corner of the main road was an upgraded

Parisian café. Not a trendy one – it had fake Louis XVI-type chairs (a homage to the neighbourhood's former resident, no doubt), and a board in the window advertising touristy stuff like *crêpes*, sandwiches, omelettes and even cappuccinos.

Next up was a juice bar, a *bar à jus*, with a toasted-sandwich menu and a few sunny tables on the pavement, all of them occupied. You see, Jean-Marie, I thought, the healthy option does bring in the lunchers.

Then came a small Asian takeaway and a focaccia/pizza place, the latter a sort of cramped, elbow-to-elbow wine bar that was also doing good business. Their menu in the window featured translations that were just as pointless as mine: a *pizza rossa* was, a footnote informed the linguistically challenged, red.

And just a few metres further on came an eatery that made me stop and stare. On a sunny street corner stood a salad-and-sandwich bar so full of tropical foliage that it looked as though people were queuing up to buy palm trees. It was, a big notice promised, *bio*, and was startlingly like My Tea Is Rich, offering soup/sandwich/drink deals, with the soup of the day a fresh courgette-and-mint *velouté* – a chic word implying that it would be much more appetising than your basic *soupe*. And the place was heaving with trendy locals wanting to spend their cash on something seasonal and healthy-sounding.

It made me think how insane Jean-Marie was to want

to change the tea room into a stodge factory – even if the stodge was tasty.

And, as if to confirm my doubts, the large café on the next corner was a trendy upgrade of the traditional Parisian *bistrot*. Unlike the new boutiquey lounge on Jake's street corner, which was a break from tradition, this place was an evolution, like the son of a faded sixties film diva popping up on screen as a fresh, unwrinkled version of his mum. It still looked like a *bistrot*, with round-topped tables, a zinc bar and old, overpainted fixtures, but the menu and the staff had been updated: the waiter was sporting an out-of-work-actor look while the waitress went for underplayed, businesslike sexiness, and the menu was overflowing with marinated vege-tables and seafood, most of them accompanying salads. To be fair to Jean-Marie, there was also a beef-only section on the menu – heavy on burgers and different sorts of steak like *bavette, entrecôte* and *tartare* – but overall the emphasis was on staying hip and healthy.

Why couldn't Jean-Marie just wise up and accept that My Tea Is Rich was a bloody good idea?

I crossed the street towards the skeleton of the Temple market hall that rose from a massive building site. Good to see they weren't ripping that down, I thought. Like the café opposite, it was a case of Paris recognising what was good about it, and renovating it with loving layers of anti-rust paint. If only Jean-Marie would see the light.

*

Amandine had told me to meet her in another renovated part of the neighbourhood: the Marché des Enfants Rouges, so called not because they used to boil children there for Sunday dinner, but because of a sixteenth-century orphanage where the kids wore red uniforms. Though it occurred to me that in those days, orphans probably weren't destined for lives much less painful than being boiled.

Amandine had said she'd be at an Afro-Caribbean place, which made me laugh – as far from Jean-Marie's diner idea as you could get. She was definitely in a rebellious mood.

I walked past an organic canteen, a couscous place, a falafel bar and a pasta café, all with outdoor seating, and found Amandine huddled in a corner by a counter that smelled of fried fish and spices. She was her usual gorgeous self in a strict-looking business suit and glossy black ponytail, but looking anxious.

We did quick *bises* and I knuckled down for the obligatory apologies. I hoped I hadn't got her fired last night, I said, by giving the game away about how much I knew.

'Apparently not. Jean-Marie was looking very happy this morning, and he just said bonjour as if nothing had happened.'

I told her what I'd noticed about the photos on the anti-English website.

'So Jean-Marie and your ex-girlfriend . . .?' She couldn't finish the sentence. It was too rich in horrific possibilities. 'Poor girl,' was all she could say.

'But you have no idea exactly what his relationship is with the people behind the website?' I asked.

'No. None.'

We chomped thoughtfully on some *accras* – spicy fishcakes.

'You know, it might not be a bad thing to get fired and go somewhere like the USA,' Amandine said. 'It's all too much for me, working here in Paris. It's not just Jean-Marie. There's also a marketing guy who's started hassling me. He comes into my office when Jean-Marie isn't there and he says, "Oh, I love your skirt," and he stares at my legs. Or he says, "Adorable shirt," and he's just ogling my breasts.'

'Haven't you told Jean-Marie about him?' I asked. 'If you complain about someone else, he might take it as a warning not to be such a lech himself.'

'No, he would just say, "But it *is* a beautiful skirt," and stare at my legs, and then go to tell the marketing guy to back off, and then the marketing guy would tell everyone in the company that I am fucking Jean-Marie.'

It was, I had to admit, a dilemma.

'What about telling the HR people?' I asked. 'They were pretty nice when I worked there. Very free with their holiday allowances.'

'No, the Ressources Humaines woman said if the guy doesn't touch me, she can't do anything. A compliment is just a compliment. So I told her I have nothing against real compliments, but this isn't about real compliments. It's harcèlement.'

'Why don't you tell the marketing guy to go fuck himself? Va te faire foutre.' This was one of the first phrases I'd learnt when I'd arrived in France.

'I can't – he's an important man in the company. One time, I asked if his wife wears adorable shirts, too, but he said, "I don't know, I never look at her any more. I prefer looking at you." There's no escape.'

Being a Frenchwoman sounded even tougher than I thought.

'Just tell him straight, then,' I said. 'Tell him, "Look, Monsieur le Marketing, I came to work in this company because I'm an intelligent woman and I want to learn the business, and I think I have the right to come to work every morning without being worried that you are going to walk in my office and spoil my day by making suggestive remarks." It might shame him into going and fouting himself.'

'Oh, Paul.' Amandine laughed, presumably at my naivety. 'When you're an intern like me, you have no power to do something like that. And it's all such a shame, because at first I really enjoyed working on this project. Sorry, but the diner seemed like a great idea. My friends and I go to American's Dream for brunch all the time. And you know, even if Jean-Marie is being a bastard towards you, in purely business terms, from what I learnt in school, he is right. You're a small player. You have no money to invest. He needs to buy you out if he wants to grow.'

'Well, I was thinking of paying for lunch,' I told her, 'but now you can buy your own.'

She laughed. 'Well, that was what I thought at the beginning, anyway. Now I'm not so sure.'

'Then let me make your mind up for you,' I said. I paid for our *accras* and led her out into the rue de Bretagne. We were just a couple of small streets away from Marsha's shop, and the trendies were out in force, with their tight shirts, carefully nurtured facial hair, jeans and high heels. And all of them were either off to lunch or heading back to their artsy work after eating.

I walked Amandine eastwards, towards the rue de Turenne, where things got even artier, and showed her what I meant. Along the way, within no more than a hundred metres, were four or five of the trendy updated Parisian cafés, like the one I'd seen at Temple. And the most successful of them all was such a faithful reworking of tradition that it was actually an imitation of an old café, with white tiled walls, a vintage wallphone and 1950s metal light fittings. We read all the menus, one after the other, and by the time we'd got to the corner of the rue de Turenne, I was almost sure I'd won Amandine over.

'You see,' I said. 'They all do burgers. The burger is in fashion, big-time. Jean-Marie's right about that. But what most people want is to eat their burger in a fashionable new version of the traditional Parisian café. A diner is a great idea for weekend brunches, but not for everyday meals. For office workers, diner food is a treat, not a daily lunch. And the cafés know this, because alongside their burgers, they all do healthy salads. You can have salad or fish four days a week, and treat yourself to a cheese-burger on Friday. If I tell Benoît at the tea room to start making burgers, My Tea Is Rich will be just about the perfect place for a Parisian, young or old, to have lunch *every day*. It would be suicide for Jean-Marie to replace it with a diner. Can't you convince him of that?'

Amandine laughed.

'Have you ever managed to convince him of anything?' she asked me.

'Not without blackmailing him,' I had to admit. 'I'll just have to hope that my lawyer is better than his.'

'Than his army of low-yahs, you mean,' she said. 'He has arranged a meeting with them for the day after tomorrow. Three of them.'

'*Three* lawyers? That's not a meeting, it's a hit squad.'

It looked like my tea room's salad days were over.

*

IV

I was striding purposefully towards Bastille when Alexa's call finally came through. Perhaps, I thought, she was stalking me on Satnav and had noticed I was on my way to her dad's apartment.

'Paul? Bonjour-er.' It was her voice number two – a business call, but an amicable one.

'Did you listen to my messages?'

'Yes. So many of them, I'm flattered.' She hadn't been speaking much English recently, I thought. Her French accent had got a little stronger.

'So what's your explanation?' I asked.

'How are you, Paul? It's been a long time.'

It was an old French trick to avoid answering the question – the reminder that polite pleasantries have not been exchanged, meaning that the other person (in this case, *moi*) was an uncool bastard.

'Très bien merci, et toi?' I said. 'Now please explain what you're up to, and especially what you're up to with Jean-Marie.'

'You sound like a jealous boyfriend, Paul.'

She actually laughed, and I had to mime smashing my head against one of the place des Vosges's historical stone columns to avoid losing my temper.

'Alexa, can you *please* just tell me why you've been helping Jean-Marie to put me out of business?'

'That's what you think I'm doing?'

'Yes, and trying to nobble my girlfriend's bookshop, too.'

'What?'

'Who's paying you? Is it Jean-Marie or these anti-English nutcases, or both?'

'Now you sound like a policeman.' A French person's ultimate insult.

'And you sound surprised by my questions, Alexa. Why is that? Didn't you listen to my messages?'

'Well, I must admit, after the first one, I sort of presumed they were all the same.'

The amused note had come back into her voice, and it only made me angrier.

'What have I done to you, Alexa, to make you so bloody vindictive? Why are you trying to screw up my life?'

Actually, now that I asked the question, it did seem hard to believe. She'd never been that sort of person.

'OK, Paul,' she said, and suddenly her voice had changed into number four – the clipped, angry one. 'I am going to hang up, and you are going to have a good, long think about these accusations you've made, and send me an email explaining why you're sorry. Then maybe we'll talk.'

'Me, sorry?' That bloody word again. 'But *your* photos are on that website, and *you* went off with Jean-Marie. What am I supposed . . .?'

I stopped, realising that she'd gone, and I was talking to a rubbish bin. It was one of Paris's transparent plastic bags, hanging limply from a green pole like a burst balloon. I felt just as deflated.

V

Marsha called to talk about the next round of the poetry competition.

'You realise that because of your boss and your ex, I'm going to have to let French poets in?' she said. More blame on my shoulders, I thought. Load it on, everyone else is. 'It might not be such a bad thing, though,' she went on. 'Bring in more people . . . Paul? You there?'

'Yes,' I said. 'Do you fancy meeting up tonight? I need to go out and have a laugh. Forget my troubles. I'm not far from the shop. I could come over now.'

'Ah, sorry, babe. I'm feeling rough myself. But I'll see you tomorrow night, OK?'

'Yes, tomorrow.'

'Bisous!' she said, kissing me down the phone.

Merde to this, I thought, I need to go out and drown my sorrows. But looking inside my wallet, I saw that lunch had practically wiped me out. Drown my sorrows? I wouldn't even be able to get them damp.

Not to worry, though. I was only a street away from a branch of the bank where the tea room kept its profits.

Until now, I'd avoided making too much of a dent in my share out of the account, but this was a crisis and I needed some euros. The cash machine grinned welcomingly at me.

It was just a pity that the account was *bloqué*.

That was wrong, surely. I took my card out of the machine, tried again, and got the same result.

It couldn't be empty, I reasoned, because the tea room was a profitable business, and this was the account where the profits were banked. But when I asked the machine for the *solde*, the balance, it told me I wasn't authorised to know.

I went into the branch and asked the woman behind the counter to give it a try with her computer. She only confirmed what I'd already read. The account was *bloqué*.

'By whom?' I asked. 'When?'

'Last week,' she told me. 'By the other signatory.'

Jean-Marie.

'Can he do that?'

'He's done it,' she said, a flicker of sympathy crossing her face.

'Is the money still there?' I asked.

'If it's blocked, I'm not supposed to give out details.'

'But I'm the *other* other signatory.'

She smiled consolingly and clicked once or twice on her computer.

'Yes, it's there,' she finally said.

'Dieu merci.' I thought it safer to thank a French god.

'But there's a transfer order set for the day after tomorrow that will empty it.'

'Where?'

'To the other signatory.'

'Can he do that?'

'He's done it.'

'Can he do that?' I repeated my chorus *du jour* down the phone at my lawyer.

I could almost hear him shrugging – a slow, expensive hunching of his no doubt impeccably dressed shoulders.

'There's probably a clause in the contract that allows him to,' he said eventually. 'I haven't looked yet. But you're supposed to be business associates, no? Why don't you just ask him what he's doing?'

Because he wouldn't tell me, I wanted to say, but it would only have been a waste of time. And anyway, my one-man legal team had given me an idea. Jean-Marie was going to meet his lawyers the day after tomorrow, wasn't he? Well, I was going to give him *une petite surprise*.

Neuf

'Dire le secret d'autrui est une trahison, dire le sien
est une sottise.'
*Giving away someone else's secret is betrayal. Giving away
your own is stupidity.*

Voltaire, 18th-century French writer, who
managed to keep secret the fact that he was the
author of a treasonous pro-British book, the *Lettres
Philosophiques*

I

I HAD A trawl through the French news. It was full
of grumbling *fonctionnaires*. As Marie-Dominique had
said, the row at the Ministry was being used as an excuse
to cause wider, national *merde*. Teachers, nurses and
train drivers were all making statements about
government spending, and the Minister of Culture was
looking decidedly non-arty in a video report I watched.
First he whinged that his projects had been planned for
years so he didn't understand all the fuss. Then he

delivered a blistering, flared-nostril attack on one of the unions for undertaking costly restoration work on its headquarters, a hideous Soviet-style bunker that was losing chunks of concrete from its façade and looking as though someone, the Minister himself probably, had been firing missiles at it.

All the more reason to get my report in quickly, I decided, and spent the next day computer-bashing for Marie-Dominique. I typed up some sample menus, most of them cribbed directly from what I'd seen in Brittany and in the Marais the day before. My favourite was a perfect mix of classic Breton and trendy Parisian, sure to please the most demanding artistic palate:

Entrées
Six local oysters
Fillets of fresh (non-salted) anchovies on a bed of local sea asparagus

Plats
Entrecôte grilled in salted Breton butter, with mixed-vegetable French fries – potatoes, courgettes and beetroot
Whole grilled local mackerel served with steamed Ratte potatoes and young spinach leaves

Desserts
Local strawberry tartlet
Far breton

It was just a shame that all I could afford to eat right now was a baguette, a supermarket Camembert and the end of a bottle of Côte de Provence rosé that was so close to becoming pink vinegar that I had to take the edge off it with ice cubes.

I also put together an essay on how to get the catering operation started in the artists' residence. It could really have been condensed into one sentence: 'Replace and/or clean the old kitchens and buy some new dining-room furniture.' But I took a French leaf out of Marie-Dominique's book and explained it with as many lists, bullet points and repetitive sentences as I could manage. All it needed was translating into French, preferably by a human being, so I sent it off to Benoît at the tea room, who helped me out with language problems now and again.

I then wrote an email to Marie-Dominique saying that she could have my full report, everything, at once, as soon as she gave me the go-ahead to send it. I'd decided to ignore her request to give her the menus early. It had to be all or nothing if I was going to get paid all the money she'd promised me.

Finally, I copied some phrases off a website about

writing official letters in French, and sent my expenses invoice to Marie-Dominique's assistant Monique with an excruciatingly polite message expressing my 'gratitude in advance for her co-operation in ensuring that I might be promptly remunerated' and hoping that she would 'agree to receive my most respectful, most distinguished and sincerest salutations'. If she didn't put the payment through *tout de suite* after that little collection of niceties, I thought, then she was what my mad neighbour would have referred to as a *pétasse de chiottes de merde*.

II

Despite all my worries about Marie-Dominique, Jean-Marie, Alexa, the tea room and my general lack of financial, professional and (yes) emotional stability, I was feeling fairly upbeat that evening as I walked through the Marais to the bookshop.

The warm spring breeze seemed to have sucked everyone out of their apartments and into the street. I'd seen lots of posters in the Métro about the end-of-season sales, and people looked as though they were showing off their newly acquired garments, completely oblivious to the fact that they were, strictly speaking, at least half a season out of fashion. *Merde* to *mode*, the groups of laughing people outside the rue de Bretagne's trendy cafés seemed to be saying, let's have a drink.

I was looking forward to a dose of alcohol, too – a free one, preferably, given the airy lightness of my wallet. And, I had to admit, I was also in the mood for some wacky poetry – English, French or a mix of the two as Jake's would probably be.

I'd been avoiding his calls all day. He'd wanted to test lines out on me, and had left messages asking if I was going to 'favourise French or English poems', but I hadn't had the energy to reply, except to one of his voicemails, which was much too dangerous to leave unanswered. It had asked me if I knew much about hermaphrodites. Or 'erm-afro-deets', as he pronounced them.

I called back as soon as I heard it.

'Don't tell me you've starting sleeping with them, too?' I asked him.

'No, but I've rotten, ratted, you know, writed . . .'

'Written?'

'Yeah, a posy on their sufferances.'

As soon as I'd worked out what he meant, I began to feel like Californians do when an earth tremor wakes them up in the middle of the night: queasy, but with a sense that things could be about to get much, much worse.

'This isn't a poem for the competition?' I asked.

'Yes, the first lines are . . .'

And before I could beg him to stop, he'd recited them:

'The only good thing about being half-woman,
   half-man,
Is that if someone tells you to go fuck yourself,
   you can.'

It took several minutes, and a heated discussion about
the artist's obligation to shock the public into awareness,
and similar things that might earn someone a grant from
the French government but would have Marsha and
Amandine reaching for their sickbags, for me to persuade
Jake to go for something less provocative.

'Less free?' he asked, defiantly.

'If you want to drop out of the contest, you're entirely
free to do so, mate,' I told him. That was how Marsha
would view things. And in the end he'd promised to read
something softer.

'But I will probably wear a black armband in honour
of my dead principles poétiques,' he told me.

Whatever else you said about him, and there was a lot
to say, Jake was always good entertainment value. He
reminded me of a linguistically challenged American I'd
once seen at the Gare de l'Est. I was at the ticket office
trying to change a reservation when a tall, bewildered
tourist came up to the counter next to me.

His train was obviously running very late, and he said
something like 'pourquoi non train à Strasbourg?' in
strongly accented pidgin French. 'Grève?' he asked. He

must have taken the precaution of looking up the word for strike before coming to France.

'Non,' the railway guy told him. 'Pas de grève. C'est juste un retard' – it's only a delay.

'Pardon?' The American didn't understand.

The Frenchman repeated what he'd said before, a bit more slowly and loudly.

'Pardon?' the American said.

I saw the railway guy writing something in big letters on a piece of paper. He held it up. It said 'RETARD'.

At which point I was forced to step in and explain why the American shouldn't punch the innocent railway worker.

Marsha was also in the mood for some punching when I got to the bookshop. Not for punching me, luckily. It felt as though I hadn't seen her for ages, but when I walked in the door, she greeted me with a kiss that almost blew my teeth down my throat.

'Great to see you again,' I told her.

'Yes, it will be,' she said, and pinched my jeans where it hurt. 'But if that Jean-Marie or your ex turn up, I swear . . .'

'They won't dare,' I told her, praying that I was right. 'Oh shit,' I added. 'I think that woman from the Ministry of Culture might be dropping by, though.' I told her that Marie-Dominique had been badgering me via email for the time and place, and I'd eventually had to give in. 'Sorry,' I added. 'I should have warned you earlier.'

'Bloody hell, Paul, sorry seems to be the easiest word with you, doesn't it? This frumpy old culture snob, a friend of your mate Jean-Marie, is coming along to pour a bit of French bureaucratic shit on my English bookshop and you *forget* to tell me?'

'She's not that frumpy,' I said. 'She told me she actually liked that exhibition we saw at the One Two Two. And if you've invited some French poets, she might even give you a grant or something. I'm sure there are bookshops who'd kill to get someone from the Ministry of Culture to come to a reading. Make her feel important, say how much you love some totally obscure poet. The French never get it when you're taking the piss out of their culture. They don't see how anyone could.'

Marsha's mood swung almost instantly back upwards again.

'You're right, Paul, I'll ask one of this lot to find me a good line to quote.'

She nodded towards the customers loafing around in her armchairs. I didn't know if they were spending much money, but she certainly had a few browsers in. There were four people reading either paper or electronic books, and two chatting over mugs of something steamy.

Just then, Amandine walked in.

'Is Rain Man coming?' Marsha asked her. Amandine

wasn't too familiar with Dustin Hoffman's filmography, so it took a short while for Marsha to explain that she meant Thomas, Amandine's socially challenged boy-friend. By the time we'd got this clear, and Amandine had told us that he was parking the car, we were upstairs, staring at Greg the soundman's naked back. He was topless again, wearing only low-cut jeans, and bending over with his backside held aloft while he did his thing with the cables and the duct tape.

Marsha briefed us.

'With the new French contestants, there are going to be so many poets that we'll be allowed to interrupt them this time. Feel free to wade in like you did before, Paul. The wader the better. And I've decided it has to be a majority vote, two to one, if we're going to keep the loony fringe in check.'

Two to one? It sounded bad for Jake. I didn't know which poem he was planning to recite, but it would have to be something that didn't send Marsha and Amandine screaming for the door.

Marsha was still talking. 'And we've got to give these French poets a fair hearing, right?'

'Right,' I agreed.

'And then we vote the fuckers off, OK?'

She gave one of her loudest laugh-screams yet, and before I could reply that I didn't think that would be such a good idea, especially if Marie-Dominique was coming, she announced that she was off downstairs to find the worst line in the whole of French poetry to quote in her opening speech.

It sounded as though the evening was going to be pretty eventful.

While we waited for poets and audience to arrive, I asked Amandine how things were going. There was nothing new on the Jean-Marie front, she told me, but her boyfriend was still getting her down. She glanced nervously at the door. A bad sign, I thought, when a girl looks nervously towards where her boyfriend is about to walk in.

'I tried to tell him about my idea of going to America and he got mad. He said I just wanted to leave him, and then started saying that I encouraged the men at work because I wear short skirts and tight shirts.'

Tonight she was doing just that, and I had to admit that a man's eyes were naturally drawn towards her.

'Yes, it must be a fine balance,' I said. 'Wearing what you want without being accused of dressing provocatively. It's something we blokes don't have to worry about. I mean Gregory over there – he obviously doesn't care who ogles him.'

We had a laugh at Gregory's shamelessly rippling muscles.

'You know what we call a stomach like that?' Amandine asked me. 'Une tablette de chocolat.' She mimed the hard segments of chocolate running down either side of Gregory's tight abdomen. He caught us looking at him and shouted across at me to show some muscle.

'Mine's more of a half-melted Twix,' I said, and lifted my shirt a few inches to show off my lack of *tablette*.

'Ah, c'est ça!' A shout from the top of the stairs cut through our laughter.

Thomas the Rain Man was looking furious. Not surprising, really. The jealous guy parks the car and then walks in on his girlfriend judging a six-pack contest.

'Thomas, on ne faisait que rigoler,' Amandine said tiredly – we were only having a laugh.

'Oh, yes, I could see that,' Thomas replied, barking across the room and injecting enough venomous sarcasm into his reply to kill a French schoolkid.

'Thomas, s'il te plaît,' Amandine sighed, looking close to exhaustion.

'Tu préfères les Anglais, uh?' he sneered, as if that might be a sin.

'Arrête,' Amandine tried to order him, but he didn't look like obeying.

'Ce n'est pas . . .' I began trying to say 'it's not how it seems', but couldn't work out how to finish my sentence. And I suspected that it'd only make things worse, anyway. So I opted for second best. 'Va te faire foutre,' I told him.

'Toi . . .' He pointed at me as if he was about to explain what he was intending to do to me instead of going away and getting himself fucked, but then seemed to think better of it. I thought it probably had less to do with my innate scariness than the fact that topless Gregory had taken a step towards the door.

'Viens,' Gregory told him. 'I love wrestling.'

Thomas opted for the huffy exit strategy, and stomped down the stairs.

'It's a pity,' Gregory said. 'He's cute. And I love jealous guys. They're so passionate.'

'You think you'd better go after him?' I asked Amandine.

'Non,' she said, but it was more of a groan.

'Sorry, it was my fault for flashing my stomach. It must have looked like a come-on.'

She smiled and kissed me. Only on the cheek, a quick Parisian *bise*.

'Ooh, am I interrupting something?'

Now there was another silhouette in the doorway. This time it was Marsha, her eyebrows raised and her eyes pointing straight at my damp cheek.

Here we go again, I thought. Will Greg's six-pack get me out of this one?

In fact, though, Marsha didn't care at all. She was a sort of anti-Thomas. And just to prove it she came and gave both Amandine and myself huge kisses. And then planted one for good measure on Gregory's naked chest. Oh well, I thought, at least it was preferable to Thomas's hissy fit, even if it was slightly more confusing.

'Time to come and hide,' Marsha told Amandine and me. 'People are starting to line up outside. We don't want them to see you two canoodling here. The judges have all got to make a big entrance when the room's buzzing.'

So down we went to be shut into what was little more than a cupboard under the stairs. Marsha was outside marshalling things, leaving Amandine and me sitting toe to toe amongst a collection of boxes: tea bags, coffee capsules, printer paper. The air was a mixture of Amandine's perfume, my deodorant and embarrassment.

'Just think what Thomas would say if he could see us now,' I said to lighten the atmosphere. 'If I leant forward half an inch, I'd be nibbling your nose.'

She let out a loud French 'pff'. 'How can you go from saying such nice things just now to something so stupid?'

'Yes, sorry. Saying exactly the wrong thing is a knack I have. Just ignore me.'

'Honestly, Paul, you're one of the only guys I've met recently who didn't put his hand on my knee or make a sexual remark. And even lifting your shirt didn't seem that sexual.'

I gathered she meant this as a compliment.

'Maybe it's because you're English. Sometimes it's

hard to imagine an Englishman being sexual,' she went on, and I relaxed. I'd heard that old chestnut a thousand times before. 'Except Daniel Craig maybe,' she said. 'And even then, as a Frenchwoman, I imagine that I would have to do a striptease and jump on him to make him react.'

'Please don't start stripping now,' I said, and she laughed.

Marsha opened the cupboard door.

'Still dressed, you two? What's wrong with you?' she said. 'Come on – showtime.'

III

It was easy to spot the language loonies in the room. For a start, they were sitting at the front, whereas for the first round, people had come in more shyly, and begun filling the room in the middle rows. The anti-Anglos were also sitting in relative silence, as though waiting for a funeral to begin.

'Has your frumpy friend turned up?' Marsha whispered to me as we three judges filed to the front, causing a babble of anticipation.

I scanned the crowd and saw no sign of Marie-Dominique's nondescript hairdo or drab, fashion-free clothes.

'Doesn't look like it,' I told her.

'Good omen,' Marsha said, and went to speak into the poets' microphone.

'Bonsoir,' she announced. 'Or good evening for those of you who don't understand French. We don't want anyone to feel left out.' She gave the front rows her most charming smile. 'Bienvenue and welcome to our poetry competition, notre concours de poésie, round two, deuxième tour.'

It was impressive. Even Jake couldn't mix the two languages like that and still be understandable.

'As the little-known French poet, le poète français peu connu, Marc Destrophes said, Paris est un fruit mûr – Paris is a ripe fruit – à cueillir et à savourer – there to be plucked and savoured. Il faut juste faire attention de ne pas tomber de l'arbre – you just have to be careful not to fall out of the tree.'

So she'd found her obscure poet. An unjustly obscure one, though, by the sound of it.

Marsha explained the rules, saying that she was *ravie* – delighted – to have French poets along tonight, and that she had one French judge – Amandine, one Brit – *moi*, and one totally bilingual – herself, so everything would be completely balanced and fair.

All this seemed to disarm the website people a little. They'd come looking for conflict and *pollution linguistique* and found only bilingual harmony.

I must point out that the people in the front rows

weren't a cross-section of the Parisian population. They were all white, and, if the opinions on their website were anything to go by, probably voted for the kind of political party that thinks immigration should have stopped in about 1789. So it was a pure joy to see the look on their collective faces when Marsha announced that first up was a young French-language poet called Fatima Al Saïd.

A tall girl sporting a bouncy henna-coloured Afro, jeans and an Algerian football shirt, whose ancestors obviously came from several different parts of Northern and Southern Africa, strode confidently up to the stage to a rousing cheer from all the audience, except the front rows, who gaped and consulted each other about what to do.

It was as I was looking out into the audience that I noticed some late arrivals: a wildly mismatched couple getting settled at the back of the room. He was tall, a head higher than most people around him, and she was the same amount shorter. They both seemed to be wearing wigs – his a sort of floppy black early-Beatles mop and hers a blonde Marilyn Monroe – as well as matching punk collars, black with little metal studs. I didn't know any fancy-dress addicts, but they were waving and nodding as if to say 'yes, it's us'. I smiled back, trying not to show that I had no idea who the hell they were.

Fatima had what even I recognised to be a strong North African accent, the kind that I'd heard French rappers use on the radio. 'Oui' becomes 'way', syllables are heavy, the voice is deep and strident. Quite honestly, I hardly understood a word of what she recited. She was chanting with the microphone practically inside her mouth, punctuating her stream of words with a thrusting arm. Her delivery was as fast as a Renault racing through a red light, and there was lots of slang. The chorus of her rap, or slam, went something like 'j'ai pésho, j'ai pésho', which was a new one on me.

I asked Amandine what it meant and she had to shout into my ear that it was *verlan*, backslang, for 'j'ai chopé', which didn't help me much.

'It means she picked a guy up, she scored.'

'I'm not surprised,' I said. She was very sexy and didn't look the kind of girl who'd take no for an answer – if you could get a word in edgeways to say anything at all.

She got a huge cheer at the end, from the rear half of the room at least, and Marsha went out to thank her and say how wonderful it was to welcome French poets. Cue another syrupy grin at the language bigots.

I voted for Fatima. The girls did, too, even Marsha, in defiance of her earlier 'vote the French fuckers off' stance. I leant across and congratulated her on her spoiler tactics.

The only trouble was that the next two poets were also French rappers. How do you vote for poems you can't understand? I had to abstain and let Amandine and

Marsha decide, which they did, voting one out and one in.

By now, the people in the front rows were grumbling loudly, obviously suspecting that someone here was taking the *pisse*. Rap, especially when performed by someone in an Algerian football shirt, did not correspond to their ideal of French poetry. The English-language spectators were growing restless, too. If they were like me, they hadn't understood more than ten words that had been recited in the last quarter of an hour.

The weird-looking couple were still smiling at me, and apparently whispering about some private joke. And as the woman turned to her partner, I remembered where I'd seen her before – she was the dominatrix I'd spotted at the *vernissage*. She was certainly being friendlier tonight than she had been then.

The next competitor, Marsha now announced, would be performing a poem called 'English City, Saturday Night', or 'Ville anglaise, samedi soir'. She told us his name was 'Mark', or 'Marc', giving the second alternative a rolled French R. This got him a confused, half-hearted round of applause.

As he walked forward, nervously holding a printout of his poem, I tried to guess which language group he belonged to. It was hard to tell. A nondescript white guy in jeans and a stripy shirt, he could have come from New Zealand, Newcastle or Nice.

It was only when he opened his mouth that everything became starkly clear. A little too starkly for my liking.

> 'Ze girls in ze street in Leever-pool,
> I was thinking, Zey are beauty-fool.
> Zey 'ad a miniskirt and false blonde 'air,
> Naked legs, and eet was Decemb-air.'

If he's joking, I thought, it's genius. If he's serious, it's tragic.

The Anglos started to laugh loudly, but the reaction down the front was completely the opposite. The sound of a French mouth (if that's what it was) speaking English words was too much for the '*Non à l'anglais*' crowd. With their backs against the wall after the onslaught of Franco-Algerian rap, they now came out fighting, howling down poor, bemused Mark or Marc with shouts of 'en français, en français!' Some of them stood up and started to clap along with their own chant, and only a swift intervention by Greg stopped one of them grabbing the microphone.

Marsha appealed for calm, and tried to make a French plea for freedom of speech and artistic tolerance, but she might as well have been asking them to sing along to a Lady Gaga song or buy shares in Starbucks. They'd been driven insane with frustration, and wanted everyone else to share it.

'Ça suffit!'

A voice with the power to knock down buildings made everyone shut up.

It hadn't come from any of the microphones, so I looked out into the crowd. The woman in the Marilyn Monroe wig and the studded collar was on her feet and glowering at the troublemakers. She was also, I now saw, wearing a tight leather bodice and a skirt with open stitching at the side that made her look like an over-decorated baseball.

'Ça suffit,' she repeated, only slightly less deafeningly, and I almost fell off my seat. It was Marie-Dominique. And if I wasn't mistaken, standing up next to her to lend her moral support was her tall, thin colleague from the Ministry, now in a black wig and studded leather jacket. So this was how they spent their leisure time – as fetishist poetry fans.

As soon as Marie-Dominique had got everyone's attention, which wasn't difficult, she began to lecture the website people about France being a cultural capital precisely because it had always welcomed art and artists from all over the world.

Or tried to lecture them, anyway. The front rows were all on their feet and shouting her down.

'Ta gueule, vieille peau!' one of them called out. Shut up, you old bag (literally, old skin, presumably a pun on Marie-Dominique's leather outfit).

'Rentre chez toi, espèce de Marilyn gonflée!' Go home, you sort of inflated Marilyn.

'C'est Laurel qui baise Hardy ou le contraire?' Does Laurel shag Hardy or the other way round?

So much for the purity of the French language, I thought. Marie-Dominique puffed out her tightly trussed chest and shook her head at them, her blonde wig bobbing from side to side.

'OK, OK!' Marsha yelled into her microphone, and her sheer volume shut everyone up. 'Vous avez gagné! You win. Le concours est annulé – the contest is off. Sorry, people, goodnight. Bonsoir et adieu.' She gave Gregory the throat-cutting sign and he turned off the sound.

There was a collective cry of no from the back rows and *oui!* from the front. I looked over to Jake who was standing in mute shock as if someone had just dropped an ice cube down his trousers.

'That's it?' I asked Marsha. 'You're giving up?'

'Don't blame me, blame these fuckers,' she hissed, smiling graciously at a middle-aged couple who'd come wearing French tricolour T-shirts. 'Now can you help me make sure they all fuck off without trashing anything?'

IV

Half an hour or so later, we sat down with a glass of wine to survey the damage.

We being the three judges, Gregory, Jake, Mitzi and Connie, and Marie-Dominique and her tall friend, whose name, it turned out, was Mathieu. Amandine's boyfriend Thomas had come up on stage at the end and tried to drag her away with the rest of the crowd, but she'd shaken him off.

Marie-Dominique was getting all the attention. She was lounging in one of Marsha's armchairs, looking much more leather-bound than the furniture or any of the books. Mitzi and Connie were cooing over her clothes as though they wanted to eat them. As well as her shiny bodice and skirt, Marie-Dominatrix was wearing viciously pointed stiletto boots and, if I wasn't mistaken, droopy silver earrings in the shape of coiled whips. Only Gregory had eyes for Mathieu and his leather suit.

'We have always been interested in the fringes of culture,' Marie-Dominique boomed as if still trying to shout down a rowdy audience. 'One can dress like this, live like this, and still have a conventional professional existence.'

'Bien sûr,' we all agreed.

'In a truly free society, we should be able to dress like this at work and be respected like any other colleague.'

Amandine nodded more emphatically than anyone.

'Well, thank you for trying to defend my competition,' Marsha told her. 'Pity it didn't work.'

'Yes, if you have another one, please contact me,'

Marie-Dominique said, pulling a Ministry of Culture card out of a pouch on her studded belt. She and Mathieu said their goodbyes, and as I shook Marie-Dominique's gloved hand, she told me she'd be in touch in the morning.

When they'd gone, we all sat back, deflated.

'I can do a reading *quand tu veux*,' Jake offered, holding up the printout of his poem. In reply, Marsha just squinted. 'But this doesn't mean that posy at the shop must end, right?' he said.

Poor bloke, I thought. The fat lady has stopped singing, taken off her girdle, gone home and fed the cat, and still he doesn't get it. Well, in fact she was probably trying to hail a taxi in the rue de Bretagne, but the principle was the same. The competition was dead.

'You must not abandon hope,' Mitzi told him, stroking his hand. 'If you believe in your work, others will, too.'

But that was the trouble with Jake's poems, I thought. As soon as you believed in them, you wished you didn't.

'How are we going to fight back?' Amandine asked.

Marsha took a slug of her cheap wine and gazed into the distance, imagining, I hoped, some kind of triumphant revenge: an English poetry contest on the steps of the Panthéon, perhaps, where the French bury their staunchest establishment figures. Or a festival of bilingual fetishist verse, hosted by Marie-Dominique, brandishing a whip to keep the crowd under control.

'We're not,' Marsha finally said.

'What?' and 'Quoi?' we all asked at once.

'No. There were a few journalists in the crowd, and when they write this up it'll be great publicity. I had a couple of people filming it, so I can post some footage on YouTube. If I can get Marie-Dominique's permission to show her speech, it'll be even better. All in all, it's not a bad result.' She looked almost pleased.

'But you're still going to publish a collection of poetry, right?' I asked. Jake leant forward, offering himself up as possible material.

'Maybe, but now I get to choose what goes in it.' She gave Jake a look that punctured even his ever-buoyant optimism. 'You're too late,' she added. 'Your friends have gone, so you can fuck off, too.'

I turned to see who she was insulting.

Alexa was standing in the shop doorway.

V

Alexa ignored Marsha, and looked at me.

'A friend texted me and told me what was going on. I think I need to explain something to you, Paul.'

'I think you need to explain to *all* of us,' Marsha said.

'No, I don't explain things to people who tell me to fuck off,' Alexa replied calmly. 'I'll wait for you at the café on the corner, Paul,' she said, and left.

There was an awkward silence. I wanted to go, of course. There was so much I needed to know. But Marsha was arching her left eyebrow at me as if it was a bow, about to unleash a hail of arrows if I dared to leave.

'I think you should go,' Amandine said, nodding to me. She wanted to know what Alexa and Jean-Marie were up to as much as I did.

'Who was that?' Mitzi whispered to Jake.

'Paul's ex-girlfriend,' Jake replied, loudly. 'French. They're all totally hysterical, you know.'

'Oh yes,' Marsha said, still in arrow-firing mode. She was glowering at Amandine. 'That's the woman who set the French-language fuckers on me and screwed up my competition. And now you reckon Paul should go and have a cosy chat with her, do you?'

'She's also trying to screw up Paul's business,' Amandine retorted, blushing with anger. 'So yes, he does need to hear what she says.'

'Well, you can send him chasing after his ex if you want to, but I don't fancy your chances with him if he goes. She hangs around him all the fucking time.'

'But I'm not—' Amandine's denial ended in a choked laugh of disbelief.

It was all very flattering watching two beautiful women fight over me, if that's what they were doing, but I felt obliged to step in.

'Listen, Marsha, all I'm going to do is ask her why she's been hanging round your shop.'

'No, you listen, Paul,' Marsha said, putting her wine glass down so she could point a pistol-like finger at me. 'You know one of the main reasons why I live in Paris?'

'To learn about French poetry?' But she brushed aside my attempt to lighten the atmosphere.

'Back home,' she went on, 'there are people who see Darwin as the devil incarnate. Here in Paris, people think of him as the guy who said that nature has to screw around till it gets things right.'

'Hey, that's good, can I use it?' Jake said, reaching for his notebook.

Marsha ignored him. 'Here,' she said, 'I'm anonymous. There are none of my parents' friends watching me, no stay-a-virgin-till-you-get-married nutcases peeping through my keyhole. I'm free. So I don't care if you want to screw your ex-girlfriend, or Amandine, or anyone.'

Amandine and I both raised a hand in our defence, but she stormed on.

'This is Paris, Paul, people don't care who fucks who.'

I had to answer that.

'You really think Parisians are that cool?' I asked. 'You tell a man or a woman here that their partner is shagging someone else and they'll get as mad as anyone in London or New York or wherever.'

'OK,' Marsha conceded, 'but I really *am* that cool. You screw who you want when you want. I do.'

This sank in slowly but very surely, like a large slab of rock dropped on to quicksand.

'You do?' I asked.

'Yeah. We're not exactly married, are we?'

'Well, no.'

'And I mean, Paris is heaving with cute guys.'

'Right, and cute girls. Though recently I've been confining my attentions to just one of them.'

'Oh, don't come over all moral on me, Paul.'

'Moral? Look, I appreciate your honesty. It's very . . .'

'Refreshing?'

'Well, I was going to say something more like brutal.'

'Oh.'

'And surprising. I'm amazed you've been able to find the time. Though I suppose we haven't exactly seen each other very often.'

'No, well . . .' Marsha picked up her wine glass and took a long swig.

'I think I'll go and talk to Alexa,' I said, getting to my feet. 'Bonne soirée, everyone.'

I avoided the *bises* ceremony and made a quick exit, with Jake's voice accompanying me to the door.

'Attention, Paul, she's French. She'll be even more hysterical than Marsha.'

*

VI

As I walked in the café and saw Alexa sitting over a glass of deep red wine, I felt a momentary stab of regret. Not for coming to meet her and provoking the fight with Marsha, but that we'd broken up in the first place. There was something so free about her as she sat there alone, looking around at the party people in the café as if she was wondering whether any of them were worth photographing. It was her sexy hippie-punk look, the stylishly unstyled way her blonde hair was cut, accompanied by the kind of figure that teenage boys dream about when they're inventing their ideal woman.

But then she saw me approaching, and the mocking look in her eye reminded me how often the sparks had flown. She'd been fun and challenging, but in the same way skiing down a black-flagged slope was – you could get a real battering during the ride.

'So you escaped from the prison guard?' she asked me as soon as we'd kissed each other's cheeks hello.

'She's a bit scary, isn't she?' I agreed.

'Yes, you prefer your women soft and submissive, don't you, Paul?'

'You mean like you?'

We shared a laugh about the good old days of blazing rows and walkouts.

'What's happened to you?' Alexa asked me once I'd settled down into a seat opposite her.

'Happened?'

'You look so trendy.'

'Oh yeah.' It was the Marsha effect. I'd gone to a gay shop in the Marais and bought myself some ridiculously expensive jeans and a pair of slightly absurd pointed shoes. If my clothes were trendy enough, I hoped she'd forget about the nipple wax.

'You look great,' I said. Alexa hadn't changed a bit, which was the best thing that could happen to her. Although, of course, there was one major change to her character: her new racist leanings. All this cosy chit-chat had distracted me from what I really wanted to talk about.

'So,' I said, 'you came to explain?'

'Yes, I was pretty mad at you when you made all those accusations over the phone, but when I heard what was happening at the bookshop, I sort of understood why you made them. But it's not what you think, OK?'

'That phrase rings a bell,' I said, and she laughed. It was the plea of innocence I'd used every time I'd done something stupid that was about to send her into a raging fury.

'It's true, though. I have nothing to do with those website idiots,' she told me. 'They stole my pictures without my permission. I've told them that if they don't erase the photos immediately, I'm going to take legal action and close them down. Well, in fact I'm going to talk to a hacker friend of mine to see if he can't close them down, anyway. Racist imbeciles.'

'Yes, but why——?' I began.

'Did I take photos of the tea room and the bookshop?' she said. 'Well, believe it or not, Paul, I do have a life, and that life sometimes sends me to the same places as you in this little city.'

'It's a bit of a coincidence, though.'

'The coincidence is in the other direction,' she said. 'I was there first. Or my family was. My grandfather was a photographer, and he died a few months ago.'

'I'm sorry,' I said.

'He was ninety and happy and he died in his sleep. Nothing to be sorry about, really. Anyway, he left me his collection of photos of Paris that he took in the nineteen fifties and sixties. My latest project is to go to the same places and reproduce his photos today. And yes, it happens that he went to the street where your tea room is, and the street where the bookshop is. And about two hundred other streets. Not such a big coincidence, Paul.'

It all sounded very credible, but there was of course one major problem with her *mea culpa* (which was, incidentally, another phrase she'd originally taught me how to use).

'So how come you leapt in the car with Jean-Marie and drove off into the sunset?'

'When I found out that he was involved with the website, I wanted to know if he was the one who'd told them to use my photos. And I've met him before, remember? I know that the only way to get any information out of a lech like him is to play the seduction game. So I jumped in his car and flattered him a bit, and when I found out what I wanted to know – that he had no idea where the website got its photos – I jumped out of the car again.'

'Ah.'

'And the one thing I did *not* do was presuppose that you and he had joined together to try and steal my work. Or call you and start making crazy accusations.'

'I'm sorry,' I said, meaning the S-word even more than I had during all of its recent cameo appearances in my conversations.

'But from what I could tell from the stupid grin on Jean-Marie's face, and from some things he said, now he's trying to do to you what he tries to do to any woman he meets?'

'Yes.' I explained Jean-Marie's plans to screw me out of the tea room. Alexa looked shocked. She'd been there when I was setting it up. She'd seen me covered in plaster dust and paint. She'd heard me grinding my teeth in frustration as I tried to stop myself suffocating my useless architect with his wrongly drawn plans. She even had it all on film.

I also told her why I thought Jean-Marie had got things so very wrong. The proof of what I was saying was all around us. At that very moment, we were sitting in one of the trendy updated Parisian *bistrots*, and I could see three people tucking into a mountainous burger, accompanied by a friend or lover eating a salad or something lighter.

'Il est con,' Alexa said, and I agreed with her.

There was an embarrassed silence. A waiter came over, but I couldn't decide what to order, or whether to order, and he went away again, saying he'd give me 'some moments to reflect'.

'Well, thanks for coming to explain,' I told Alexa. 'And sorry I got things wrong about you and the website.'

'No problem.'

'Sounds like a fascinating project, revisiting your grandad's photos.'

'Yes, it's going to take me a year at least.'

'Well, if you have an exhibition, let me know.'

'Of course. You must come.'

'To the vernissage maybe?'

'Yes, I'll send you an invitation.'

We were starting to scrape the bottom of the barrel as far as pleasantries went. Soon she'd be asking me what films I'd seen recently and where I planned to spend my summer holidays.

'You know, I'd like to talk but I ought to go,' I finally

said. She didn't object. 'It's been a long day and tomorrow I'm going to confront Jean-Marie and his lawyers.'

'Confront them?'

'Yes. They're going to have a meeting about our business contract. I think they're going to invoke some get-out clause and freeze all our profits to avoid paying me off. So either I confront him before he can do it, or I go totally bankrupt.'

'Wow.' She looked genuinely concerned.

We both stood up and did a *bise*, the fingertips of our right hands barely brushing each other's left shoulder in a politely choreographed Parisian goodbye. But even as we performed our sexless dance, I was acutely aware of one of her breasts pressing against my heart, and of the perfume on her neck, where I used to bury my head and breathe in whole lungfuls of the hypnotic, exotic scent.

Oh *merde*, I thought.

Dix

'Les ennemis, ça n'existe pas. Ce sont des gens avec
qui l'on n'a pas encore déjeuné.'
*There is no such thing as enemies. They are just people with
whom one hasn't yet had lunch.*
Jean Nohain, 20th-century French writer, who was
obviously anybody's for a *steak-frites*

I

THERE IS nothing like a night of dreams populated
by curvaceous but unavailable women, and waking
to the sound of a crazed neighbour barking 'enculé' out
of the window at the honking traffic, to fire you up for a
meeting with a business rival and his lawyers. Jean-Marie
might have hired the best sharks Paris could offer, but I
was feeling as dangerous as a starved killer whale. Sharks?
They were my *apéritif* snacks.

I hadn't been to the VianDiffusion offices for a couple
of years, and pushing through the revolving doors
brought back a mixed bag of memories: my shy first

entrance when I couldn't speak French and managed to convince the receptionist that I was a congenital idiot. And my stomping last exit when I got fired for 'abuse of my computer', as the severance letter put it (I'd been receiving anti-French jokes from friends in the UK, and hadn't deleted them from my hard drive, even though most of them were so feeble they ought to have faded away naturally).

Now I marched up to reception and said a loud *bonjour*. It was, I knew, the only way to get the attention of the woman behind the *accueil* – welcome – desk, who was famous in the company for trying to make every new arrival as unwelcome as possible.

She'd been busy reading a celeb magazine, but looked up and instinctively answered my greeting.

'I have an appointment with Amandine . . .' Dammit, I didn't know her surname. I'd arranged with her to get me in the building just before Jean-Marie's meeting with his lawyers. We'd discussed every detail of our covert operation, and it hadn't occurred to me to make sure I knew her bloody name.

'Amandine?' the receptionist asked. She'd spotted a weakness in my approach and was on the verge of returning to her double page of famous French people in their beachwear.

'Amandine, Monsieur Martin's intern. It's Paul West, I worked here?' I tried to adopt the expression that had been on my company ID card, a sort of 'hello France, please be gentle with me'.

'Amandine,' she repeated, the fingers of one hand tapping on her desk, next to the keyboard that would instantly reveal who I was talking about if she just keyed the name into her computer. It wasn't that common a first name.

'I have her direct number,' I said, waving my phone around in the hope that this might speed things up.

'Oh, très bien,' she said, and was already staring back at some famous person's thighs.

I called Amandine and asked her to come down and rescue me. She arrived less than a minute later, looking nervous, as well she might. Once I'd had my unplanned meeting with Jean-Marie and his goons, she was bound to get the blame for letting me into the building. She shook my hand from the other side of the low glass barrier that separated VianDiffusion employees from the outside world.

'Could we have a badge for Monsieur West, please?' Amandine asked the receptionist with just the right amount of servitude.

'Of course.' She handed me a plastic clip-on wallet, with my name and time of arrival already written in by hand. 'I remember you, Monsieur Wess,' she told me, and actually cracked a smile. 'How are things going?'

'Very well, thanks, and you?'

'Oh, comme d'habitude,' she said, with an expression that could have implied anything from mild boredom to terminal syphilis.

She buzzed me through the glass barrier, and I followed Amandine to the lifts with my head reeling from the way French people can mess with your mind.

'Jean-Marie is already in with the lawyers,' Amandine told me as we sped upwards. New lifts, I noticed. Business was obviously good.

'Thanks,' I said. 'Sorry to do this to you. You were my only hope, apart from abseiling down from a helicopter. And right now I couldn't afford the rental.'

'That's OK. Though I don't really understand what you think you can achieve. On your own like this, without a low-yah. What can you do?'

I didn't answer. I was still waiting to find out.

II

Jean-Marie had revamped his whole floor. When I worked there, it had been like a greenhouse: all glass and plants. You expected a herd of cows to come wandering down the corridor, on their way to be turned into burger meat. Now he was going for corporate chic, with thick carpets, wooden panelling and art. The corridor outside his office was decorated in a style that said: 'I may be a successful businessman, but that doesn't stop me helping blind modern artists by paying good money for their crazed daubings. And yes, I can afford a leather sofa that no one will ever sit on.'

'They're in the meeting room.' Amandine pointed to a pair of steel-handled doors.

'OK, wish me luck.'

I gripped a cold metal handle in each hand and tugged. Nothing happened. I tugged again, harder this time.

'They slide open,' Amandine told me.

The surprise factor was only partially lost. When I finally appeared between the sliding doors, four faces were staring towards me. One, Jean-Marie's, registered shock, the other three only faint interest, as though I might be bringing a refill of coffee.

'Bonjour,' I said.

I got only three replies.

'Ceci est Monsieur West,' Jean-Marie announced, and now the lawyers were examining me more closely.

Jean-Marie was looking very old-school today. Sober grey suit, crisp white shirt, and even a pair of half-moon reading glasses to make him look more studious. His legal men were three very different types. Nearest me, and having to turn almost completely around to face me, was the young legal eagle, barely out of university, probably wearing his first flash suit and the large gold cufflinks that his dad gave him when he graduated. On his face, the enquiring look of a guy who still thought he had plenty to learn from the world. Next to him, only a couple of years older but a decade wiser, the hired gun. About my age, but trying to look more mature, dressed in classic Parisian chic and sporting a long haircut that suggested he would use the law like a Musketeer, fencing with his opponents and then stabbing them legally through the heart. And closest to Jean-Marie, the old, trusted confidant: seen it all, done it all, probably owned at least four Rolexes bigger than the one on his wrist, fifty-something years old and able to smile on the world with the utmost condescension. With Jean-Marie's amused grin setting the tone for the whole group, I felt like a virgin prostitute stumbling into her first *soirée*.

'I told Amandine you had asked to see me,' I said, in French.

Jean-Marie shrugged, not even bothering to accept or refute my lie.

'So you have come to sign your agreement?' he asked me, motioning me towards the table.

'No, I have come to show you why you're wrong.'

Jean-Marie gave a self-loving laugh of disbelief. Why he needed a wife and mistresses, I didn't know. He got more than enough adoration from himself. He appealed to the others to share his hilarity. The two older men sniggered pityingly at me.

'Come and sign the agreement we are drawing up. It

is inevitable,' he said, all kindness, like a benevolent farmer leading his prize cow to the slaughter.

I had intended to challenge him about freezing the bank account, but it didn't seem worth it any more. I had to cut to the essentials.

'Why are you doing this, Jean-Marie? Why in secret? Without discussion?' My limited French didn't let me get many verbs in there.

'Without discussion?' Jean-Marie pulled off his reading glasses and turned his full glare on me. 'We had discussions, and you wouldn't listen. And now we have no more time. I have the opportunity to obtain more premises, to buy the diner we visited, and you have no money, so I have to act alone. It's all very clear in our contract.' He held out a hand towards the hired-gun lawyer who had a pile of papers in front of him.

'Monsieur West,' the lawyer said, 'in the event of one partner being unable to back the investment plans of the other partner, the contract can be annulled, with the richer partner able to purchase the business at the initial price, plus a small rate of interest.' He shrugged. This was the law, not his fault.

'So you see, Pool, you'll get some money back,' Jean-Marie said. 'Not much, but enough to keep you in the style to which you are accustomed.' He and the lawyers shared a chuckle at this. 'I think maybe we should ask your friend Amandine to come in,' Jean-Marie went on.

'She needs to hear this, too.' He leant across to a phone and called her in. She was there in seconds, as though she'd been expecting the summons, and seemed to be even more intimidated by the gathering than I was. I understood why – every man in the room except me was undressing her. Even the young apprentice had a glint in his eye.

'We were just explaining,' Jean-Marie said, 'that Pool has no money and must therefore cede his half of the business so that I can expand. As you obviously invited him here today, Amandine, I thought you would like to witness the signature of the legal documents.' He shot her an oily-smooth smile.

'Why are you doing this?' I repeated, calling him *tu*. 'It's just because you can, n'est-ce pas? Because no one can stop you?'

'No,' he said. 'It is, my dear Pool, because you don't know anything. Where did you study? A top business school? No – some anonymous English university. And you defend this tea room as though it is a toy that you can't bear to throw away. You know nothing about business, especially Parisian business. I can't work with such inexperience. Let's end this now before someone starts crying.' He gave Amandine and me a pitying look.

Somehow, I managed to laugh. The guy was such a total fraud. He was the one acting like a spoilt kid because he couldn't get his way.

'Sorry, Jean-Marie,' I said, 'but you know nothing about Parisian food. You think diners are the new fashion here? You're wrong. Go to the rue de Bretagne and count them. Zero! Count the salads, like the ones at My Tea Is Rich. Millions!'

I realised that my primitive French was making me sound like a cross between a bad politician and an advert for the lottery, but at least I had the lawyers' attention, and Amandine was nodding her assent.

'What would be really fashionable, at My Tea Is Rich, would be a burger menu to go with the salads. You're right – the burger is fashionable in Paris. VianDiffusion's product is fashionable. But in a place like My Tea Is Rich, not an American diner. You are wrong to close it. Tu as tort,' I repeated. 'Tort.' And I rolled my R like Edith Piaf warbling 'Je ne regrette rien'.

'He's right,' Amandine said. 'He showed me the menus on these trendy cafés. They're—'

'Oui, merci, la stagiaire,' Jean-Marie snapped. Thanks, intern. He was obviously more pissed off with her than he had been showing. Amandine flushed, and held her mouth open in shock.

'And that's another thing you're wrong about,' I said. 'Your brand of sexism is out of fashion, Jean-Marie. Women in the office want more than your hand on their knee. After all, Amandine studied at one of the famous business schools you love so much. Is it even legal, the way you treat her? Why don't you ask your lawyers?'

At last, Jean-Marie's façade was down.

'Va te faire foutre,' he growled at me. 'Sorry, maîtres,' he apologised to the lawyers, 'but this petit con . . .' He stared at the ceiling as though it might give him some advice on how to deal with small English twats.

The fact that he'd lost his rag somehow made me feel icily calm.

'If you try to take the tea room, you will have a surprise,' I told him, doing my best to add a trace of menace to a sentence that sounded as if it had come out of a grammar lesson about the future tense. 'Une grande surprise,' I added, and turned on my heel. 'Sorry, Amandine,' I whispered as I marched out of the double doors and into the corridor.

Truth was, the only surprise Jean-Marie was going to get if he tried to take away the tea room was that I would put up absolutely no struggle. I couldn't even afford to phone my lawyer and ask if I could afford him. I was like a prizefighter with no money to pay for his gloves, his gumshield, or his shorts for that matter. If there was going to be a fight, it would be bare-knuckle, and I'd be naked. My only hope was that my nudity might put Jean-Marie off his aim.

*

III

I was in the Métro when Amandine called me.

'How was he afterwards?' I asked her.

Amandine puffed into her phone.

'He was weird. Silent. He's gone out. But I had a quick chat with the youngest low-yah before he left. I think they're going to finalise things tomorrow and send you a lettre recommandée.'

'Bastards,' I said.

The middle-aged woman sitting opposite me tutted.

'I hope I won't get you into too much trouble,' I told Amandine. 'Sneaking me into the meeting like that could count as a *faute professionnelle*. You could be fired.'

'Don't worry about me,' she said. 'I have my insurance.'

'Your what?' I must have said this loudly, because the woman opposite me, who was trying to concentrate on a French crossword without any black squares, tutted again and raised her eyes despairingly towards the rue de Rivoli.

'I'll show you sometime,' Amandine said.

This, under almost any other circumstances, would have been my cue to suggest meeting up for a drink. Which, I realised, was something I'd like to do. Yes, it would be really good to go out for a drink with her. But how could I say so? I make a speech to try and protect her from her lech of a boss and then I ask her out? It felt all wrong.

'What will you do?' Amandine interrupted my thoughts.

'About Jean-Marie? For the time being, panic.' We managed to share a laugh. 'Thanks for calling me,' I told her. 'You've stopped me panicking for a few minutes. Feel free to call again anytime.' But I heard myself starting to sound like a guy in full chat-up mode, and stopped.

'Well, I just wanted to tell you not to worry about me,' Amandine said. 'Give me a call if you need to discuss any ideas about Jean-Marie.'

'I will, thanks.'

'Fini?' Madame Mots Croisés asked as I stowed my phone.

'With him, never,' I told her.

Back at the garret, I found Jake lounging on the sofa bed.

'Hey man,' he greeted me. 'How did it go with Alexa? You two bezzing again?'

'No.'

'Don't say she's bezzing Jean-Marie?' His whole body screwed up in horror at this idea.

'No, of course not. She just wanted to find out if he had anything to do with giving her photos to that loony website. Which he probably did.' Right now, I'd be willing to believe anything about him. Who really shot JFK? Ask Jean-Marie where he was in 1963. Jack the Ripper? Look no further.

I would have asked Jake to move over so I could collapse on the sofa bed with nervous exhaustion, but he was looking troubled.

'What's up with you?' I asked him.

'They stole the dream, man,' he said. 'I had the poem. And they stole the dream.'

I could tell that his emotions were running high by the way he actually got a verb right. Personally I never believed he stood a chance of getting through the two-to-one vote with Amandine and Marsha there to censor him, but at least he could have put up a fight. The anti-climax of it all had hit him hard.

'Yeah, they were a bunch of salopards,' I sympathised.

'And Marsha, man. I mean, I know she was your girl-friend and shit, but what a salope.' Meaning the female version of a *salopard*. 'She refuses to try a new concourse . . .' I guessed he meant *concours*, the French word for competition. 'And what was all that about bezzing lots of guys in Paris? She refused to have sex with *me*,' he complained. 'I told her I once had a girl from North Island, but never from South Island. And she *refused*.'

'Well, shave your nipples and you might be in with a chance.'

'De toute façon, it's too late now,' Jake said.

'What is?'

'Marsha. I don't want sex with her. Because I think I only want sex with Mitzi.'

'What?'

This time, I *had* to sit down. Jake was contemplating some kind of monogamy? It was like a dolphin giving up swimming, or Johnny Hallyday deciding not to wear leather trousers.

'Yeah, you know what Mitzi's doing just maintenant?' he asked. I shook my head. 'She's out there visiting her business contacts, trying to get sponsors for another concourse.'

'Another poetry competition?'

'Yeah. What a femme, right?'

'But why doesn't she just get sponsors to print up some poetry books for you?'

He sat up straight – a mean feat on his sofa bed – and there was the fire of a born-again monogamist in his eyes.

'Oh no, man. I'm going to *win* this. When my posy is published, it will be because the public demands it.'

Poor guy, I thought, last night's disappointment has driven him to hallucinations.

'Well, good luck,' I told him. 'You deserve it. You have more determination than anyone I know. Except perhaps Jean-Marie, who is determined to screw my life up once and for all.'

Jake asked for details, and I gave them, until the whole sofa bed was creaking under the strain of my anger. Now I understood what sent my mad old neighbour swearing out of his window. Paris, in the form of Jean-Marie, had driven me to the verge of Tourette's.

'Sorry, Jake,' I told him, 'but if you do manage to set up another competition, I won't be there to judge it for you. I'm getting out of this place. Just as soon as I've sent in my report to the Ministry and made sure their payment is coming through, I'm on the train back to England.'

'The Ministry of Culture?' Jake said. 'This morning, didn't they start a grève? You know, a strike?' He smiled, pleased with himself at remembering an English word.

I was already on my way to the window.

IV

I had received several emails from the Ministry, most of them circulars about photocopier use, not sending out unnecessary emails, and similar subjects that were just a waste of electricity. One, though, looked relevant.

The heading was '*Zéro pour Bretagne 1 et 2*', an obvious attempt at some kind of numerical wordplay.

The email itself was less punchy, but I managed to wade through the dense French officialese, and translated the core of the message as something like 'how can the Ministry be planning to spend so much money on a concert hall and an artists' residence when the government is cutting civil-service jobs and raising the pension age?' It was what I'd been wondering myself while knocking back the free wine at the One Two Two's state-subsidised pornography exhibition and spending hours in pointless meetings with Marie-Dominique's numerous colleagues.

The worrying thing was that the writers of the email were the unions, who were calling for an out-and-out boycott of both Bretagne projects: the concert hall and my residence. They were demanding 'an instant and definitive annulation of these elitist outrages'. Any attempt to push the projects forward would be seen as 'the worst political provocation'. To discourage this, the Ministry was, as Jake said, on a one-day strike, with more action threatened if the Minister didn't back down.

I called Marie-Dominique, and wished her a hearty *bonjour* so that I could adjust the volume on my phone according to the decibels in her reply.

'Ah, Paul,' she foghorned. 'Thank you again for a most entertaining *soirée*. Such a shame it ended in anarchy.'

'Anarchy, yes,' I said. 'Like at the Ministry today?'

'It's true, it's true,' she replied in what other people would have called a bark but for her was a whisper. 'There is a protest picket outside the Ministry. You know, the *fonctionnaires* are very tense at the moment. This kind of high spending on culture – even if justified – is very sensitive.'

'But my report . . .'

'Don't worry, soon they will pass their attention on to something else like education or health, and forget us. Then we can start again.'

'Start again? But I would like to be paid for my work maintenant, tout de suite,' I said, constructing my French as carefully as I could.

'Sorry, but the project is frozen.' All our solidarity about poetry and SM leatherwear seemed to have disappeared.

'That doesn't stop me sending my report and being paid for my work,' I said.

'Non, non!' Her voice was back at blast force. 'Please, on no account send in your report. Any progress with the project now would be disastrous. We've promised the unions.'

'*You* are working, though, n'est-ce pas? And officially it's a strike day.'

There was a silence and I knew I'd gone too far. I'd turned it into a case of us and them, and I was most definitely one of them.

'I am working on other projects,' she said, as if declaiming it to the crowd of protesters outside her window. 'And in a moment I will be going out to join the strikers. I must order you not to submit your report or engage in any work towards Bretagne Deux. One sign that we are ignoring the unions' demands, and there will be an open-ended strike at the Ministry. It could escalate into a national strike of fonctionnaires. You could bring the whole of France to a standstill. You don't want that on your conscience, do you?'

V

'The French love strikes,' Jake told me. 'You'll be doing them a favour. Hey, that's the right English word, isn't it?' He had agreed to come to the Ministry with me, or rather announced that he was coming, and he was in upbeat mood. 'Cause a strike, Paul, you'll be a hero. If you get beaten up by the police, you can call Alexa and she'll take some photos of your, how do we say? Wounds?'

'Well, as usual, thanks for your advice, Jake,' I told him. And I meant it. It was bollocks of the most bollock-like kind, but at least it was getting me in the right mood for the scene that I was about to cause. So there was a demo right outside the Ministry, was there? The perfect place for a showdown. Instead of a placard, I was carrying a crisp white A4 envelope addressed to Marie-Dominique.

We walked past a Métro entrance apparently made of coloured beads, along the side of the Comédie Française theatre, which had large '*En Grève*' stickers pasted over the posters for its latest production of Molière's *Bourgeois Gentilhomme*, and into the square decorated with a petrified forest of toothpaste. Just beyond the modern art, I could see a large crowd of people filling most of the Palais-Royal gardens, several of them holding banners on which the commonest word seemed to be '*Non!*'

By the Ministry entrance itself there were a dozen or so picketers facing out as though they were expecting Wellington's army to arrive and declare war on French culture. Little did they know that one of the Iron Duke's countrymen was on his way. Standing to one side, trying to look inconspicuous, was a small group of riot police in their black gladiator gear, long batons by their sides in case anyone decided to start damaging state property.

I gripped my envelope and marched forwards, not quite sure yet what I was going to say.

But before I reached the picket line I was hit by a broadside in the shape of Marie-Dominique.

'Why are you here?' she demanded, her voice louder than any cannon. She was with her tall, thin friend Mathieu. Both of them were in everyday working clothes, and looking much tenser than they had when they were trussed up in their leathers. Mathieu gestured at someone to come and join us – a small, thickset guy with a long haircut that officially became extinct in 1972. I recognised him as the union rep who had had a go at me in the corridor of the Ministry, telling me he 'knew what I was doing'.

'What's he doing here?' the rep demanded.

No one seemed to know the answer.

'And who is this?' the union guy asked, pointing at Jake.

'My lawyer,' I said.

'Ah.' To anyone except a union man with a seventies haircut, the idea that Jake, in his un-matching trainers and a pair of small pink sunglasses that he had borrowed from Mitzi, could be a member of the French legal profession was totally insane. But French union activists are open-minded people.

'I've brought this for you,' I told Marie-Dominique, and held up the envelope.

'What is it?' she demanded.

Before I could answer, several other strikers arrived, and were told who I was – 'le consultant anglais' who was working on 'la résidence d'artistes de merde', the Minister's elitist project that was causing all this friction. There was a general rumble of discontent. In the background, I could see the cops staring, on the lookout for trouble.

'I've come about my reports,' I announced, 'and my bill.'

'If he delivers them . . .' one of the pickets said, looking nervously at the envelope.

'If he *tries* to deliver them . . .' the union rep said.

A woman with a video camera came over, followed by a guy with a microphone and another pointing his phone at me. Journalists, I guessed. The union rep turned to stand between me and the nearest camera lens.

'Deliver what?' the camerawoman asked, and the rep explained, more or less accurately, what I was doing there.

'What's your name?' the guy holding up the phone asked me.

I told him.

'Pol Wess?' he said, as they always did.

'And what are you doing here?' the camerawoman said, focusing on my face.

'I told you,' the rep said, 'he's come to provoke a national strike.'

'Really?' the camerawoman said, and pulled her face away from the eyepiece to get a good look at the bloke who was about to make her job a lot more eventful for the next few weeks.

'He's an emmerdeur,' the rep said, meaning a person who covers everything in shit.

Suddenly I noticed how bright the sun was, and how high in the sky. Perfect lynching weather.

VI

'I have come to the Ministry because I have rights,' I told the protesters, Marie-Dominique and the cameras.

'Yes, the right to go and fuck yourself,' the union man

heckled. Of course, he didn't actually *want* to go on a prolonged strike. That's not what French workers want when they take industrial action – they'd prefer the government to give in to their demands so that life can go back to being cosy and koala-like again.

'Look,' I said, 'I know that you fonctionnaires are suffering because of la crise économique. I know that it's not really true any more that you are koalas in France's eucalyptus tree.' Here I lost my audience a bit, perhaps because koala ('kwa-LA') and eucalyptus ('erkalip-TOOSS') are hard to pronounce properly in French. 'I am not a fonctionnaire,' I went on quickly. 'I'm only a contractuel, I don't have the same rights as you. If I present my report, you will go on strike and I won't get paid for months. You will probably get money from the union. I will get nothing. But if I don't present my report, and the project is annulled, I don't get paid at all, ever. So I have decided that there is only one thing I can do. I have come to present this envelope to the Minister, or his representative if he himself is busy.' I looked down at Marie-Dominique, who was glowering as though she wished she had one of her whips handy.

'I won't accept it,' she said, trying to back off, but unable to because of the crowd hemming her in.

'If he offers it to you, you have to accept it,' the camerawoman said. She was obviously hoping for a big story on the evening news.

I held the envelope out towards Marie-Dominique.

'Open it,' I told her.

She clutched her hands to her chest, not wanting to give her fingers the chance to touch the envelope.

'Trust me, Marie-Dominique. Have you forgotten last night?' I tried to whisper this, but several people picked it up, and eyebrows were raised.

Marie-Dominique reached out slowly and took the envelope from my fingers. The union rep said a loud 'hoh!'

'But if I open it, the whole country will be on strike,' Marie-Dominique said.

'Open it, please,' I told her.

She did so, and pulled out the contents.

'Voilà, c'est la grève,' the rep said, and started to comb his hair with his fingers in readiness for his national TV interview.

Marie-Dominique read the first page quickly, and then handed it to the rep, who frowned.

'Tu es tenace,' she told me.

'Tenace, that's the French word for a slug, isn't it?' I whispered to Jake, who was standing by my shoulder, grinning into the camera.

'No, that's limace,' he replied. 'Tenace is, you know, tenace.' A great help. Then I worked out that it probably meant tenacious. Much more appropriate in this case.

The union guy was knitting his brows at me.

'You must explain,' the camerawoman said. True, suddenly the whole scene had turned into a silent movie.

'I have read the rules,' I said. 'I know my rights. In French employment law, anyone can go on strike for reasons of conscience. If they think their employer is asking something wrong, they can go on strike. The Ministry has asked me to write a report for a project that is unjust to French workers, so I am now on strike.'

Marie-Dominique shook her head. 'You can't do that. You're a contractuel, you're self-employed.'

'But in French law, the self-employed can go on strike,' I said. 'I am on strike against myself. And in this envelope is the announcement of this, and my application form to join the union and ask for strike pay. Until the conflict about the project is ended,' I added, just in case anyone thought I was asking for only one day's money.

It was all true. As a newly qualified expert in reading officialese French, I'd managed to battle my way through the relevant section on the government website and, unbelievably, it was totally legal. I, the consultant, could refuse for reasons of conscience to work for myself, the consultancy. And if the union supported me, I was entitled to strike pay.

'So, will you support him?' the camerawoman asked, swinging round to face the union rep.

'Well . . .' he said.

'We need an answer,' she told him. 'It's for the eight o'clock news.'

He finger-combed his hair frenetically, gazing into the lens. 'We must, I think, respect the accords governing such cases.'

'Does that mean oui or non?' the woman asked him, telescoping her lens for a close-up.

'Well, in the light of . . .' He looked at the faces around him, and then back at the camera. And, taking a deep breath, said, 'Oui.'

I reached out and shook his hand before he could change his mind.

'Le chèque est dans l'enveloppe,' I told him. A year's union sub worked out at less than the daily rate of strike pay. And it was hardly my fault if the cheque was drawn on an account that Jean-Marie had frozen.

Onze

'Les femmes ont une place d'honneur dans notre société. Elle est juste en-dessous de celles des hommes.'

Women have a place of honour in our society. It is just below that of men.

> Napoleon Bonaparte, apparently annoyed that Josephine was taller than he was

I

THAT EVENING, Jake announced that his mission was 'to stop me fermenting in my merde'.

He was Mitzi-less – she was at a fashion event – and he took me to a bar in the 20th, a sort of industrial-era cave with silver air-conditioning tubes snaking across the black-painted walls and ceiling.

It was, Jake shouted in my ear, one of Paris's fashion weeks. It seemed to me that these came around almost weekly, and always decorated the city with ten-foot-tall girls whose biggest curves were their cheekbones. It was a sad irony: here they were in the capital of the creamy *pâtisserie* and yet they were forced to go on a starvation diet. Poor girls, I thought. One of Jean-Marie's burgers would give them indigestion for a week. If they still had a digestion, that is.

'This is why Mitzi has her meeting ce soir,' Jake told me. 'They prepare the collection hiver,' meaning winter. We were now on the cusp of summer and enjoying Mediterranean heat, so I guessed it was logical. Winter in summer, skeletal bodies in an age of obesity: it was an industry that did everything backwards.

'So why didn't you make them all go en grève?' Jake asked me as we sipped beer from squashy plastic glasses.

'My problems are with Jean-Marie, not with France,' I told him. 'And I agree that the Minister of Culture is insane to build arty-farty palaces when the country has no money. So I didn't want to cause merde for nothing.'

Jake nodded. 'There would have been no space for poets at the residence anyway. It's all about painters. No one respects poets.'

And for good reason in some cases, I thought, but it would have been unkind to say it.

'So what will you do now?' Jake asked.

'Oh, the union guy says I should get some money before the end of the month. And by the looks of it, I'll get Jean-Marie's pay-off sooner than that. So I'll probably take the money and run.'

'Run where?'

'Somewhere sunny.'

Jake was only half listening. He was watching a pair of particularly stork-like models stalk past on their stilt legs.

'You know, it is a liberation,' he said. 'Because of Mitzi, for the first time ever, I don't give a merde where all these girls come from.'

It was true. At any other time, he would have left me to cope by myself while he worked the room looking for obscure nationalities, especially amongst the models, many of whom had been plucked from their country's gene pool to feed the fashionistas' appetites for new faces.

'Too bad you are without a woman,' he said, making it sound like a medical condition.

'Yes,' I agreed, and two faces flashed before my eyes: Amandine and Alexa. But before I could work out what this meant, a voice began yelling into the PA system, blasting any thoughts out of my brain.

'Bonsoir, bonsoir!' Up on stage, a tattoo-plastered guy in combat shorts, combat boots and a T-shirt printed with metallic muscles was grinning into a microphone.

Jake had brought me along to watch the French air guitar championships, and the guy with the mic went on to explain the concept of air guitar, which, given that the only thinking behind it is that you pretend to play guitar while listening to someone else doing so, didn't take very long. After that, a series of French people got up on stage and mimed to backing tracks of soaring guitar solos, most of them morphing into wild animals for the duration of the song, hacking and biting at their imaginary instrument like crazed termites. But there were a couple who were overcome by shyness, and one who tried to play a joke – 'I've snapped a string' – and ended up getting booed off by the crowd. The booing was all part of the fun, though, a long way from the spoiler tactics we'd had to put up with at our poetry contest. The only downside was the judges themselves, who seemed to think that their job was to show how much cooler they were than the people on stage. For the most part they poured scorn on the poor, guitarless heroes. I felt a flush of guilt. Once or twice I must have been like that with the poets.

At the end of it all, the judges chose a guy who had dressed up as Jimi Hendrix – Afro wig, psychedelic jacket, skin-hugging silk trousers – and practically shagged his invisible guitar to death. He came on to receive his award, and then performed his act again, with even more mimed string-licking.

'You know, Paul, I think that I have took, er, toked, a grand decision,' Jake shouted in my ear over the sound system. 'I will e-pooz Mitzi.'

'You'll do what?'

'You know, épouser, marier.'

'Marry? You?'

'Yes. When you find something you want, you must keep it.'

It was not the most romantic of declarations, but coming from Jake it was as earth-shattering as 'I have a dream'.

'Good on you, Jake,' I told him, and we even had a quick man-hug as, on stage, fake Jimi finished his miming and got a huge cheer from the crowd.

'Yes, now all that is missing from my life is a concourse of posy,' Jake said. 'What is missing from your life, Paul?'

I coughed a laugh. Like the recently crowned French air-guitar champion, there was something very obvious lacking from my life.

'Pretty well everything,' I told him. 'But hearing you talk, one thing has jumped to the front of the queue.'

II

To the untrained eye, the *boulangerie* down the road from Jake's apartment probably looked timelessly French. By the door, there were the usual *Ticket Restaurant* stickers announcing that office workers could buy their takeaway lunches here. Before weekday lunchtimes, the long cold cabinet next to the till was always heaped with wrapped baguette sandwiches, the ham, Gruyère and lettuce poking out the end of long paper bags. Alongside them would be neat stacks of salads in their plastic tubs: lettuce, tomato, olives, boiled egg and sweetcorn, with a beige splash of vinaigrette. And at all times, the cabinet nearest the shop window was a parade ground of pastries, lined with ranks of glistening strawberry tarts, fruit-topped *charlottes* and bulbous *religieuses*: the snowman-shaped double-ball éclairs filled and glazed with coffee or chocolate cream. Apart from the prices and the focus on salads, it all looked like something out of the nineteenth century.

But this *boulangerie* had moved with the times. The bakers working at the ovens on the other side of the glass partition were North African, as were the women serving, and in addition to the racks of traditionally French loaves, the shop also sold flat, round North African bread and an array of deliciously gooey bite-sized *pâtisseries*. Dripping with honey or coated with icing sugar, these were the perfect comfort food, so next morning I bought myself a selection and climbed upstairs to wonder how I was going to fill the gaps in my life. Cake would be a good starter.

It didn't take me long to get settled. I beat the more visible lumps out of the sofa bed, opened up the window to get some relatively fresh air into the oven that the apartment was becoming as the spring wore on, and then leant out to yell a couple of *connard*s to make the old nutcase downstairs shut up. Finally it was time to lie back, close my eyes and get my fingers sticky, my teeth gummed together and my palate caked with sweet, chewy pastry.

Not a good time for my phone to start buzzing. Half determined to ignore it, I looked at the number. It was a VianDiffusion extension. Oh shit, I thought, here we go.

'Ago,' I said, as close to 'hello' as my glued jaw could manage.

'Monsieur Wess?' a woman asked.

'Oui.'

'Bonjour. Monsieur Martin would like to meet you this morning,' she told me in clipped French. It was Jean-Marie's new fire-breathing dragon of a secretary.

'Ah.'

'He has asked me to invite you to a meeting at eleven.'

'Où?' I asked – where?

'Matty's Ridge,' she said.

'Où?' I repeated.

'Le salon de thé. My Tea Is Rich?'

So simply humiliating me wasn't enough for Jean-Marie. He wanted me to go along and watch the execution of the tea room? No, he wanted me to perform it. The very act of signing my name on his forms would be like injecting poison into its veins.

'No,' I finally said. 'Not at the tea room. I'll come to your office.'

'Non, non. It must be the salon de thé. Monsieur Martin insisted. It is a convocation.'

This, I recognised, was a legal word. It was like a summons. So it was his lawyers who'd concocted the plan. Typical.

'D'accord,' I said. 'Eleven o'clock.' I thanked her for calling. It wasn't her fault she was working for a shit. After all, I'd worked for him myself.

III

It was months since I'd been to the tea room. The last time I'd seen it had been in Alexa's photos. Stupid, really, I told myself. I should have popped in more often, kept in touch with the place. If I had, maybe I would have spotted that it needed updating – with a burger menu, say.

Looking around at the people walking in this chic neighbourhood, I couldn't imagine a single one of them going into a diner. The middle-aged bourgeois couple, dressed like a throwback to the 1940s. The trotting fashionista, a rake-thin young guy in a suit delivering what looked like a couple of dresses to a show somewhere. The two concierges, Portuguese probably, chatting as one of them wheeled her green bins back into the open double doors of a fancy apartment building. Admittedly, the office workers were still at their desks. They wouldn't come streaming out for an hour or so, but as I'd tried to tell Jean-Marie, they wouldn't want to sit in a booth and eat stodgy comfort food every day. It just wasn't chic enough. Even the kids of that middle-aged couple weren't around often enough to make a diner work. They'd be here at weekends and holidays, but their school was miles away.

And there, right outside My Tea Is Rich, shamelessly occupying a *livraisons* (delivery) space, stood Jean-Marie's Jaguar, its top down and its vintage leather seats glistening in the sun.

He was taking no chances, though. I could see him silhouetted in the window, keeping an eye on his baby. I couldn't resist it. I got out my keys and scratched 'Buy yourself a Renault' on his bonnet. Or pretended to, anyway. From the way Jean-Marie gesticulated through the window, I could tell that for a satisfying few seconds, he thought it was for real.

Sitting opposite him, I could see Amandine, which was a surprise. I thought she would have been excluded from all this.

I walked in and was hit by the smell of my recent past. Toast, coffee, the vapour from a spicy soup. Benoît was busy setting out the bowls of salad that the customers would choose from as they moved along the counter – potato, Greek, Niçoise, sausage and haricot bean, grated carrot and beetroot – four portions with a soft drink for 8.50, almost exactly the price of an average *Ticket Restaurant*.

Benoît was looking his usual self. Cool T-shirt, jeans,

mild-mannered smile behind his soft growth of beard. The exact opposite of his dad, in fact. We shook hands, but he kept one eye on the figure of Jean-Marie behind me, as if he was worried about being too friendly with the condemned man.

Four or five of the ten tables had people sitting at them – not bad for mid-morning – and Jean-Marie had commandeered the two in the window, one apparently just for his briefcase. On the other stood two mugs of coffee, diner-style.

For once, he had actually let Amandine sit more than an inch away from him. She was looking great, but I noticed that she'd dressed down, with a loose black cardigan camouflaging her top half.

'Bad joke, Pool,' Jean-Marie said, nodding towards his car.

'Bonjour, Jean-Mary,' I replied, holding out my hand to remind him of the need for civility. 'How do you know it was a joke?'

Amandine shook her head.

'Can't you two stop the Pool and Jean-Mary thing?' she said, in French, and stood up to give me a *bise*. I wondered what had happened to make her so assertive.

'Comment ça va?' I asked her, and for once it wasn't just a greeting. I needed details. Something had happened.

'Great,' she said, switching back to English. 'Jean-Marie has made me an offer, and I accepted.'

With almost any other woman who'd had to work with Jean-Marie, the obvious question would have been: Was she to be a full-time mistress with luxury apartment or just a business-trip squeeze at a luxury hotel? Not with Amandine, though.

'A job?' I asked.

'Of course, what else?' She laughed.

I turned to study Jean-Marie, who was smiling inscrutably.

'You are surprised, Paul?' he asked me.

'Yes, I wasn't sure you two – how shall I put it? – would be able to work together any more.'

Jean-Marie gave a chuckle worthy of Santa Claus.

'Oh, that's all in the past,' he said. 'We had a frank exchange of opinions. It was very educational. Explain, please, Amandine.'

I turned towards her, fearing the worst.

'Jean-Marie is going to start a campaign against sexual harassment in the workplace,' she said. 'He wants me to make VianDiffusion into an "entreprise phare". You know, a sort of role-model company.'

'And you *believed* him?' I asked.

'Yes. Our slogan will be: "We sell meat, but we don't treat our women employees like it." We are going to put ads in the magazines.'

'Is this true?' I asked Jean-Marie.

'Oh yes. I invented the slogan. Good, no?'

Gross, I wanted to say, but brilliantly so. For some perverse reason, his sudden turnaround was all too credible. It was typical of Jean-Marie to turn his failing into a virtue and, meanwhile, make all his friends in high places suffer the same fate as him – I'm not allowed to touch up the interns any more, so why should you? He was probably going to get himself appointed Minister for Sexual Equality.

But there was a problem with all of this: if Amandine and Jean-Marie were in each other's good books again, where did it leave me?

'Sit down, Paul, have a cup of tea,' Jean-Marie said. 'The other person will join us in a moment.'

Ah yes, I thought, there were no lawyers present. Which one would it be, I wondered: the old guy, the hatchet man or the young apprentice? The young one, probably, to rub it into me that I was a mere minnow in Jean-Marie's big pond.

'I hope I'll be walking out of here with a cheque,' I said. 'Just because you two are best friends again, it doesn't mean I've forgotten why we're here.'

A frown crossed Amandine's face and I saw that she wanted to tell me something, but Jean-Marie gave an almost imperceptible shake of the head, and she sat back in silence.

'It's self-service here, or have you forgotten?' Jean-Marie said. 'Maybe you should go to the bar and order. This place needs its profits, after all.'

I got up.

'Maybe I'll just keep half the tea money so I can be sure you won't freeze it in some bank account,' I said, and went to see Benoît.

'Benoît, please don't discuss business with Paul, OK?' Jean-Marie called over my shoulder, and his son nodded meekly. It was shutdown time.

What I really fancied was a coffee with a double shot of whisky, but I ordered a cup of Darjeeling for old times' sake, and watched Benoît steam the small teapot, then fill it with boiling water and drop the bag in, just as I'd taught him to do. It had taken a while to convince him that it was a good idea to depart from the typical French café custom of handing the customer a pot of water with a teabag on a saucer. That was a recipe for tasteless tea that no one would ever want to reorder.

'Milk, Paul?' Benoît asked, and I nodded. He poured a splash into the mug. Again, not a French thing to do. They'd have given me a little jug. Extra cost, extra washing up.

'Non, non,' he said when I tried to give him money. 'Papa was joking. He says he will pay.'

'I hope you got a lawyer to witness that promise,' I said.

When I turned around to walk back to Jean-Marie and Amandine, I almost poured the hot tea and cold milk down my shirt. Three faces were staring at me, enjoying my reaction, which for the moment was mute shock. I could do nothing but gape.

'Is that tea for me, Paul?' Alexa asked.

'Sorry, but I think I need it,' I told her. There are times in life, even in these days of espressos and caramel lattes, when an Englishman's only refuge is a cup of tea. I sat down. 'Is someone going to explain?'

'You have a problem, Paul,' Jean-Marie began. There, at least, he was on safe ground.

'No, that's not a good way to start,' Alexa interrupted him. 'What you need to know, Paul, is that My Tea Is Rich is not going to close.'

'It's not?'

'And it will stay a tea room.'

'It will?' This had to be a hallucination.

'Your problem was—' Jean-Marie began again, but Alexa cut him off a second time.

'No negativity, please,' she said. 'Paul, I have offered to buy Jean-Marie's half of the business.'

'You have? But how?'

'You remember I mentioned my grandfather left me some photos? Well, he also left me some money, and when you told me that the tea room might be closed in favour of a diner, I decided this was how I would spend the money.'

'And you agreed to this?' I asked Jean-Marie. He

shrugged benevolently, as though it was the most natural thing in the world. 'But yesterday . . .' I said, trying with outstretched hands to conjure up the disaster that had been imminent less than twenty-four hours before.

'Yesterday afternoon, I contacted Alexa and told her what was happening,' Amandine said.

'But you didn't know each other.'

'There aren't many photographers in Paris called Alexa,' Amandine went on. 'And when Jean-Marie's lawyers returned to the offices at the end of the day to finalise the contracts, Alexa and I went to the meeting to discuss things.' The way she said 'discuss', and the way Jean-Marie flinched ever so slightly as she said it, made me feel that the discussions must have been what politicians call 'frank'.

Jean-Marie saw me staring at him in disbelief.

'Let's just say,' he said, 'these two ladies showed me that the best course of action for my business interests was not to replace the tea room with a diner.'

In the past, a sentence like that would have been accompanied by a hand on a female knee. Now, though, his hands were above the table and pressed together, as if in prayer.

'And with this, I must leave you,' he announced. 'I must go and buy American's Dream. Whatever you think, Paul, that diner is a good business, and will do well.'

'Yes, great, perfect,' I said, still not quite able to believe that all this was really happening.

Jean-Marie stood up, shook hands all round, and went to say a few words to Benoît, presumably to commiserate with him that he was soon to be the employee of an Englishman and a mad hippie woman.

As soon as he'd left, all resemblance to a business meeting ended.

'You two are fucking geniuses,' I told the grinning girls. 'You're my fairy godmothers.'

'No, Paul, I don't like the idea of being your god or your mother,' Alexa said, though she had a smile on her face.

'But how did you do it? Am I allowed to kiss you?'

We all stood up and did a group hug across the table.

'How do you *think* we did it?' Amandine asked. 'Blackmail, of course. I told you I had my insurance.'

She picked up her phone, pressed the screen, and a grainy film began. The sound was bad and the picture overexposed, but the action was unmistakable. It was Jean-Marie being smarmy and over-tactile.

'I started recording and filming him as soon as he started harassing me,' Amandine said. 'And yesterday, after you walked out of the meeting with the low-yahs, I decided it was time to show him.'

'Wow,' was all I could say as I tried to imagine how Jean-Marie would have reacted to a humble intern, and a female one at that, squaring up to him. 'But was he really worried about blackmail?' I asked. 'He usually just passes off all this kind of thing as being charming and French.'

'No,' Amandine said. 'Times are changing, even in France. A compilation of his best lines on YouTube and he would look like a macho idiot.'

Of course, the internet was powerful enough to sweep away even some of France's oldest traditions. I had to laugh. Jean-Marie the power freak, obsessed with staying one step ahead of everyone's game, had been well and truly nailed.

'What did he say?' I asked.

'At first, nothing. Like he was scared I was filming his reaction. But about an hour later, he came and told me it was a difficult time at home for him, and all the usual married men's merde. He said he was sorry and I had nothing to worry about. And he offered me a job in marketing.'

'Bloody hell. Great.'

'Well, no, I told him I didn't want it, because of the lechy guy who keeps bothering me. You know, the one who comes into my office all the time. And Jean-Marie walked out, and when he came back he told me the lech had been fired.'

'Fired?' I couldn't believe it. The last man to be fired for sexual harassment in France was probably a Napoleonic general who winked once too often at

Josephine. 'Yes, so we had a talk and he offered me this job presenting VianDiffusion as a leader in gender equality.'

I had to laugh. Until yesterday, the last place Jean-Marie had wanted to lead a woman was towards equality.

'He is a changed man,' Amandine said solemnly.

I was sceptical. Jean-Marie might change his suit and get his teeth bleached, but that didn't alter the man inside. But if he was willing to leave Amandine and her female colleagues in peace, then that was the best the world could hope for.

'And she called me,' Alexa cut in, 'and told me what was happening with the tea room. She knew Jean-Marie had been working with this anti-English website, and she thought I could come in and blackmail him about opening American diners while campaigning against Anglo culture.'

'I just hoped we could stop Jean-Marie forcing you out of the business,' Amandine said.

Alexa nodded. 'But I'd been thinking about it ever since you told me the tea room might close, and when I got Amandine's call, I decided that that was what my grandfather's money was for. This was one of the streets where he took his photos, after all. It was synchronicity. So when Jean-Marie's lawyers came back, we were ready with our new blackmail and my offer.'

'And they advised him to accept?' I asked.

'No, they advised him to fight,' Alexa said. 'They're *lawyers*, Paul.'

'Benoît repeated your arguments about the kind of food people eat at lunchtime,' Amandine said. 'I described what we saw in the rue de Bretagne. And he listened to me. I think his personal feelings against you had stopped him listening to you. It was a shame, because you were right.'

'Maybe I was, but you two are geniuses,' I said. 'I'd like to marry you both.'

'That doesn't sound like gender equality to me,' Amandine said.

'I'd do all the housework,' I promised. 'Well, the cooking, anyway.'

'Yes, housework isn't your thing, is it, Paul?' Alexa laughed. 'It never used to be, anyway.'

Suddenly the laughter had stopped. With one remark, we'd switched from being three comrades in arms to a bloke, his ex and a witness to their private jokes.

'Anyway, from now on, we'll be partners, but in a purely business sense,' Alexa added, which if anything only made things worse. 'And I intend to be active – what do you call it? A hands-on partner. Though not literally, right?'

'I think I'd better get back to the office,' Amandine said.

'No, you stay,' Alexa told her. 'Explain things to Paul.

I have to go to my bank to warn them that they're going to get a bit poorer.'

When she said goodbye, I allowed myself the liberty of giving her an extra hug, purely out of gratitude for saving my bacon, as well as my potato salad, my tea and cake and, well, everything.

'You still like her, don't you, Paul?' Amandine asked me when we were alone, sitting face to face.

'Of course. She just saved my life. I love her.' Which was, I thought, a brilliant way of avoiding the question.

'Do you like staying close to your exes?'

'Well, you were the one who called her,' I said, then regretted it when I saw Amandine blush. 'Sorry, that sounded really ungrateful. You saved my life, too. You made it all happen. I've never seen anyone get the better of Jean-Marie like that.'

'You're glad she's back in your life?'

I tried to laugh. 'Well, she has tended to pop in and out of it. A friend of mine once said that we ought to remember the "ex" in the middle of her name. Not that we still . . .'

Oh fuck it, I thought. The day had started out so well and now I was screwing it up. Amandine was right – it was weird having Alexa so close to me again. She'd disappeared from my life, then she'd popped up as some kind of shadowy stalker, and now, suddenly, she had a front-row seat. The driving seat, even. It was all very confusing.

'Well, you and I won't be working together any more,' Amandine said.

'No.' I thought about the consequences of this. No more excuses to call each other. Would we still do so? And what would it mean if we did?

'It was fun, though, wasn't it?' I said, and looked up to see Amandine blushing as though she'd just got the brush-off. 'But on the upside, now we can meet up without talking about Jean-Marie. Well, not unless you want to, of course. Obviously, you can talk about whatever you want, including your job. Gender equality and all that.'

She nodded, staring at me as though I was slightly bonkers. Which I probably was. I knew that what I ought to have said was: 'Of *course* I want to keep seeing you, Amandine. I really like you, and not only because you managed to outwit Jean-Marie and save my tea room. You're beautiful, and really easy to get along with – laid-back and fun, much less touchy than Alexa. But it's just so complicated with her shadow hanging over us like this . . . Even so, I think that what I really want to do right now is kiss you, Amandine, but your seat is quite a long way from mine, so I'd have to lean right across the table, in fact I'd have to actually stand up and bend over you, which might freak you out because I'm not sure we've got to a kissing stage, and you've had all these guys trying to force themselves on you, although I'd quite like to sort of force myself on you too, without the force, if you see what I mean.'

But all I did was smile and say she had to let me invite her out for a celebratory drink.

'Yes, give me a call,' Amandine said. She stood up. 'I must get back to the office.'

'I'll call you later today.' I stood up, too.

'Yes, great.'

She smiled, but it looked slightly forced, and she didn't look back as she walked out of the door.

Benoît came over, smiling.

'Would you like some more tea or coffee to celebrate, Paul? Or some gateau?' he asked.

No need, I thought. I'm baking my own cake here. A *merde* cake with *merde* filling and *merde*-flavoured *merde* on top.

Douze

'Les diamants sur une bague de fiançailles doivent
être juste assez brillants pour éblouir la demoiselle
par rapport à vos vraies intentions.'
*The diamonds on an engagement ring should be just bright
enough to blind the girl to your true intentions.*

The Marquis de Sade, who certainly wasn't locked
in the Bastille for being too romantic

I

THE SCULPTOR Auguste Rodin didn't seem to
have any women troubles. He would have got on
really well with Jake, I decided. In fact, he was probably
one of Jake's inspirations. Rodin would draw or sculpt
women in some of the most sexual poses I'd ever
seen outside of a Russian website, sleep with most
of them, and then get paid for the drawings and sculptures. What's more, he was also heaped with praise as
a serious *artiste*. Nice work if you can get it. If you
want it.

I was in Rodin's museum in the posh 7th *arrondissement*, a chateau-like mansion in a leafy urban park, looking for Jake. I'd called him up after my meeting at the tea room. Against my better judgement, I thought it might be good to talk things over with him, even if I ended up doing the exact opposite of what he suggested.

Some of those sketches of Rodin's were hot stuff, and I couldn't stop myself uttering a few loud puffs of frustration, attracting the unwelcome attention of visitors who were frowning at the pictures of splayed legs and raised buttocks as though they were just lines on a page.

In the end, I had to leave the house and wait in the garden. Staring at Rodin's sexploits was not at all good for my brain.

A few minutes later, Jake wandered out, still scribbling in a notebook.

'Hey, man,' he said when he'd finished jotting. 'Good news? Bad news?'

I gave him the good news about the tea room first, and he gave me a victorious high-five. Then I told him how Amandine and Alexa had engineered it all, and as I described the scene after Jean-Marie had left, he began looking at me with ever-narrowing eyes. By the end of it, he was shaking his head.

'C'est la merde, man,' was his verdict. 'French girls. That's why they call them femmes fatales – because they kill you. You know how they used to execute people in

France? They tied a horse to their arms and legs, and then the horses went in different directions. They pulled them in pieces. It lasted hours. And now you're doing it to yourself with two women – two *French*women. And one of them your ex? Oh man.'

It was all very well for him to talk, I told him. He was, for the first time in his life as far as I could see, in a monogamous, love-based relationship, and it just so happened that she was from Kazakhstan or Tajikistan or somewhere, rather than France.

'And somehow I suspect you might have had a hand in making your French girlfriends murderous,' I told him. 'They're not all like that. My problem is, am I just fantasising about Alexa because she must still like me a lot to buy half the tea room? And if she wasn't there, would I find it easier to make a move on Amandine? And are either of them really interested in me, anyway?'

'I don't know,' Jake said. 'They're French. You have to work it out for yourself. What do we say in English? You made your cake, now lie on it.'

Thanking him for his wise words, I followed him into the museum's cafeteria, a chalet on one side of the park. As we perused their selection of sandwiches, I asked Jake what was new with him.

'Oh yeah, man, it's formidable,' he said, punching his tray and scaring a couple of aged art-lovers. 'Mitzi has decroched some sponsoring for a concourse.'

'She has?' I asked, only half sure what he was talking about.

'Yes, she is a member of a Paris businesswomen thing, and they will give sponsoring for a soirée of posy.'

'Another poetry competition?'

'Yes. All we need is a place, a time and some other poets. They will pay for the microphones, the posters, and the publication of the winner.'

'That's brilliant. Have you asked Marsha about using the shop?'

'Ha!' was all he said, so I could guess what her answer had been.

'No problem,' I said. 'We can do it at the tea room. We'd have to take out all the tables, but it'd work.'

'You're a genie!' Jake told me, meaning not that I was a kind of bottled wizard but a French genius. Suddenly he was hugging me and leaping up and down.

'This is the poetic destiny, man,' he said. 'And I have promised myself, if it works, if we have a new concourse, I will write a poem for Mitzi, and ask her to epooz me on that night.'

'Great idea.'

'But only if I win.'

'You'll only propose if you win?'

'Yes, we must let the poetic destiny decide.'

I couldn't believe it. Did he honestly think that the audience were going to vote for his obscenities? Or that

Mitzi would say yes once she'd heard the poem? The wedding was off before he'd even proposed.

II

The French have a thing called *la théorie de l'élastique*. It's a subtler version of playing hard to get. The idea is that instead of chasing around after someone, you get them to chase you. For example, where some people might be tempted to ask what their potential loved one is planning, you say instead, 'I'm going to see a film, are you coming?' Off you go, and the theory is that the elastic will bring them pinging after you. Alexa was an expert at this. 'Qui m'aime me suive' was one of her favourite sayings – 'anyone who loves me will follow me' – and you were expected to traipse off after her. Either that or she'd go silent and you'd have to track her down to prove that you were still fascinated by her.

Well, I have always been useless at twanging the *élastique*. If you're interested in someone, why bother playing games? You're not going to make someone like you more by just ignoring them.

And anyway, I had plenty of good reasons to call Amandine. For a start, I owed her that celebratory drink. And then I wanted to pass on the good news about the new poetry competition, and invite her to be a judge. We were hoping to get it organised for the coming Saturday.

Short notice, but Mitzi was apparently saying that the timing was perfect. Fashion Week would be over, but there would still be lots of journalists on the lookout for quirky Paris culture stories. She was already putting together a press release, which to my mind was way beyond the call of duty, given that she was also meant to be launching her and Connie's new store. By some miracle, Jake had landed himself a real pearl.

Anyway, I called Amandine that same afternoon and, after raving yet again about how brilliant she was, started out by asking her when I could take her out for a thank-you glass of champagne.

'I'm going to stay with my parents for a couple of days,' she told me. 'It's my birthday, and they've organised a party with my sisters and my grandparents.'

'It's your birthday? When?' I felt guilty for not knowing, even though she'd never told me.

'Next Monday, but the party is on Saturday. Can you imagine? Saturday afternoon,' she laughed, 'with my grandparents, at my parents' place, en province.' This being the withering Parisian term for anywhere not in Paris.

'So are you having a proper party in Paris sometime?' I asked.

'Yes, like last year – I had a canal cocktail party. You know, everyone brings some alcohol and some ice, and we mix as many cocktails as possible before the ice melts, and then throw some pétanque balls around. But it will be a Monday, so I don't know if many people will come.'

'Well, I'd love to come, if I'm invited?'

'Of course, I'm going to send out an email. You're already on the list.'

On the list? Wonderful. Then it struck me that maybe she was playing the *élastique* game – not mentioning her birthday or her party, and waiting to see if I'd find out. Well, if that was the case, it had worked.

'Do you think you might be back in Paris on Saturday night?' I asked her. 'Mitzi has managed to get sponsorship for another poetry competition. They want to hold it on Saturday.'

'Great. Where?'

'At the tea room. Providing Jean-Marie agrees – he's still part-owner till the buyout goes through.'

'And you'll have to ask Alexa's permission, too,' Amandine said. 'You promised to consult her on everything.'

'Yes, I suppose so,' I said, wishing that Alexa and Jean-Marie hadn't butted their way into our conversation. 'But anyway, if it does happen on the Saturday night, I hope you'll be able to make it?'

'Oh, I don't know. It's more than an hour by train. And I'll be with my grandparents, you know . . .'

Here, perhaps, a French bloke would have said he'd carry her away on a white horse and gallop back to Paris with her clinging on to his suit of silver armour. But I preferred to let her choose whether she stayed an extra night with her gran and grandad. She probably didn't see them that often. Who was I to make hoofmarks all over their lawn and kidnap their guest of honour?

'Sure,' I said. 'But if you can't come on Saturday night, we'll see each other on Monday, right?'

'Yes, Monday.'

'Great. Enjoy yourself with your family. Don't get your grannie too drunk. She might fall off the table.'

She laughed happily and we said goodbye. What more would you want from a phone call?

Next call, Alexa, who was actually answering me today.

'Don't tell me, Paul,' she said before I'd had a chance to open my mouth, 'you've decided that you don't want to be in business with a woman and you've sold out to Jean-Marie?'

'I have no problems working with women,' I said.

'Working with us, yes. It's just all the other stuff you have problems with, right?'

'Very droll. Anyway, thanks again for playing white knight,' I told her. 'I'm assuming white knights can also be female,' I added quickly.

'I don't know, Paul. Joan of Arc was accused of being a witch for wearing men's armour.'

'Yes, well, times have changed, thankfully. Which is

338

why I'm calling. I wanted to consult you on something, in your new role as co-owner of My Tea Is Rich.'

'You want the waitresses to be naked?'

'There are no waitresses. We only do counter service, as you would already know if you were a conscientious owner.'

'OK, topless bargirls, then.'

'I can see our meetings are going to be fun, Alexa,' I told her. 'And very long.'

'Sorry. Please go on.'

I told her about the plans to hold a poetry competition in the tea room.

'Your girlfriend's not going to be there, is she?' she asked.

'Girlfriend?'

'Yes, you only have one, I presume. The mad Australian.'

'New Zealander,' I corrected her. 'Marsha's not my girlfriend any more. If she ever was. We split up the other night, remember, when I came to see you after the last poetry competition?'

'You split up? I knew you had an argument with her, but I didn't know you split up. Honestly, Paul, if you split up with a woman every time you had a row, you'd *never* have a girlfriend.'

While she was laughing at her satirical jibe, an idea dawned on me. A rather disturbing idea.

'You mean', I said, 'that you thought I was still in a relationship with this woman who was aggressive as hell towards you, who insulted you . . .?'

'If you remember, Paul, you insulted me too, by saying I wanted to close down the tea room with my racist friends.'

'OK, but even though you thought I was still going out with Marsha, you decided to step in and save the tea room?'

'Yes, I don't see the connection.'

Bloody hell, I thought. And I'd accused her of being a vindictive ex. She wasn't a white knight, she was a business angel, in the truest sense of the word.

III

When I turned up at the tea room on Saturday afternoon, Benôit welcomed me with a rare burst of emotion. He wasn't the most outgoing of blokes, no doubt a reaction to his dad's main characteristic of putting it out as much as possible. Or *former* characteristic, I should say. All that was finished now, *n'est-ce pas?*

'I'm so happy that we're not going to become a diner,' he told me in French, pronouncing diner 'dine-AIR'. 'It would have been a cata-stroff, une idée complètement stupide,' he added, looking over his shoulder as though he was frightened his dad might be recording the conversation. 'But I am wondering, if we start doing burgers, must we translate "burger" into French? It is "un burger", so customers will think we are treating them like idiots. But if we don't, will the government fine us again?'

'That's exactly the kind of thing that will be dealt with by Alexa from now on,' I told him, and we began decorating the place for a poetry competition.

I hung a few festive balloons and 'Poetry Nite' posters over some arty close-ups of vegetables sunbathing in an idyllic English garden, and then went to help Gregory, who had double-parked outside the tea room with his sound gear. It was a sultry day, so he was of course showing off approximately 80 per cent of his skin, the only parts covered up being the soles of his feet in his flip-flops, and his groin and buttocks (well, the bottom half of his buttocks, anyway) in tight khaki shorts. Here in the posh *huitième* I was tempted to suggest he tone it down a bit. But most of the people passing by ignored him – just another body delivering something – so instead I thanked him for coming along, and carried my share of speakers, amps and cables.

Jake was a less welcome addition to the team. As soon as he arrived, he began hopping about like a frog on caffeine, asking if he could sound-test the mics with his poem, complaining about the lighting, worrying that the packed rows of chairs might distract him – if people got up and down to order drinks, it might 'derange the concentration on my posy', he said. Deranged was right.

'If you want to make yourself useful,' I told him, 'why don't you check that all the pens work?'

One of Mitzi's businesswomen, the boss of a company called Prévisions Funéraires, had sent us a boxload. I wasn't sure how many of our audience would be interested in prepaying their funeral, but we needed the pens because I'd decided to scrap the judges. There are enough dictators in the world, I thought, without setting up a panel of them here. So this competition was to be run as a democracy: a pen, a voting slip, and you wrote down the name of your favourite candidate. And if anyone got five hundred votes and there were only a hundred people in the tea room, we'd know that there had been foul play.

Jake had suggested I set up a phone line to charge people a euro a time to vote 'like à la télé', but I'd decided it might ruin the suspense on the night if I had to spend an hour reading text messages.

So I left Jake doodling with a pile of black ballpoints and went out into the street to put in a call to Amandine.

'Happy pre-anniversaire. I hope you're coming along,' I told her. Or her voicemail. It was six o'clock, so I figured she was either finishing up her birthday cake with Grand-mère or sitting on a train. No way to find out which.

I went back in to help Jake, and he showed me the engagement ring he was planning to give to Mitzi – if he won the contest, of course. It was a remarkably sober gold band with three white stones. I congratulated him on his good taste.

'Oh, I got it bon marché,' he said, meaning cheap. 'From an ex. She's a hostess of the air, and she always buys her bijous in the Gulf. She says you know they're real because otherwise the jeweller gets his hand cut off.'

'I don't think Mitzi needs to hear that story, Jake. But well done on getting an ex to sell you an engagement ring.'

'Oh, yeah. Well, she wasn't too content that I asked. We didn't have a great separation.'

I could imagine – Jake's separations were often uncannily like having a hand cut off. But it was a cute ring, and the way he wanted to give it to Mitzi was even cuter. He outlined his plan, and it was impossible to believe it was the old wham-bam-merci-madame Jake talking.

'That's incredibly romantic,' I told him. 'You should do it even if you don't get first prize.'

'No. It's tout ou rien. All or anything.'

'Hey, you're not going to tell the audience what's at stake?' I had to ask. 'You can't tell them you'll propose if you win.'

Jake banged his fist on the counter, snapping the point off the pen he'd been testing.

'You insult me, Paul. I'm going to win this thing and get my posy published because people *love* it. If it ain't sincere, it don't count.'

Coming from a man who'd spent half his adult life getting women into bed just for the sake of crossing their nationality off his world map, this declaration of sincerity was quite a statement, but I apologised and assured him I'd be ready to play my part if – no, *when* – he won.

'OK, and just so we're clear, Paul, I know you're not a judge any more, so you only get one vote, but I want you to promise that you won't vote for me.'

Sadly for him, it was one of the easiest promises I've ever had to make.

IV

We were expecting a small, personal-invitation-only crowd, so I put up a '*Soirée privée*' sign, and went outdoors to play bouncer. I figured that potential hecklers would be easy to spot – the berets and tricolour T-shirts would give them away.

To my surprise, bouncing turned out to be fun. I imagined that people would be swinging bottles at my head or trying to knife me. But this wasn't England, it was Paris, at a venue that hadn't been plastered all over the social networks, so things at the door went as smoothly as a kiddies' tea party without the hysterical parents.

One of the arrivals was less welcome, though: Marsha.

'Hi, Paul,' she said, with the grin of a gatecrasher who doesn't give a damn whether they were invited or not.

'This is a surprise,' I said, meaning, 'How did you even know about this evening?'

'Don't worry,' she said, 'I'm . . .' and she held out an arm towards the advancing figure of Brick or Stick or whatever his name was, the hunky rapper with the dreadlocks and a bass guitar slung over one bare shoulder. 'I'm his other,' she said, and gave him the sort of kiss that proved beyond all doubt that there were no lingering emotional scars from her break-up with me.

'Hey, man,' Rock or Stack said, and gripped me in one of those man-hugs where they clasp your right hand and pull you in for a touch of chests with their left. I had to admit it was a very rock-like chest.

'You don't mind, do you?' Marsha asked me.

'No, but just be nice to Alexa, OK?' I told her. 'It's half her tea room now.'

'Yes, so I hear. Ex marks the spot, eh?'

A few minutes later, Jean-Marie arrived in a taxi. The flashy cars were staying in the garage tonight. He went to open the other rear door of the taxi and held out a hand to the lady who was accompanying him.

And out popped Marie-Dominique, in full leather regalia: bulging bodice, lace-up skirt, vicious stilettos, this time with her own hair gelled to her head like a black helmet. Holy shit, I thought, Jean-Marie's gone from macho predator to total submissive. I was just grateful he was dressed as himself, in a chic suit, rather than coming trussed up with one of those zipped SM masks.

I greeted them both as though they were royal guests of honour, and Jean-Marie hung back to let Marie-Dominique make her entrance first.

'Merci,' he whispered.

'What for?' I asked.

'Your speeches to me about sexism in the workplace. They have changed my life.'

'But I thought it was Amandine's speech that really made the change?' I said.

'Yes, yes.' He patted my arm as if to console me for my excess modesty. 'But I am the one who is glad. You know, it is so much more efficient to be anti-sexist. You touch a girl's leg, and half of them will detest you. You give them a big talk about sexism, they all love you. Merci, Paul. I had no idea you were so intelligent.' He slapped me on the shoulder and went inside.

Typical Jean-Marie. His gender equality in the workplace scheme had smelled like bullshit, but I'd only just realised exactly how much *merde de taureau* was involved. Though if it kept his hands off Amandine and her colleagues, why not? They didn't necessarily want sincerity, just to be left in peace.

Neither Amandine nor Alexa had arrived when Benoît came out to tell me it was time to start my second job as MC, but I still held out hopes for later on. Now it was time to get things rolling.

The rows of chairs were packed tightly facing the far end of the tea room, and there was barely space to squirm along the counter and get to the microphone stand. The place was crammed – about a hundred people, with Benoît on the door to stop any undesirables adding to the crush. He had instructions, of course, to let Amandine and Alexa in even if everyone else inside was passing out for lack of oxygen.

'Bonsoir!' I yelled into the mic, and got a loud reply. Parisians, even expats, are so polite. I explained the rules and why we were there, and expressed my hope that tonight, we'd actually be able to listen to the poems instead of the protesters' chanting. If anyone wanted to protest, I said, I knew some people on picket lines who would be glad of their support. This got a major cheer, even though I suspected that I was the only one in the room who was actually part of the French civil servants' campaign for a fairer France.

'Let the games begin,' I announced, and introduced our first poet of the night: the annoying American 'bling of the past' guy.

He left his row of friends and squeezed his tubby frame towards the front.

'Thanks, I'm Laurie, vote for me,' he shouted, prompting someone to remind him he hadn't actually recited his poem yet.

'The playwright Oliver Goldsmith once wrote,

"What shall we do if Comedy forsake us",' Laurie said.

'Is this part of your poem?' a girl called out. It was obviously going to be a tough night, even without French-language lobbyists.

'No, it's just a thought that I want you to keep in mind as I perform.' He nodded to Gregory, who hit a button. A booming rap rhythm started bouncing off the walls. Laurie swayed to the music for a few beats, then began to recite his poem. Or rather, a series of non-rhyming one-liners, like his earlier 'bling' effort.

> 'I told my mum and dad, When I grow up, I
>   want to be a memory man,
> They said, Forget it.
> I said, In that case I'm going to be a maths
>   teacher,
> They said, Don't count on it.
> I told them, I want to be a singer in a soccer
>   stadium,
> They said, You've got no chants.
> I failed the exam to be a roadroller driver,
> I was crushed.'

He went on in the same punning mode for a minute or so, and then ended with the worst of them all:

'And so I became a poet,
    Is that such a heinous rhyme?'

Despite its almost physically painful ending, it went down well with the crowd. With the Anglos, that is – the French were completely baffled, and from what I could see, their English-speaking friends were making little attempt to translate or explain. Jean-Marie was staring at me as if to say: 'I bring a dominatrix from the Ministry of Culture to your soirée and this is all you can manage?'

But this time I wasn't judging, so I simply thanked Laurie, who was on his way back to his table, and seemed to have made lots of new friends.

And he wasn't the only one, apparently. Because I looked towards the door to see Alexa smiling at me, and shaking her head in apology for being late. She was looking wonderful in a tight button-up T-shirt and battered jeans, which were being admired from the rear by a bloke. A handsome nerd – unkempt hair, glasses, a week's beard – was following her into the tea room, and sat next to her at the back of the room.

Logical, really, I thought. She's a beautiful woman, living in Paris. Of *course* she has a bloke. Though they're not holding hands or kissing or anything. Does that mean there are no fireworks between them?

But it was time to introduce the next poet, a French

guy called Samuel, who had given me a printout of his poem. And if I understood it correctly, it was a self-loathing little ditty about being a rent boy. Not that Samuel had anything to self-loathe – he was cute-looking, about nineteen, with an adorable head of curls, golden fleece on his chin and cheeks, and clothes straight out of Fashion Week.

He came up to the mic and almost whispered, in a heavy French accent, 'Zis is ma pwem. I was calling it at first "Je suis une pute" – "I Am a Whore". But now I call it "I Am Not a Playboy, I Am a Payboy".'

This got a big cheer from everyone except one guy, about halfway back, just behind Marsha and Rock/Stack/Brick, who stood up and shouted, 'Non!'

Oh shit, here we go again, I thought.

'Tu es français, parle français!' he barked at poor Samuel, who was looking as though he'd been slapped. The heckler hadn't been at Marsha's shop, I was sure of that. He was in his late twenties to early thirties, dressed in a trendy sweatshirt and wearing thick black designer glasses. He'd come with a group of friends who weren't joining in with his protest.

'Je vais parler français,' Samuel objected. 'If you let me speak,' he added in English, earning a round of applause from the crowd.

'Voilà!' the heckler replied. 'English pollutes everything. You want an English poem, I have one.' He pointed at me. 'Paul West, you are a pest, so leave France and give us a rest,' he recited in a surprisingly good English accent. I was flattered. It was the first time anyone had written a poem for me since I was at school and a girl called Jackie had penned a few words to tell me we were splitting up: 'Let's call it a wrap, because you're crap.'

I was just wondering whether to ask Marsha's Hunk/Block/Rock to throw the guy out when help came from an unexpected quarter.

'T'es nul!' This shout, meaning more or less 'You are crap', had come from Jean-Marie, who was on his feet and pointing at the heckler. 'What world are you living in?' he demanded. 'I am a French businessman. For my business, I speak French, English, Italian sometimes.' He treated the whole room to a blinding display of his expensive dentistry. 'And I am about to acquire an American diner, where I will—'

He was interrupted by a loud creak of leather as Marie-Dominique stood and told him to shut up. He sat down meekly and she turned towards the heckler, who guffawed at her. Oh no, I thought, she's going to get a faceful of French insults again.

'Is not Paris a cultural capital precisely because it has always welcomed art and artists from all over the world?' she began, but this time her elegant French rhetoric was met by an intrigued silence. 'Is the city not at the forefront of artistic activity because it has always embraced innovations like abstract art, jazz, rap and fetishism?' Still the French guy didn't reply, probably because she was declaiming at a volume that brooked no interruption. 'Can we not express ourselves freely here? Do you think we are in 1940 again?' She pointed her armoured boobs at the heckler, and if I'd been him, I'd have run for it there and then. 'If you don't like our world, the real world, then you can just' – she inflated her frightening bodice – 'fuck off. Va te faire foutre,' she told the guy, and the shock of it provoked a howl of laughter. 'Go on,' she said, easily drowning out all noise from the crowd, 'go and get yourself fucked, if you can find anyone to do it, and leave us to enjoy our evening of intelligent, cosmopolitan entertainment.'

All eyes turned to the heckler, who clearly didn't know what to do in the face of this menacing ball of leather. In the end, he decided to cut his losses and stalk towards the door, which Benoît opened for him.

'And I bet your grandfather was a collaborator,' Marie-Dominique called out at the guy's back. If she had managed to say a few words in rhyme right then, she would have won the competition, but she simply bowed to acknowledge the applause, and then poor Samuel coughed into the microphone to remind us who'd caused all the rumpus.

'I am not a playboy, I am a payboy,' he said, and began to recite. Personally, I kind of wished he hadn't. It was all based on the fact that *paix* means peace and *paie* is pay, and that *pédé* (pronounced 'pay-day') is the French equivalent of queer – a word that's an insult unless gays themselves use it.

By the end, Alexa was clapping loudly, shouting her approval into the nearest ear of her bloke, who came back with what looked like a funny riposte. Must be French, I thought.

Meanwhile, Marie-Dominique was on her feet, shouting, 'Bravo!', Samuel was giving us all his cute smile, and I began to think that Jake was looking less and less like ending the evening as a fiancé.

Next up was Rake or Rod or whatever, doing his rapping, slapping thing that drove everyone orgasmic despite the fact that they couldn't understand, or even hear, what he was saying. As he came off stage, Marsha leapt on him to show people where his heart, or at least parts of his body, lay. Then came the punky girl who'd given us her poignant poem about kids with not enough chairs to read Baudelaire. She did a new one from the point of view of a French policeman who secretly dreams of grafitti-ing walls and smoking weed, and who crashes his car into the scooter of a *banlieue* kid he's chasing because the kid had been spotted grafitti-ing walls and smoking weed. Tough urban realism, in English peppered with French, and everyone loved it.

As she was returning to her seat, I saw Benoît step outside. Not to confront the heckler, I hoped, returning with his hunting rifle.

The door opened again, and in came Amandine, whose first sight as she walked in the room was me grinning stupidly at her, a microphone held to my mouth and no words emerging. She was looking flushed, as though she'd dashed from the railway station. I waved hello and pointed her towards the front where I'd saved a seat, and where Jake was fidgeting for me to call him up on stage. Mitzi was whispering in his ear like a trainer sending her boxer into the ring. I knew, though, that as far as she was concerned, tonight was just about poetry. She had no idea that if Jake won, she was going to be offered the chance of becoming Madame Baudelaire, the official muse.

If he won, which had to be one of the biggest ifs pronounced in Paris since February 1912, when an Austrian tailor called Franz Reichelt said, 'What if I were to leap off the first level of the Eiffel Tower wearing my homemade parachute suit?' After which the poor bloke plummeted to his death.

Jake threaded his way towards me and the microphone. Shit, I thought, I hope it's not all about to go horribly wrong.

'Bonsoir, I'm Jake, and this is called "To Beurk or Not to Beurk".'

Beurk is the French word for yuk. So 'horribly wrong' was going to be about right, even if his title did get a titter from one or two generous members of the audience.

'It's a bilingual poem,' Jake went on, 'about the French and English noises that women can provoke.' He began to recite, and it was even worse than I'd feared. *Au revoir* to wedded bliss and poetic immortality.

> '*Paf* in French, in English is *pow*,
> As I learnt when being punched by a girl from
>   Cracow.
> *Ouch*, I yelped, et j'ai crié *aie*,
> When I was slapped by a furious Thai.
> *Huh* was what I got, and a scornful *pah*,
> For a lame excuse to a Mexicana.
> *Bim* in français – in anglais that's *bang*,
> Was the door being slammed by a girl from
>   Penang.
> And when I read a poem to an uptight Turk,
> All I heard was *yuk*, and a long French *beurk*.'

Jake paused for dramatic effect and turned to point at Mitzi – rather undiplomatically, I thought, considering what he'd just said. I braced myself as he carried on.

> 'But the words that rhyme with Kyrgyzstani,
> Are in a totalement différente catégorie,

They're things like *youpi*, which is French for
   yippee.
Or as the Français and the Anglos say – *hurrah*,
That you came to Paris from Central Asia.
Because since you arrived from the city of
   Bishkek,
The only sounds that I want to make,
Are ones like *wow* – nothing to do with Cracow,
And *aah* – way sweeter than any señorita,
And most of all, pleasure's hum,
A softly murmured bilingual *mmmm*.
A sound that's used in French and anglais too,
The only sound I've made since meeting you.
Mmmmmmitzi.'

He mimed smooching Mitzi, who turned beetroot-red
while her semi-identical twin Connie grabbed her for a
python-like hug.

I was struck totally dumb. This was Jake, for God's
sake. He didn't do romanticism. Coming from him, this
beat 'a rose by any other name' into a hat. It was like
stumbling across a long-lost Amazonian tribe quoting
Keats, Byron and Barbara Cartland.

Everyone in the room was chanting, 'Kiss, kiss, kiss!'
Jake obliged them, and Mitzi emerged from the clinch
even more crimson than before.

I had to interrupt the love-in and ask people to start

voting with their little bits of paper and the pens kindly provided by Prévisions Funéraires, the specialists in prepaid burials.

As ballpoints started to scratch on paper, I went to say a proper hello to Amandine.

'I'm really glad you got here,' I said. 'I was afraid you wouldn't.' I was definitely turning on the wit tonight.

'Merci, Paul. Are you going to give me a *bise*? It is traditional, you know.' She offered up her cheek for me to kiss.

'So is a glass of champagne,' I told her, when I'd *bised* her on both cheeks. I went into the kitchen, where there were limited supplies of bubbly for VIPs only. Here, like elsewhere in France, the voting was democratic but the drinks weren't.

Jake was already in there, hovering by the fridge.

'Well, you really are a man of surprises,' I told him, shaking his hand. 'And I don't just mean when you hire building-site vehicles instead of cars. Congratulations.'

'Yeah, merci, man. Voilà the ring,' he said, crushing it nervously into my palm.

'Let's do it anyway. It doesn't matter if you don't win.'

'No, man. Only if I win. And I'm going to, I can feel it.'

Right, I thought. Every time I buy a lottery ticket I can feel myself winning millions, but it hasn't happened yet. I pocketed the ring and went out to give Amandine her champagne. We spent a few minutes chatting about her family get-together. Her mum had given her a French bestseller on how to be lazy at work, she said — a great start to her career.

'That reminds me, I've got you a present,' I told her. 'I'll give it to you after we've finished the voting.'

'Ah, c'est gentil,' she said, and gave my hand a squeeze.

'Careful, I might be filming you,' I said. Exactly the wrong thing to say. A mind-blowingly stupid thing to say. And she looked shocked, as well she might.

Fortunately, I had an excuse to get out before I said any more stupidities. I went round collecting up the votes, and withdrew to the kitchen to do the count. To ensure total openness, all the poets were gathered around me as, one by one, I stacked their handwritten names on little piles between the bottles of ketchup and boxes of tea.

At first, it was skewed, because gangs of people had voted for their friend, but then things began to even out. The names came in random order, and it got much too tight to tell who had won. I took an order pad down from a peg and wrote out the names, then counted up each poet's votes.

'If there's only one or two votes' difference, we'll do a recount,' I told them.

But in the event, it was worse than that. After two recounts, it turned out that three poets all had the same number of votes: seventeen. They were punky Suzie, the girl who wrote about the *banlieue* policeman, Laurie the unrhyming rapper, and Jake.

'You get the deciding vote, Paul,' Laurie said. 'And we know who you're going to vote for.' He gave Jake a withering look.

'No,' Jake blurted out. 'I told Paul not to vote for me. We have to ask the public. Maybe someone hasn't voted.'

This sounded like a dodgy plan, but I couldn't think of a better one, so I went out and asked if there was anyone who hadn't voted yet.

Amandine raised her hand, naturally enough, but then she'd missed all the poems except Jake's. No one else reacted except to shake their heads, until a shy hand went up just along the row from Amandine. It was Mitzi. Presumably Jake had ordered her not to vote for him, either.

'Yeah, right,' Laurie groaned. 'His girlfriend.'

Shit, I thought, I *am* going to have to vote. Then a movement by the door caught my eye. Of course, I thought, and picked up the microphone again.

'Benoît?' He looked slightly startled as everyone turned to stare at him. 'You didn't vote, did you?' I asked him.

'Non,' he replied.

'So who would you vote for?' I gestured towards the row of poets standing beside me along the counter, who also included all those not in the tie-break. Merde, I thought, one more vote for Brick or Bat, or whatever

Marsha's bloke's name was, would bring him up to the same score, too.

'Oh . . .' Benoît looked along the line of expectant poets, apparently not realising the full importance of his choice. He shrugged. 'Him,' he finally said, pointing towards the counter.

'Moi?' Laurie said, thrusting himself forward.

'Non, the next one, him, yes, you, the mmm guy.'

Jake.

To look at him, you'd have thought he was about to explode, or at the very least lift off and smash through the ceiling on his way into orbit. *Le public* had voted, and they'd voted for him. Baudelaire's home town thought he was the best poet it had ever heard. Tonight, anyway. Everyone in the room except Laurie and too-cool Jean-Marie was howling at him. Jake seemed to be almost in pain with the pleasure. Then suddenly his arms shot up and he double-punched the air. This also caused him to punch the ceiling above the serving counter, but luckily it was a false one, and buckled rather than pulping his knuckles.

As the cheering went on, I listed his prizes: not only was there the gold-plated funeral-fund pen to help him write more poetry, there was also a publishing contract with one of Mitzi's business associates. It was a company mainly used to publishing books on women's issues, but Jake didn't seem to mind. And after all, he was a bit of a women's issue himself.

I shook his hand and gave him the microphone so he could make his acceptance speech, but he lowered it and mouthed at me: 'The ring.'

'Right, yes.' I went back into the kitchen while Jake thanked everyone who'd ever helped him, fortunately without listing all the women who'd inspired his poems.

My job was a tried-and-tested one. Jake had gone the whole hog in his conversion to *homo romanticus* and his surprise for Mitzi was to be the old ring-in-the-glass-of-champagne trick. So I filled two *flûtes*, dropped the ring into one of them, and went back out to join Jake.

'Ah!' He welcomed me with a huge grin. 'Mitzi, one of these is for you.' He took the glass with the ring in it and beckoned to her. 'Drink it, *avec prudence*,' he warned as he handed it over. They clinked glasses. Mitzi saw what was inside hers and gasped.

'It is a bag,' Jake announced to the confused audience. In the excitement, he'd reverted to French and called the ring a *bague*. 'When she has finished the champagne, I will pose her a certain question.'

There were whoops of encouragement as Mitzi drank with pursed lips, doing her best not to swallow the ring at the bottom of the glass. Finally, she tipped it into her hand. At which point it was her turn to look confused – the diamonds had disappeared, leaving three gaping holes at the top of the ring.

Mitzi clutched her throat, afraid that she'd swallowed

them. Ominously, the ring was also looking much less golden than when I'd put it in the glass. Now it was more of a dark grey.

'How cheap was it exactly?' I whispered to Jake.

But he was holding Mitzi up as she staggered around holding her windpipe.

'Ça va, ma chérie?' he said.

'I don't know,' she croaked.

'Will you e-pooz me?'

'If I survive,' she wheezed.

'You'd better get her to hospital for an X-ray,' I told him. I wanted to add that he might want to take the precaution of having her tested for toxic metal colourings and soluble crystals, but it didn't seem like the right time.

Marie-Dominique's leather-bound form appeared by my side, trailing Jean-Marie in her wake like a plain-clothes bodyguard.

'Come,' she said. 'Our taxi is waiting outside. It will take you to hospital.'

She led Jake and Mitzi away, all the while saying how much she had loved the 'naked sensuality' of Jake's poem.

'You don't have any about SM, do you?' she asked.

Once the excitement had died down, it was time for me to make a final announcement.

'Excuse me, but you have to listen to one more poem,' I told everyone. 'It's for my good friend Amandine, here.

On Monday it will be her twenty-fifth birthday, but she's celebrating it tonight.' There were cheers and a short burst of the usual song. 'It's also thanks to Amandine that we could all be here this evening, because she was the one who called my other good friend Alexa' – I held out a hand towards my sardonically smiling business partner – 'and told her that it was possible to save this tea room from being turned into an American fast-food place.' This earned a satisfying round of anti-fast-food hissing. 'My present to Amandine,' I went on, 'is a little poem of my own. I know it's too late to vote, but anyway, only one vote counts.' I smiled over at Amandine who was blushing and getting a rather over-hearty birthday kiss on the cheek from Hunk or Lunk or whatever, much to Marsha's obvious irritation.

'Happy twenty-fifth, Amandine,
You're new on the scene,
Looking like you're sixteen.
The thing is to stay keen,
Don't get blasé like a has-been,
Don't give in to French spleen,
Just keep living the drean.
I ran out of rhymes, but you know what I mean.'

The last two lines earned me huge groans from the audience. As had, to be honest, several of the other lines.

But Amandine was giving me the kind of look that you'd receive if you went to the desert during a drought and offered to build a brand-new oasis.

She walked over to the serving counter, and turned her face up towards mine to give me the traditional French thank-you kiss. But as she brushed her hot cheeks against mine, and hugged me, I saw Alexa zigzagging her way through the crowd, her bloke following in her wake.

'That was one of the worst poems I've ever heard in my life, Paul,' she announced. 'But a nice gesture. I'm just glad you never tried to write one for me. Nothing rhymes with Alexa.'

'Sexer?' said her bloke, who was hovering at her shoulder.

'That's not a word, is it? By the way, this is Simon,' Alexa told me. 'He's the guy I was telling you about.'

'Telling me about?' She hadn't mentioned any boyfriend to me.

'Yes, the one who' – she lowered her voice – 'is going to hack the anti-English website.'

'Oh, the nerd?' I said, much more bitchily than I'd intended.

'Well, he's not my boyfriend, Paul. I can talk to men without sleeping with them, you know. You, for example.'

She gave a laugh that was probably meant to be gently teasing, but to me it sounded as though she was shattering all the illusions that had been trying to crystallise in my head. She was right, I realised, we weren't going anywhere romantic together. The idea that an ex-girlfriend being friendly meant that she wanted to start up again was a male fantasy, and I'd been wallowing in it right up to my neck. Pointlessly, too, because when I thought about it, I saw that I wasn't really interested in going back in time. The future looked much more promising. Suddenly I found myself laughing along with Alexa.

'Drinks, everyone?' I asked.

So while Benoît sold glasses of beer and wine to the remaining members of the audience, a select group jammed themselves into the kitchen. Select, that is, but large enough to make it hard to breathe in that confined space: all the poets who weren't at the hospital, plus Marsha, Amandine, Gregory, Alexa and her friend Simon. We toasted the evening, the continued existence of the tea room, and our absent friends who were probably queuing up in A&E, with the loud dominatrix harrying the nurses into hurrying things along.

I did my best to play host and chat to everyone, but this only made me increasingly aware that my poetry moment with Amandine was slipping into the past. It was being crowded out by the sheer number of people in the room with us. Whether we'd have been canoodling together if we'd been alone, I really didn't know, but how could you canoodle when every word you said emerged from your mouth at a maximum distance of six inches from three other people's ears? And when two of your exes – one recent and fleeting, the other more distant but now your business partner – grinned half mockingly at you every time you looked in their direction?

At one point I tried to twist my way through the crush towards Amandine, but I was hijacked by Laurie.

'OK, Paul, so just admit one thing,' he said, sweating at me. 'You fixed it so Jake could go last, right?'

'Quite honestly,' I told him, 'I was expecting his poem to be dire, so going first or last really wouldn't have changed a thing.' As always, when a person starts their sentence with 'quite honestly', I wasn't being quite honest. I'd calculated that if Jake's poem was half-decent, it had to be an advantage for him to go last. But was that really so wrong? After all, this was a French competition, meaning that even if you didn't break or bend the rules, you could still massage them until they relaxed a little.

'Hm,' Laurie conceded. 'And what did you think of my poem?'

'Quite honestly, I thought it was very funny.'

Eventually Amandine squeezed her way towards me and said she was going to leave.

'Thank you so much for the poem, Paul,' she said. 'Will you give me a copy?'

'Of course. I'll have it framed. If you don't think that's

too arrogant. It's not really a work of art, just a present. And an amateurish one at that. I mean, DIY poetry . . .' I realised I was starting to talk rubbish and stopped.

'That'd be great,' she said. 'Bring it on Monday to my canal party. You are coming?'

'Yes, tell me where and when and I'll rustle up some cocktail ingredients.'

'Great. And I'm not inviting *everyone*,' she said, shifting her eyes right and left to indicate the other people in the room. Particularly, I guessed, Alexa and Marsha.

'Very wise,' I said. 'Are you taking a taxi home or getting the Métro? I'll walk you.'

'No, you're the host, I don't want to make you leave your own party.'

I wondered if she was applying the *théorie de l'élastique*. Was I meant to say: Balls to convention, I'll walk you to the taxi rank? Or would she really think it was impolite to leave my guests? She was a well brought-up *Parisienne*, after all. This could be a test of my politeness or my manliness.

I felt a tickling sensation in my groin, and realised it was my phone.

It was Jake. I could hardly tell what he was saying, but gathered that Marie-Dominique had blitzed them through A&E, and that Mitzi was fine. The 'diamonds' had been non-toxic. More to the point, she'd accepted the offer to wear a better-quality ring.

'On arrive!' Jake shouted above the background noise. They were on their way to the party.

'I'll walk with you to the Métro,' I told Amandine. 'I've got time before Jake and the others arrive.'

'No, you must stay. See you on Monday night.'

And she *bised* me goodbye.

V

So there I was, on the Monday evening, walking along the canal path from Stalingrad, possibly the least romantic Métro station name in Paris, on my way to Amandine's party.

I had no idea what sort of cocktail I was going to receive when I got there. Almost certainly not a Sex on the Beach – there was no beach for a start, and Sex on the Canal Bank sounds just plain creepy. Knowing my luck, it was probably going to be a few random English and French ingredients sloshed together in a frantic Parisian shaker, and it was anyone's guess what would come out – sweet or sour, fizzy or flat.

These thoughts were mixed up in my head as I walked past groups of trendy Parisians playing *pétanque* in the evening sun. And they weren't negative thoughts. It was like I'd told Jake. The exciting thing about life is not knowing. Not being sure what would happen in an hour or two, or three, when – if – I finally managed to manoeuvre Amandine away from everyone else for a private *tête-à-tête*. Having no idea what she'd say, or what I'd say, or where I'd end the night. Alone on a sofa bed, *à deux* somewhere more comfortable, or alone but still hoping that the *à deux* might happen? I hadn't a clue. The only thing that really mattered was that my glass would be full. *Merde* to the choice between half full and half empty – I was looking for a whole slice of life, not a *demi-portion*.

Of course I was worried that I'd get the cold shoulder, all the more so because at that moment I was literally suffering from one. I was carrying a ten-kilo bag of ice cubes like a pillow jammed against my right ear. In my free hand I held two carrier bags. One contained Amandine's poem, which I'd framed with the help of the local DIY shop. The other, some ingredients to tip the balance of fate in my favour: a bottle of chilled bubbly, a miniature of raspberry liqueur and a punnet of long, scarlet Gariguette strawberries. I've always found that with a drop of liqueur in a *flûte* of champagne and a slice of strawberry to make the pink liquid fizz, the world can usually be relied upon to look a little brighter.

But there was always the *merde* factor to be reckoned with. *Merde* can, as the French will tell you, be a good or bad thing. It can mess up your new shoes or bring you luck.

Jake, for example, had merded seriously with his cheap

ring, but the trip to A&E had given him some time with Marie-Dominique, who'd fallen in love with his poems as a form of what she called 'art brut', and was now promising to wangle a grant for him to go and write in a *résidence d'artistes* somewhere in the south of France.

And despite all the *merde* I'd caused at the Ministry, Marie-Dominique had also decided to help me. She said that if I handed in my report with a non-*Bretagne*-related title, she would be able to pay me the full fee. In any case, she'd told me, the Brittany residence wasn't going ahead. The latest plan was to turn the former monastery into a boarding school to teach French to the children of deposed dictators.

Meanwhile, the Minister of Culture was up to his ears in it, because although the massed ranks of civil servants had agreed to call off their walkout, a wave of self-employed French accountants, lawyers and plumbers were following my example and claiming all sorts of strike benefits. The last Marie-Dominique had heard of Monsieur le Ministre, he had 'accepted the President's offer to become France's ambassador in the key strategic city of Pyongyang, North Korea'.

As soon as Marie-Dominique's money came in, I intended to go and find myself an apartment where I could sleep with my legs outstretched. And maybe where I could sit by an open window without being subjected to a chorus of French swearing. In Paris, though. Now that my path had been cleared of *merde* by Alexa and Amandine, I'd decided to stay on and give the place another chance.

My only lingering doubt was whether I'd leapt completely clear of the brown stuff, because with me, there's always the danger that I'll hunt out some more to tread in. A *pétanque* party by a canal with a load of French people was a potential minefield. I might end up telling the wrong joke, or trying for a compliment and achieving an insult. I might fracture Amandine's toe with a badly aimed *boule* or a ten-kilo bag of ice. There was always the possibility that I would get so nervous that I drank too much and fell in the canal. I might even be capable of pretending to push Amandine in, and then accidentally pushing her in. And if one or all of those disasters did happen, she could either write me off as a lost cause or think it was the funniest thing that had ever happened in her whole life. I simply didn't know. In the end, like everything else, it would all be up to the *merde* factor.

But when I got to the picnic spot, I realised there was one eventuality I hadn't even considered – that absolutely nothing would happen.

No one was there.

I was at the right place, I was certain of that. Just past the bridge, she'd said, the first stretch of canal bank after the children's playground. She was going to get there early to be sure of a good pitch. And I was almost exactly on time.

But the only people sitting by the canal here were a couple of guys swigging from tall cans of beer. And there were no signs of any full-blown picnics further down the bank.

Cold shoulder was right. I dumped my ice bag at my feet and reached for my phone. Perhaps she'd had second thoughts about it all. Or maybe she was applying the *théorie de l'élastique* – though not turning up for your own birthday party was a pretty extreme form of it.

'Are you looking for me?'

I turned and saw a female form emerging from the shadows. She must have been sitting on a bench under the trees.

'Oh, Amandine.' I felt a rush of relief. 'Am I the first to arrive?'

'No.'

'Sorry, I mean the second – after you, of course. I wasn't trying to deny your existence or anything like that.'

Calm down, I told myself, you're screwing it up again.

'No, Paul, I mean you're the last.'

'The last?'

'Yes, I thought that it might be good for us to be alone for once. Away from Marsha, Jake, Alexa, Jean-Marie and all the rest. So I didn't invite anyone else.'

'I see. Wow. Great,' I said, feeling the smile grow wider on my face with every word.

'Do you like my idea of a picnic *à deux*?'

'Oh yes. It's the best idea I've heard since, well, since your scheme for saving the tea room. You have a natural gift for ideas, you know. This is for you.' I held out the framed poem.

'Merci. Is it my birthday present?'

'Yes, and as you're French, I think it's traditional for you to give me a thank-you kiss. If you don't mind.'

'If I don't mind,' she said, laughing as she walked the last few steps towards me. 'You're so English, Paul.'

Sometimes, the *merde* factor gets the cocktail exactly right.

Available exclusively as a digital short:

The much anticipated next instalment to
1000 Years of Annoying the French

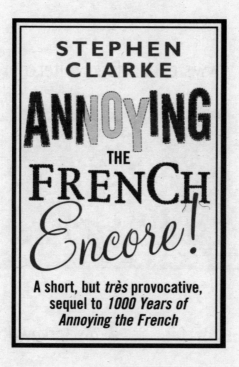

Stephen Clarke reviews everything the English-speaking world has been doing recently to ensure that France hangs on to its national inferiority complex.

For the French, the *merde* never ends...

Find out more about
Stephen Clarke
at

www.stephenclarkewriter.com

Follow him  @sclarkewriter

Read his weekly Telegraph blog at:
http://my.telegraph.co.uk/expat/
tag/stephen-clarke/